Palace
of
Mirrors

Also by Margaret Peterson Haddix

Full Ride
Game Changer
The Always War
Claim to Fame
Uprising
Double Identity
The House on the Gulf
Escape from Memory
Takeoffs and Landings
Turnabout
Leaving Fishers
Don't You Dare Read This, Mrs. Dunphrey

THE PALACE CHRONICLES
Just Ella
Palace of Mirrors
Palace of Lies

THE MISSING SERIES
Found
Sent
Sabotaged
Torn
Caught
Risked
Revealed

THE SHADOW CHILDREN SERIES
Among the Hidden
Among the Impostors
Among the Betrayed
Among the Barons
Among the Brave
Among the Enemy
Among the Free

The Girl with 500 Middle Names
Because of Anya
Say What?
Dexter the Tough
Running Out of Time

MARGARET PETERSON HADDIX

Palace
of
Mirrors

The
Palace
Chronicles
Book 2

SIMON & SCHUSTER BFYR

NEW YORK   LONDON   TORONTO
SYDNEY   NEW DELHI

SIMON & SCHUSTER BFYR

An imprint of Simon & Schuster Children's Publishing Division
1230 Avenue of the Americas, New York, New York 10020

For information about special discounts for bulk purchases, please contact Simon & Schuster
Special Sales at 1-866-506-1949 or business@simonandschuster.com.
The Simon & Schuster Speakers Bureau can bring authors to your live event.
For more information or to book an event, contact the Simon & Schuster Speakers Bureau
at 1-866-248-3049 or visit our website at www.simonspeakers.com.
Also available in a SIMON & SCHUSTER BFYR hardcover edition
Book design by Chloë Foglia
The text for this book is set in Perpetua.
Manufactured in the United States of America
First SIMON & SCHUSTER BFYR paperback edition April 2015
2 4 6 8 10 9 7 5 3 1

The Library of Congress has cataloged the hardcover edition as follows:
Library of Congress Cataloging-in-Publication Data
Haddix, Margaret Peterson.
Palace of Mirrors / by Margaret Peterson Haddix.
p. cm.
Summary: Fourteen-year-old Cecilia has always known she is
the true princess of Suala, but when she and her best friend, Harper,
decide to speed up her ascendancy to the throne, they find danger
and many imposters who challenge her claim.
ISBN-13: 978-1-4169-3915-3 (hc)
[1. Princesses—Fiction. 2. Identity—Fiction. 3. Best
friends—Fiction. 4. Friendship—Fiction. 5. Orphans—Fiction.
6. Fantasy.] I. Title.
PZ7.H1164Pal 2008
[Fic] —dc22
2007034090
ISBN 978-1-4814-2022-8 (pbk)
ISBN 978-1-4424-0250-8 (eBook)

For
Hannah, Jenna,
and Megan

Palace of Mirrors

1

Somewhere in the world I have a tiara in a little box. It is not safe for me to wear it. It is not safe for me to know where it is. It is not safe for me even to tell anyone who I really am.

But I know—I have always known. Perhaps Nanny Gratine sang my secret to me in hushed lullabies when I was a tiny, squalling creature. Perhaps Sir Stephen began his weekly visits even in my first months, and whispered into my ear when it was no bigger than an acorn, "You are the true princess. We will protect you. We will keep you safe until the evil ones are vanquished and the truth can be revealed. . . ."

I can almost picture him kneeling before my cradle, his white beard gleaming in the candlelight, his noble face almost completely hidden by the folds of a peasant's rough, hooded cloak. This is how he always comes to visit us—in disguise.

I am in disguise too. I think if I had not known the truth about myself from the beginning, it would be hard to believe. To everyone else in the village I am just another barefoot girl who carries buckets of water from the village well, hangs her laundry on the bushes, hunts berries and mushrooms and greens in the woods. Nobody knows how I study at night, turning over the thin pages of Latin and Greek, examining the gilded pictures of kings and queens—my ancestors—as if staring could carry me into the pictures too. Sometimes, looking at the pictures, I can almost feel the silk gowns rustling around my ankles, the velvet cloaks wrapped around my shoulders, the gleaming crown perched upon my head. It is good that Nanny Gratine has no mirror in her cottage, because then I would be forced to see that none of that is real. I have patches on my dress, a holey shawl clutched over the dress, a threadbare kerchief tying back my hair. This is strange. This is wrong. What kind of princess wears rags? What kind of kingdom has to keep its own royalty hidden?

I don't know why, but ever since I turned fourteen, questions like that have been multiplying in my mind, teeming like water bugs in the pond after a strong rain. Last night, as Sir Stephen was giving me my next reading assignment in *Duties and Obligations of Royal Personages*, a thought occurred to me that was so stunning and bizarre I nearly fell off my stool.

I gasped, and the words were out of my mouth before I had time to remember Rule Three of the Royal Code. ("One must consider one's utterances carefully, as great importance is attached to every syllable that rolls from a royal's tongue.") Even though I know that the Great Zedronian War was started by a king who said, "Dost thou take me for a fool? Art thou a fool thyself?" when he should have hemmed and hawed and waited to speak until he could find a wiser way of expressing himself, I still blurted out without thinking, "Great galleons and grindelsporks! Are you *her* teacher, too?"

Sir Stephen scratched thoughtfully at his chin, setting off tremors in the lustrous curls of his beard.

"Eh? What's that?" he said, blinking his wise old eyes at me several times before finally adding, "Whose teacher?"

Sir Stephen is entirely too good at following Rule Three of the Royal Code, even though he's only a knight, not royalty.

But then I hesitated myself, because I'm always loath to speak the name. I stared down at my hands folded in my lap and whispered, "Desmia's."

Desmia is the fake princess, the one who wears my royal gowns, the one who sits on my royal throne—the one who's saving my royal life.

Sir Stephen did not reply until I gathered the nerve to raise my head and peer back up at him again.

"And why would I be Desmia's teacher?" he asked, raising one grizzled eyebrow. He wasn't going to make this any easier for me than conjugating Latin verbs, solving geometry proofs, or memorizing the principle exports of Xeneton.

"Because you know how to train royalty, and—"

"She's not royalty," Sir Stephen said patiently.

"But she's pretending to be, and if she has to keep up appearances, to throw off and confuse the enemy—then doesn't she have a tutor too?"

I cannot remember when I found out about Desmia, any more than I can remember when I found out about myself. Perhaps, by my cradleside, Sir Stephen also crooned, "And don't worry that your enemies will ever find you. They won't even look because we've placed a decoy on the throne, a fake, a fraud, an impostor. If the evil ones ever try to harm Desmia, we will find them out; we will roust them. And then we can reveal your existence, and the kingdom will ring with gladness, to have its true princess back, safe and unscathed. . . ."

When I was younger I used to playact the ceremony I planned to have for the girl Desmia when the enemy was gone and the truth came to light. I'd play both roles, out in the cow pasture: kneeling and humble as Desmia, standing on the wooden fence to attain proper royal stature when I switched to playing myself.

"I, Princess Cecilia Aurora Serindia Marie, do hereby proclaim my gratitude to the commoner Desmia, for all the kingdom to see," I'd intone solemnly, balanced on the fence rails.

Then I'd scramble down and bow low (though keeping a watch out so that neither my knees nor my forehead landed in a cowpat).

"Oh, Princess," I'd squeak out, as Desmia. "It is I who ought to be thanking you, for allowing me the chance to serve my kingdom, to ensure your safety. I have wanted nothing more than your safe return to the throne."

Back to the fence rail. Back to my royal proclamation voice.

"It is a fortunate ruler who has such loyal subjects. In honor of your service, I grant you a tenth of the royal treasury," I'd say. Sometimes the reward was "land on the Calbrenian coast" or "my best knight's hand in marriage" or "the services of your favorite dressmaker for a year." But somehow it never sounded right. What was the proper reward for someone who had risked her life to save mine? What was the proper reward for someone who'd already gotten to wear silks and satins while I wore rags, who'd gotten to feast on every delicacy in the kingdom while I ate porridge and gruel, who'd slept in a castle while I slept on a mat on the floor? Wasn't it reward enough that she'd gotten to live the life that was rightfully mine?

Last night, when I asked Sir Stephen if he was Desmia's tutor too, he finally shook his head and said, "Of course I'm not Desmia's tutor. She doesn't need to learn the same lessons as you."

It was a perfectly clear answer—straightforward and to the point. But it left me wanting more. Long after Sir Stephen had shifted into a lecture on the Eight Principles of Royal Governance, I was still thinking of more questions. *Then who is her tutor? What lessons does she learn?* And, most of all, *When? When will we trade lives? When will I ever get to use all this nonsense I'm learning?*

When will my real life begin?

2

I'm awakened by a cry down the lane. "Cecilia! Eely-eel-yuh! Time to go!"

Even yanked from deepest sleep, I know instantly that it's Harper calling for me—Harper, my best friend. I'd like to say that he's the only person who calls me Eely-eel-yuh (or Eels, Eelsy, or the Eel-Eyed Wonder) but alas, the nickname has caught on in the village. And no, I don't look anything like an eel. I don't think.

When I don't rush out of the cottage instantly, Harper takes to pounding on the door.

"Eelsy, come on! Sun's almost up. The fish are biting *now!*"

Laughing, Nanny Gratine slides my fishing pole into my hand.

"Best go on," she says. "Before he wakes the entire kingdom."

"But—"

I'm thinking breakfast would be a good idea, maybe

along with a good long spell sitting at the table over a mug of Nanny's herb tea. As if she's read my mind, she bustles over to the kitchen table and begins bundling chunks of oat bread into a kerchief. She ties it firmly and slips the knot over the end of my fishing pole.

"There," she says. "Everything you need."

Harper's still pounding at the door.

"Can't you wait a blessed moment, until I'm dressed?" I holler. And then I blush. A year ago—maybe even a month ago—I could have yelled that at Harper and neither of us would have thought a thing of it. But now . . . well, at times like this, sometimes I actually remember that he's a boy and I'm a girl and those are different things. I don't need Sir Stephen around to tell me that a true princess shouldn't be discussing her state of undressedness with a peasant boy.

I spring out of bed and lean the fishing pole against the wall long enough to exchange my nightgown for the simple shift and apron that pass for my day clothes. I grab the fishing pole again, accept a good-bye kiss from Nanny, and jerk the door open fast enough to surprise Harper mid-knock.

"Took you long enough!" he growls. "I could have caught fifty fish in the time it took you to put on that dress."

"Oh, yeah? And if you're that good at fishing, how come you have to sit there all day, sometimes, just to catch one?" I spit back.

Somehow, now that we're face to face, that whole boy-girl thing doesn't seem weird at all anymore. Harper is just

Harper again. Even if I'd never touched a geometry book in my life (as everyone thinks I've never touched a geometry book in my life), I still would say that Harper is all angles: jutting cheekbones and ears, his pointy elbows and knees sticking out of his tattered sleeves and pants. And he's got freckles sprinkled across his face, freckles the same sandy color as his hair, as if he dunked his whole head in the pond and the silt stuck everywhere.

"Wouldn't it be nice?" Harper says wistfully, as we start off down the overgrown, brambly path that leads from Nanny Gratine's cottage down to the pond.

"Wouldn't what be nice?" I ask absentmindedly. We're at the point in the path where there's a break in the bushes, and I'm watching the mist rise over the meadow, a mysterious glow in the dim light of near dawn.

"To spend a whole day doing nothing but fishing."

"Maybe we could do that sometime," I offer. "I could ask Nanny to let me out of chores for one day."

"*I* couldn't," Harper says. He kicks angrily at a rock in the path. "You know. Mam would never let me miss harp practice."

Harper's name isn't just a name. It's his destiny, his mother's hopes for him, his one chance to live a long life. There's a war on—there's been some sort of war going on in our kingdom forever, it seems—and Harper's father was called away for soldiering before Harper was even born. When the king's men came to tell Harper's mother that her husband was dead, she grabbed one of them by his velvet coat and demanded, "And how is it that you live? How can any man survive in this land of killing?"

The story goes that the man sputtered out, "I—I'm just a court musician. They don't send court musicians into battle."

So her plan was hatched. Nobody knows how she got the harp, or how she learned to play so she could teach Harper. I do know there is harp music at every soldier's funeral in the village. And ever since Harper was old enough to stand, he's had to practice every day. The older he gets, the longer his mother makes him play. Practice time for him is all afternoon nowadays, from the noon meal until it's time to get the family cow from the meadow.

And of course what Harper dreams of, what he longs for and plans for and aches for, is . . .

To be a soldier.

"Fish don't bite well after noon anyhow," I tell Harper helpfully, though I don't really know this. By afternoon I'm always helping Nanny scrub out her pots or beating laundry on the rocks by the stream or gathering eggs from our chickens or doing one of the other million chores that make up my days.

Harper gives me a little shove.

"Fish would bite well for me," he says. "You're just not ever quiet enough."

"Am too!"

"Are not!"

I giggle and run ahead of him, splashing through puddles and ducking under branches.

"See—that's just what I mean!" Harper shouts behind me. "You're going to scare every fish in the pond!"

I stop suddenly, not because Harper's yelling at me, but because there's a shadow across the path, in the exact spot where there should be a clearing. The shadow darts away, mixing with other shadows, like someone dodging behind a tree.

"What's wrong?" Harper says, catching up with me. "Goose walk across your grave?"

"Hush," I whisper. I tiptoe over to the clump of trees, gather my nerve, and peek through the leaves. It's dark and dusky behind the trees, so I have to creep farther from the path, farther into the woods, just to see anything. I'm looking for a different kind of shadow now, not like a man standing tall and proud, but one small and squat, a man crouching and hiding. . . .

Suddenly a dog leaps out at me, three of his muddy paws skidding down my dress, the other one striking me square in the face. The dog whimpers and howls and runs off toward the village.

Harper falls to the ground laughing.

"That—was—so—funny! You—should—have—seen— your—face!" he manages to say, between guffaws.

I spit out mud, snort mud from my nostrils.

"I'll get you for this!" I yell, whipping back branches, finally getting a good view behind the tree.

There's nobody there.

"Eelsy!" Harper laughs, still rolling on the ground. "The dog went thataway. Better start running if you're going to get him!"

"I don't mean the dog," I say, with as much dignity as I can muster with mud caked on my nose and lips. "Somebody threw that dog out at me."

"You're crazy," Harper says. "Who'd throw a dog? That was Pugsy, Jasper Creech's dog—you know, that big cowardly mutt? Pugsy probably just saw his own shadow, and got jumpy. Or, no—I know—maybe he saw a skunk, and now you're going to get sprayed, and—"

"It's physically impossible for a dog to jump in that manner," I say frostily. "He was thrown. *Flung.*"

"But why?" Harper asks. "Why would anybody do that?"

Because my enemies found out where I am. They're lurking around, waiting to kill me. But the moment wasn't right, so they just wanted to get away without being seen.

Of course, I can't tell Harper that. I'm not even sure I believe it myself. Maybe it is physically possible for a dog to jump like that. Maybe there was never anybody there except a dumb dog. Maybe I'm the coward who's scared of shadows.

"Maybe someone was following us," I say, even though it's illogical. The shadow was ahead of us on the path, like someone was lying in wait.

Harper just shakes his head.

"Who'd bother following us? We're not anybody important."

"I—" I have to choke back the words. It's strange how badly I want to tell Harper everything all of a sudden. Partly just to wipe that smirk off his freckled face, to make him know that *I'm* important. Partly because . . . I don't know. We're best friends. It almost feels like I'm lying to him, not telling. I want him to take my fear and the shadow seriously. I want him to take me seriously.

"You were really scared, weren't you?" Harper says softly. He stands up, brushes the dirt from his breeches. He steps a little closer, and I remember again that he's a boy and I'm a girl. This is so weird. It wasn't that long ago that we used to arm-wrestle and play leapfrog and chase and tackle, and it didn't mean a thing. But now I can see that he's thinking about putting his arm around my shoulder, to comfort me. He lifts his arm a hairsbreadth, lowers it again. Chickening out. For now.

"Really," he says huskily, "if there was any danger, if someone was following us . . . I'd protect you."

"With what?" I say. "Your harp?" I'm just trying to make a joke, trying to make it not so weird that he's standing so close, that he's offering to protect the same person he used to tackle and wrestle and pummel. But he recoils, just like I've punched him. The expression on his face crumbles. That was the worst thing I could have said to him. It's probably the worst thing I've ever said to anyone in my entire life.

Harper drops his fishing pole.

"You know what? I don't think I feel like fishing today," he says. "Maybe I'll just go back to bed. To sleep. Maybe I'll just sleep until noon, and then I'll spend my every waking hour playing that stupid harp!"

"I'm sorry," I whisper. But he's already stalking away from me, throwing up clumps of mud up from his heels with every angry step.

I pick up Harper's fishing pole, and then I just stand there. I'm too scared to move. But I'm not afraid of shadows and phantom men and enemies anymore. I'm afraid that Harper will never forgive me.

3

Eventually I force myself to walk the rest of the way to the pond. I cast both fishing lines and reel in big ugly catfish, smaller sunfish, humble monkfish. I'm having an incredibly lucky fishing day, but it's no good without Harper. Still, when I'm done, I divide the fish into two baskets. I leave one of the baskets with his pole propped against the door of the hut he shares with his mother. I can hear ripples of harp music coming from inside. I rap hard against the door— pound, Pound, POUND!—then dash away.

Nobody jumps out at me from behind any of the trees, neither dog nor human. Nobody reaches out to drag me into the bushes and muffle my mouth, bind my arms, stab my heart. Nobody even glances at me twice.

"How was the fishing?" Nanny asks, when I shove my way into our cottage.

"Fine," I say.

It's funny. I used to tell Nanny practically every thought

that flitted across my mind. I told her what kind of dress I wanted to wear to my coronation; I told her every single time I got a mosquito bite, and exactly how messy each mosquito looked when I squashed it. I told her how my quill pen squirmed in my hand and shot out blots of ink when I least expected it, and how Sir Stephen couldn't possibly expect me to memorize twenty pages of *A Royal Guide to Governance*, not when just one page of the book put me to sleep. But lately my jaw seems to lock up even when there's something I really want her to know. And I *don't* want her to know what I said to Harper. Because of that, I also don't tell her about the shadow I saw on the path, the dog that was thrown (or jumped) at me, the possibility that my enemies know where I am.

Am I foolish? Foolhardy? Or just "keeping my own counsel," as royals are advised to do in the addendum to Rule Three of the Royal Code?

"Have you forgotten what to do with fresh-caught fish?" Nanny asks.

I realize I've been just standing there, staring at Nanny as she cuts up potatoes for the expected fish stew.

"Uh, no. Sorry. I was just . . . thinking. I'll get the knife."

We have a special knife for scaling and deboning fish. I take it down from a hook near the fireplace and carry the basket of fish back outside. The wooden knife handle feels cool in my hand as I make the first slash through fish skin.

I could defend myself if someone jumped out at me now, I think. *There's no need to tell Nanny or Harper or anyone else about what I saw, what I suspect. I can take care of myself.*

The knife slides across the slippery fish, and before I can stop it, the blade nicks my thumb.

"Ow! Blast the dark one's sneezes!" I shout, which is the worst curse I've learned from Harper. I drop the fish and the knife and clutch my bleeding thumb in my apron. Nanny appears instantly in the doorway of our cottage. She's got her own knife held high over her head, clasped in both hands, ready to attack.

"I cut myself," I say sheepishly. I peel back the apron and look. The wound has already stopped bleeding. "Just a little."

Nanny lowers her knife instantly.

"You were screaming like a stuck pig," she says. She walks briskly over and inspects my thumb. "Humph. Doesn't look much worse than one of those paper cuts you get from all that reading."

I'm staring at the wound too—it is worse than a paper cut. (Really. I wouldn't scream over a paper cut.) But out of the corner of my eye I can see that Nanny's trembling. There's a quaver in her voice, too, that she's trying to hide with brusqueness. My mind flashes back to the image of her standing in the doorway, knife held aloft, her normally gentle face twisted into a fierce expression. A murderous expression.

Nanny's scared of something too.

"Why'd you do that?" I ask.

"Do what?" Her voice is still a little wobbly. She's actually scanning the woods around the cottage, as if she still believes there's some great danger out there.

I take the knife from her hand, and do an imitation of her pose. I could be an illustration in one of my books: "Warrior with Weapon Ready." Except the warriors in the illustrations never wear dresses and aprons.

"The way you were screaming, I thought you were being attacked by a wild boar," she says lightly. Too lightly. "I thought I'd kill it, and then the whole village could feast on pork chops."

I don't believe her. She's so tenderhearted about animals that if I ever really got attacked by a wild boar, she'd probably scold me for provoking it. And wild boars are low to the ground. You don't hold your knife that high to fend off a wild boar.

You hold your knife that high to fend off a human.

Nanny has always been the one who's not worried about my fate. Sometimes, when they think I'm not listening—when they think I'm fully engrossed in *Court Protocol for Everyday Use*, or when they think I've fallen asleep in my corner of the room—I can hear her and Sir Stephen whispering about current conditions in the countryside, the suspected movements of our enemies, the various speculations about what might happen next. There are advantages to living in a tiny cottage. When Sir Stephen comes for his weekly visits, there's nowhere for him to stay except in the same room as Nanny and me. And there's nowhere for him and Nanny to go to whisper in private. Unfortunately, Sir Stephen always has all the interesting information, but he whispers so softly that

I usually hear only Nanny's side of the conversation. And she always says things like "Well, no matter how hard they try, they'll never find Cecilia here" and "Who would think to look in this village? Why, I'd wager we're not even named on most of the maps in the kingdom."

But now, if Nanny's scared too . . .

Something's changed. I can see it in Nanny's eyes, that there's some new threat, some new turn of events. Maybe she's heard news from Sir Stephen, or rumors from down in the village.

"Tell me," I demand. "Tell me the truth." I will my voice to sound imperial and queenly, truly royal. I picture myself with a crown on my head, a ramrod-straight spine, a fur-lined robe engulfing my body. I want *that* kind of voice. But it's my usual voice that comes out, just a little squeakier and whinier. I sound like a spoiled little child begging for penny candy at the village store.

"I'll tell you to wash and bandage that cut, I will," she says, half laughing. But she trumps up an excuse to stay outside, pretending to weed the already weed-free vegetable garden while I finish cutting up the fish. She doesn't leave me alone the rest of the day.

And so there's really no need to tell her about the shadow and the dog, about my own fears and worries and mistakes.

Is there?

4

After I'm done cutting up the fish and the stew is bubbling in its pot over the fire, I bury the fish bones in the garden for fertilizer. Then I feed the chickens and gather eggs and bring in firewood and do my usual other dozens and dozens of chores, all under Nanny's watchful eye. And then somehow it's late afternoon, time to bring the cow in from the pasture. I can practically see Nanny deliberating about this, trying to decide if it's safe to let me go. Just as i'm about to make another embarrassing plea—*"Please* tell me what's going on! Please! You have to!"—she surprises me by asking, "Harper will be going after his mam's cow today, won't he?"

"He always does," I say.

Nanny takes the last split log from my arms.

"Then run on now and meet him at the path. You two go together, you hear?"

We always do. Going after the cows is one of my favorite chores. Harper's always in a good mood, because he's done with his music practice for the day. And for me it's the moment that divides my day as hardworking, ragged peasant girl from my evening as secret princess poring over gilded texts. The studying is no easier than the chores, but it's more promising. Each page I turn whispers, *Someday ... Someday ...* And though I can't tell Harper about it, of course, sometimes when we're going after the cows together, I figure out a way to share some of the interesting tidbits I've learned: "Did you know that the tallest waterfall in our kingdom is equal to the height of fifty men, standing one on top of the other?" "Did you know that King Guilgelbert the Fourth never wore his crown, because it made his head itch too much?" I always pass off the knowledge as something Nanny has told me, or something I've heard down at the village store. And Harper tells me what he's heard: that the Riddlings' ewe gave birth to a lamb with two heads, that One-Eyed Jack at the gristmill jumped into the river from the top of the waterwheel just to prove it could be done.

I can't tell Nanny that Harper might not want to get the cows with me today, after what I said to him this morning. The thought is too piercing.

"Run along," Nanny urges again, as if she's afraid that Harper might pass on by our cottage without stopping.

Today he might.

I whirl around and rush down to the place where the path from our cottage meets the path from the village. The village path is wide and deeply rutted by wagons and all the horses, cows, goats, sheep—and, oh yeah, humans—who have traveled over it. The path from our cottage is barely a space between trees. In fact you have to weave right, then left, then right, then left, over and over again. It's so complicated that Nanny named our cow Dancer in hopes of encouraging her to dodge the trees gracefully instead of balking at every new tree trunk looming before her face.

"But it's just a name," I can remember complaining when I was younger. "Cows don't understand words like that."

"Never underestimate the power of a well-chosen word," Nanny shot back. "Or the intelligence of a well-chosen cow."

Never mind the cow—I'm wishing that I'd chosen my words more wisely this morning. Harper *isn't* waiting for me down at the bottom of the hill, where the paths meet. I stand there for a few moments, remembering the shattered look on his face this morning. My own mocking words echo again in my mind.

With what? Your harp?

I blush red, embarrassed and ashamed. It was such a stupid, cruel thing to say. It didn't even make sense—he wasn't carrying his harp this morning, just the fishing pole.

I push the memory back to a few seconds before I opened my big mouth: to the moment when he was almost ready to put his arm around my shoulder, to comfort me. The expression on his face then . . . well, his face was still covered with freckles, of course, and his sandy hair was sticking up in all directions, as usual, and he had a little brush of mud across his cheek (probably flung there by that accursed Pugsy's paws). But somehow, even with the freckles and the messy hair and the mud, he'd almost looked romantic, almost like one of the courtiers bowing to their ladies in one of my royal books.

Romantic? A courtier? Harper? Now, that was ridiculous.

Annoyed with myself I stalk out into the center of the path to the pasture, turn toward the village, and bellow, "Harper?"

No answer.

"Fine. Be that way," I mutter.

I stomp off toward the pasture. Dancer and Harper's cow, Glissando, are the last ones left there, standing in the buttercups chewing their cud. (Harper's mother named the cow, obviously. Harper usually calls her Grease.) Seeing Glissando/Grease makes my heart do an odd little plunge. Maybe I should have waited for Harper just a little longer. Or maybe he was so mad at me this morning that he ran off and joined the army. Maybe I'll never see him again. Ever.

"Come on, Dancer," I say in a choked voice, slapping her rump. "Time to go home."

The trip back down the path seems to take three times longer than usual. The shadows are starting to creep across the path, and I shiver, remembering how Nanny was so insistent about wanting me to walk with Harper.

It's not my fault he didn't show up. What was I supposed to do— issue a royal decree demanding his presence? That wouldn't have helped!

Except, maybe it would have, because then I could just explain to Harper about who I really am, and why I did have reason to be worried this morning, and maybe, just maybe, he could understand how I could have been so mean to him, by mistake. . . .

Dancer flicks her tail in my face, as if trying to alert me to a dark figure standing ahead of us on the path, almost exactly where I need to turn off for our cottage.

"Thanks, Dancer," I mutter. "You're a great guard cow."

It's not like I can plunge into the woods and hide, not with an eight-hundred-pound cow strolling beside me. I wish I'd brought the fish knife with me. I wish Dancer were a steed I could hop onto and gallop away. I wish Harper were with me, with or without the harp.

Then the dark figure moves, and turns into someone familiar: Harper.

"What—you didn't even wait for me?" he shouts at me indignantly.

"I—I thought you weren't coming," I stammer. "You were so late."

"Mam made me practice extra, because I kept messing up," Harper says. He glares at me, and even in the dying light I can see the fury in his eyes. "I wasn't *that* late."

He's right. On a normal day I would have stood there where the paths split forever, if that was what it took to get to walk to the pasture with Harper. He's had to practice extra before. And I've never minded leaning against a tree, waiting. Sometimes I braid flowers into my hair, or fill my apron pockets with acorns to throw, or just ponder which new fascinating fact to share with Harper. Once or twice I've even walked down to the village myself to fetch him, freeing him from his musical torture with the excuse, "Really, Mrs. Sutton, the sky's getting so dark, and Nanny says her bones feel the rain coming—don't you think we should bring the cows home before it storms?" Harper loves it when I do that.

"I'm sorry. Today—it just—I—," I sputter.

"Never mind," Harper says, brushing past Dancer and me.

"Wait! I—"

"Grease is going to founder on all that grass if I don't get there soon," Harper says impatiently. And then he takes off running, his bare feet slapping hard against the dirt.

I think about tying Dancer to a tree and chasing after him, or just standing there for another eternity and ambushing him when he comes back with Grease. But what am I supposed to say? How can I excuse myself? How can he understand anything if he doesn't know that I'm the true princess?

How can I stand here in the near dark, alone, when I know someone might be lurking in the trees, ready to get rid of the true princess?

5

The Great Xenotobian War started because of a dispute over a shipment of tacks.

The Second Sachian War began after King Gertruvian the Third overheard King Leolyle of Sachia insulting his wife's taste in flower decorations.

As for the Alterian War—there's been only one so far, and, admittedly, it wasn't all that great, but still—it started mostly because King Gustando was a little sensitive about his height, and the Alterian ambassador mockingly suggested that he should wear shoes with a thicker sole and heel.

I used to giggle over those details. Even when Sir Stephen stared disapprovingly at me and intoned, "The art of foreign relations is a delicate thing. One must learn from the past, rather than mock one's ancestors," I could do little more than duck my head and hope he couldn't see that I was still laughing. What kind of idiots fight over tacks? Who cares about flower decorations or shoes?

But now, spooning up Nanny's delicious fish stew without even tasting it, I've lost my sense of humor. I keep thinking, *How can Harper and I be fighting over a musical instrument?*

I remember a long, long time ago when Nanny and Sir Stephen had an argument about me. I can close my eyes and relive the awful feeling of listening to the two most important adults in my life fighting above my head. It all began because Sir Stephen arrived early for his weekly visit, and Nanny and I weren't waiting at our cottage.

"Where have you been?" Sir Stephen demanded, as soon as we stepped through the door. "I was beginning to believe that our enemies had found the princess, found her and carried her away. . . ."

"We were in the village, buying flour," Nanny said, giving him a glare that even I, a little child, could read: *Don't go talking about Cecilia being carried away when she's standing right here listening! Do you want to give the girl nightmares?* Nanny plopped the sack of flour onto the table, and it sent up a puff of white, which then settled back over the sack and the table and Nanny's skirt like snow.

I wanted to say that I wouldn't have nightmares—that I knew they would keep me safe. But I was distracted by Sir Stephen's reaction. He was clutching his heart in alarm.

"You took the princess with you?" he asked in such a horrified voice that I wondered if there were some rule about princesses avoiding flour, just like there was about princesses not being allowed to fidget or twirl their hair around their

fingers or yawn without covering their mouths. Back then Sir
Stephen had only begun teaching me about what it meant to
be royal.

"You let the villagers know the princess is here?" he raged.
"You let them see her?"

"What would you have me do?" Nanny shot back, her
voice nearly as sharp as his. "Leave her alone in the cottage
while I'm out? A young girl like her, curious about fire,
curious about the bottles on my shelves?" It was true—I
was curious about everything, especially the bottles of herb
potions and tonics and cures lined up around the cottage like
jewels behind glass.

"I know not to touch your bottles!" I defended myself
shrilly. Both of the adults ignored me.

"Can't you just stay home?" Sir Stephen asked, almost
pleadingly.

"Aye, if you hire me a man to bring me foodstuffs and
other goods from the village, to bring in the cow from the
pasture and such like—surely there's a knight you can spare
for that," Nanny Gratine replied, her tone cutting even though
this was a funny thought. A knight couldn't go after the cow,
I thought. He might step in a cowpat! Wouldn't that make his
armor rusty?

Sir Stephen furrowed his caterpillar eyebrows together,
missing the humor.

"Of course we don't have a knight to spare for that.
Knights don't do chores for peasant women." He shook his

head disdainfully. "That'd be like hanging a sign on your door: 'This place isn't what it seems. The princess is here.' It's the same reason we can't risk posting a guard here, because people would notice. I thought you could keep Cecilia safe and out of sight—your cottage is so perfectly remote, apart from every other human habitation. That's why we chose you."

"And was that the only reason?" Nanny asked, with a fury I didn't understand. "Would you have let any slattern raise the princess, as long as her cottage was isolated? Do you care how Cecilia turns out, as long as she can stay alive and look the part and curtsy properly and spout the right genteel phrases?"

"I—," Sir Stephen tried to interrupt, but Nanny wasn't finished.

"You would have a princess sit upon the throne who doesn't know anything about her kingdom? Who doesn't know her own people? Who's never had a friend—or been a friend? Who doesn't care about anyone but herself?" Nanny asked. "Is that what you want?"

Sir Stephen blinked.

"What do the villagers know about Cecilia?" he asked, sidestepping her questions. "Who do they think she is?"

"They think she's just an ordinary orphan child I've taken in," Nanny said. "Plenty of orphans in the kingdom nowadays."

Her dark blue eyes dared Sir Stephen to argue with that. But he backed away.

"Well, then," he mumbled, looking down at the dirt floor of our cottage. "No harm in that, then, I suppose."

"Oh, there's plenty of harm in children growing up without their parents," Nanny said, still angry. "Plenty of harm in all your murderous wars, leaving widows and orphans in their wake—"

"That's enough," Sir Stephen said sharply. "Princess Cecilia, you will open your book and begin reviewing your letters. Now."

But I'd been infected with some of Nanny's fury. I didn't understand everything they were saying—I'm not even sure I remember it all correctly now, or if I've melded this argument in my mind with other opinions they've expressed, other times. But I understood enough. I knew what Sir Stephen wanted to take away from me.

I pushed back the book he handed me, and it skidded across the table, coming to rest against the flour sack, getting showered with its own dusting of white.

"If I don't go to the village, I can't see Harper!" I said stoutly. "And he's my friend! You can't stop me from being friends with Harper!"

Back then our friendship consisted of dropping pebbles in puddles together, scratching out pictures in the frost on the village store window, making faces at each other while Harper's mam and Nanny shopped. But I already knew Harper was worth fighting for.

Nanny and Sir Stephen laughed off my defiance.

"Aye, she's a true princess, all right," Nanny said, her own anger gone. "Already trying to boss us around!"

Now, as I bite down on an unyielding sliver of fish—oops, left some scales on that one—I turn over a new question in my mind. If I was willing to defy Sir Stephen when I was five, just for the chance to drop pebbles into puddles with Harper, what am I willing to do to save our friendship now?

Am I willing to tell him the truth?

I carefully remove the fish scales from my mouth and glance across the table to see if Nanny has somehow noticed that I'm contemplating the ultimate disobedience. But Nanny isn't watching me. She's watching the door, then the window, then the door again, her eyes darting back and forth. There's a faint rustle outside—a squirrel stepping on a twig, maybe, or the wind blowing branches against the thatch of the roof—and she leans forward, her eyes narrowed, her hand cupped against her ear. She sees me watching her, and puts her hand down. She attempts a laugh.

"I'm an easily spooked old woman tonight," she says. "I'm sure that was just Dancer brushing up against the wall."

Dancer's "barn" is just a little shed attached to our cottage, so that's certainly another explanation.

"Why?" I ask. "Why are you easily spooked tonight?"

For a moment I think she's going to tell me. Her eyes meet mine, and they're so deep and wise and kind that I can tell she regrets keeping secrets from me. But she shakes her head.

"You'll understand when you're my age," she says. "Old women like me—we've seen too much. We worry too much."

"But what if I want to understand now?" I ask. "What if I *need* to understand now, for my own safety?"

I am proud that I've managed to keep my voice level. I may not sound imperial and queenly, but I think maybe I sound like an adult, calm and rational.

Nanny rewards me with a half smile.

"If you needed to know, I'd tell you," she says. "But you don't, so . . ." She reaches across the table, clasps my hands between her own. "Stay a child. Enjoy your daydreams and wishes, your fun and games . . . Sir Stephen and I can do the worrying about your safety."

Nanny's hands are soft and warm and comforting. I can remember a thousand times she's soothed away my fevers with those hands, wiped away my tears, held me and hugged me and calmed me. But right now her hands feel like a cage, overly confining. I jerk mine back, and I'm ready to scream out angrily, *But I'm not a child anymore! Stop treating me like a little girl!*

Just then something else happens. The door bursts open, shoved so hard that it slams back against the wall. Both Nanny and I jump up. I'm casting about for a suitable weapon to use to defend myself—the fish knife's too far away; would the stew pot do in a pinch, slammed down over somebody's head? Then I hear Nanny say, in a puzzled voice, "Nobody's there. It was just the wind."

Both of us rush over to stand in the doorway. A strong breeze tugs at us, teasing my hair loose from my kerchief, sending Nanny's apron strings dancing behind her. But this isn't exactly a gale-force wind. The door has withstood much stronger gusts before; it's held tight against storms when the rain slashed sideways, beating ceaselessly against the wood.

Nanny seems to be thinking along the same lines.

"But why . . . ?" she murmurs. She reaches up for the leather latch we've always used to fasten the door at night. It fits tightly over a wooden peg near the top of the door. I remember feeling very proud when I was first tall enough to reach the peg, when Nanny trusted me enough to fasten the door at night all by myself. Now Nanny yanks the leather latch away from the wall.

"Ah," she says, sounding artificially cheerful. "It's just that the latch broke. I should have known it was getting too old and worn."

She crumples the leather in her hand, but not before I've gotten a good look at it. The latch isn't stretched and worn at all. It's shiny and fairly new, and the tear is as straight and clean as a knife's slash.

As a knife's slash . . .

Whatever Nanny wants to pretend, I know the truth. That latch didn't break. Somebody cut it.

6

Nanny bustles about, cleaning up our supper things, then fashioning a hasty replacement for the latch. She insists that I follow my usual evening routine, So I pull out the books hidden behind my sleep mat, spread them across the table, prepare to stare at them until the candle sputters out. But I can't concentrate on verb conjugations or the geographic features of countries halfway across the globe.

"Don't you think it's odd that the latch could just snap like that?" I begin. "With no warning? Maybe—"

"The world is full of odd occurrences," Nanny says, in a tone that discourages further speculation.

"But—"

"Cecilia. This is your study time. Sir Stephen will be quite upset if you don't have that royal genealogy memorized by the time of his next visit. Or those geometric theorems. Or those Latin verbs."

I'm a little startled that Nanny knows so precisely what

I'm supposed to be studying, but she is always sitting right there in the cottage during my lessons.

"But don't you think—"

"Study!" Nanny points sternly at my pile of books. I give up and bend my head over the books.

I can't shut out the questions from my own mind, though. *Why would someone cut the latch? How did they do it? Did they slip the knife in through the crack between the door and the wall while Nanny and I were eating supper, and then run away as soon as the door swung open?* That didn't make sense. If that was the plan, why didn't they just rush on in and attack us?

I take time to read one Latin word—*occultus*, "secretly"— and then I think of a different scenario. What if someone had sneaked in and cut the latch only partway through—not enough that Nanny and I would notice, but enough that my enemies could come back later tonight, easily open the door, and steal me away? What if no one had intended the door to come open during supper, but the breeze just gave us an unexpected warning?

I shiver. And then I can't stop shivering. Nanny sees this, and in no time at all she's crouched beside me, wrapping her own shawl around my shoulders.

"There, there," she says, patting my back. "No need to worry. I had some extra leather and fixed us a new latch. We're shut up tight for the night now. You're safe." She gently shuts the book on the table before me. "Maybe just this once, it'd be all right to go on to bed without studying."

"Will you send for Sir Stephen?" I ask. "Will you let him know . . . ?"

"That the wind blew our door in?" She scoffs. "He'd laugh himself silly if I acted like that much of a ninnyhead."

Once again I want to scream, *Stop treating me like a little girl! Tell me the truth!* I know Nanny is pretending. Maybe she even knows I know. But I let her lead me over to my sleeping mat, pull my quilt up to my chin.

She's so rattled she doesn't even realize I still have my dress and apron on. Her shawl is still on my shoulders. I don't remind her.

"Good night," she calls, blowing out the candle. "May the Lord bless you and keep you, this night and every other."

"You too," I say, because that's our bedtime routine. We've said those words to each other every night since I was old enough to talk.

But I don't plunge into sleep immediately. I lie there, wide awake, and it's like I can feel Nanny's wakefulness—her watchfulness—on the other side of the room.

She wanted the light out, I think. *So nobody could see in our windows, see that I was studying. . . .*

Or was she just trying to calm me down, so I'd stop thinking of all the worst possibilities? Surely she really is planning to get word to Sir Stephen somehow. Isn't she? Isn't that what she'd do?

A new thought strikes me, one that makes my entire body stiffen under my quilt. If Sir Stephen finds out that I'm in danger here in our village, he'll whisk me away. He'll take Nanny and me off to some other village, maybe on the other side of the kingdom, some place that shows up on even fewer maps.

Harper . . . I think, and it's like a sob in my head, a sob or a wail or a prayer. I couldn't leave Harper without saying good-bye. I couldn't let this be our last day together, not when I mocked him this morning and snubbed him this afternoon. I'd have to apologize first, apologize and explain.

Am I willing to tell him the truth?

That question has been hanging around at the back of my mind since before the door blew open, jolting me to think of other things. Somehow all the questions in my mind are jumbled together. *Am I really in danger—more danger than usual, I mean? What's Nanny planning to do? How much should I tell Harper? What would be the problem with telling him everything, anyway? He'd never betray me, and he could help me watch out for my enemies. . . .*

I try to untangle my thoughts the way Sir Stephen has taught me to plan my strategy playing chess. Sir Stephen began teaching me the game years ago, about the same time he began teaching me to read. I can still remember my awe the first time he pulled the carved ivory pieces out of his sack, unwrapping them and naming each one in turn.

"Rook, knight, bishop, king, queen, pawn . . ."

"Where's the princess?" I asked when the pieces were all lined up on their squares.

Sir Stephen pointed to the queen.

"This is the princess, all grown-up," he said. "This is what princesses become. She's the most powerful piece on the board."

I liked that, and so I liked chess right away. But it took me a while to understand Sir Stephen's explanations.

"The trick to chess—the trick to strategy—is to keep track of each piece individually, and also in relationship to every other piece. You have to see the board as a whole, and each individual piece alone, all at the same time." He talked about trees and forests, drops of waters and rivers, soldiers and entire armies. I said I thought forests were made up of trees and rivers were made up of water and armies were made up of soldiers, so what was the difference? And anyhow, weren't these chess pieces made of ivory, not wood or water or real people? I drove him to tug on his beard in exasperation and threaten to put the game away until I was older. But I was hooked, and eventually I understood well enough that he stopped both the tugging and the threats. And now I see how everything is connected, how a chess queen's fate can depend on a pawn, how the questions in my head are all related. The danger I'm in, Nanny's pretense, Sir Stephen's response, Harper's outrage—I can't do anything about any of those situations without affecting all the others.

So I lie there, wide awake, without saying or doing a thing. I feel like Sir Stephen playing chess: When he's thinking about his own strategy, he can sit there for ages without taking any action at all. "Move something!" I urge him. "Anything!"

"Nothing before its time," he always says, and then seems to deliberate even longer, just to prove his point. When he finally takes his turn, I'm so frustrated that sometimes I grab the first piece I lay my hand on, sending my bishop dashing across the entire board, or shoving my knight forward without counting spaces or gauging risks. And then he swoops in to defeat me, chiding, "This is why one must not act too hastily. . . ."

I cannot act hastily tonight, because Nanny is wide awake over on her side of the room. Just as nobody could sneak into our cottage without her knowing, I could not sneak out undetected.

But that is the plan that's growing in my mind now, cobbled together out of worry and fear and regret and some of the same rashness that always endangers my chess pieces. If there's even a chance that Sir Stephen will carry me away from our village tomorrow, or the next day or the day after that . . . if there's a possibility that Nanny will confine me to our cottage until she thinks it's safe to let me out of her sight (which might be never) . . . if it's likely that my enemies know where I am and they're planning to murder me in my sleep . . . then of course I need to go to Harper now, tonight, and tell him everything, so that I can go in peace to my new home or my confined exile or my death. I get a little sniffly thinking about my death—*Poor thing,* people will say. *She never even got to wear her own crown.* . . . Then I realize that I am sniffling so loudly that surely Nanny will hear me and rush across the room to comfort me once more.

I stop sniffling and listen. Nothing. Nothing except the thin edge of a snore coming from across the room.

Nanny's asleep after all.

Finally, I think. *We can't be in such great danger if Nanny went to sleep so fast. Can we?* I wonder. But I'm not sure how long I've been lying there, plotting and planning.

I silently shove the quilt aside and stand up and listen again—still nothing. I tiptoe over to the door. I'm in awe of my own daring. It's one thing to fling chess pieces across a board without regard for their safety, quite something else to take chances with my own life. *For Harper's sake,* I tell myself firmly. I ease the new door latch off its peg, take a deep breath, and step outside.

7

It's a moonless night, the darkness as thick around me as cotton batting. I find this comforting. Even if someone is watching Nanny's cottage, waiting for the right moment to attack, they wouldn't be able to see me slip out the door. And really, I argue with myself, if my enemies know where I live, I'm safer outside the cottage than in.

The darkness is not so comforting when I stumble forward, vines slithering against my ankles, brambles snagging my dress. My bare feet discover the hollowed-out path between the trees, so I inch forward, feeling my way with my toes. If I touch packed dirt, that's good and I take another step; if I touch grass or leaves or brambles, I'm off the path and I have to try again. That's all I let myself think about: *Dirt or grass? Dirt or leaves?* So I'm stunned when my toes plunge into water, squish down into mud. It doesn't make sense— there's no water anywhere near the path to the village. My mind reels; for a moment it seems possible that the world becomes an entirely different place at night, water flowing in the daytime's dry paths, lakes and forests trading places. I'm picturing a sort of musical-chairs game of mischievous geographical features. Then logic returns, and I remember where I've seen mud puddles before.

Oh. Then, *Oh, no.*

In the disorienting darkness I've started down the path to the pond instead of the path to the village. I've just stepped into one of the same mud puddles that I splashed through this morning when I was with Harper, right before I saw the shadow. I freeze in fear, but the whole night is a shadow now; I'm in no greater danger here than anywhere else. When the fear ebbs, I'm just weary: It's taken me so long to get this far, and now I'm going to have to edge my way back to the cottage, through the trees along the proper path, and then all the way to the village. Or . . . maybe it'd be quicker to keep going toward the pond and then—if I manage not to fall into the water—turn and go to the village from there. I can picture a triangle in my head, the points formed by the pond and the village and Nanny's cottage. And because of all of Sir Stephen's lessons about hypotenuses and the Pythagorean theorem, I'm pretty sure that I've chosen the longer distance. But I'll pretend I don't know any geometry if it means that I don't have to turn around and go back.

Because if I go back, I'm afraid my courage will give out, and I'll creep back into Nanny's cottage, crawl back into bed, pull the quilt over my head, and just let someone else make all the decisions about my fate. And then maybe Harper will never know . . .

"Harper, you had better appreciate this," I mutter under my breath, stepping forward through the mud.

I'm not worried about being heard, because the night is already such a noisy place, what with crickets sawing away and bullfrogs calling from the pond. And mosquitoes buzzing—soon I'm working out a ratio of two steps forward to every mosquito I slap away. I almost begin hoping that my enemies are lurking somewhere along this path, because if they are, they're being eaten alive.

Finally, I reach the pond and turn toward the village, and the mosquitoes thin out a bit. Then I see a bit of light glowing in the distance—it's the village watchman, swinging his lamp.

"Three o'clock of the morning," he calls, his plaintive voice just loud enough to reach my ears. "All's well. All's well."

I don't really know the village watchman—given his job, I'm guessing he probably sleeps during the day, which is the only time I've ever been in the village before. But I feel a slight moment of kinship: the night watchman and me, both out on important missions while the whole rest of the world sleeps. Still, I'm careful to stay back until he walks on. Then I follow on tiptoe, using the light dying behind him to guide my way.

I hesitate when I get to Harper's. I haven't thought this out clearly. How am I supposed to tell Harper my whole

long, convoluted story—dating back to my very birth—
without waking his mother? Like Nanny and me, the Suttons
have only one room in their cottage; Harper and his mam are
probably even more crowded in their sleeping space, because
they have to make room for the harp and music stand. For that
matter, how am I supposed to get past the harp and the music
stand in the dark, without knocking them over and setting
off such a clatter that I wake the whole village? I stand there
deliberating long enough that the gleam of the watchman's
lamp comes back into sight. I calculate: When he's close
enough that his light will illuminate the Suttons' cottage—
but not so close that he'd see an open door and investigate—
I'll push the door back, get a quick glance, memorize the lay
of the cottage, dash in, shut the door, whisper Harper awake,
and then, when I'm sure the watchman's past, bring Harper
back outside to tell him my story.

It's a lot to do very quickly, but I don't have time for
another plan. The light's coming closer. And closer . . .

Now!

I try to shove the door open, but it's blocked by something
bulky. Er—no. Something wearing a white nightshirt.
Someone. Harper.

By the time I finally realize that it's Harper himself
blocking the doorway, he's already got his mouth open, ready
to scream. Quickly, at the last possible moment before he
stops drawing air in and starts sending out his loudest bellow,
I reach down and clamp my hand over his mouth.

"Shh! It's me, Cecilia. Don't wake your mam. I have to tell you something," I whisper into his ear.

He's still flailing about, uncomprehending. The watchman's light is getting brighter behind me. I have only a few seconds left.

"It's Eelsy!" I hiss a little louder. Harper stops flailing and nods. I take my hand off his mouth, grab his hand, and pull him out the door, then yank the door shut with my other hand. "The watchman's coming! This way!"

I jerk Harper around the corner of his cottage, but the light reaches even there. I'm debating the pros and cons of diving into the bushes at the edge of the woods—the dangers of bumps and scratches versus the value of a good hiding place—when Harper tugs on my hand.

"No, this way! Into the cowshed!"

I decide his idea's better than mine. Seconds later we're inside the shed, crouching in clumps of straw—rather strong-smelling straw.

"Ugh! Don't you ever clean out this place?" I demand of Harper.

"Never have time," he says. "Harp practice, remember?"

I try to forget that it's not just mud squishing between my toes now. Poor Glissando.

"Anyhow," I say, "what were you doing, sleeping right on top of the door, practically?"

At the same time Harper asks me, "What are you doing, waking me up in the middle of the night?"

We're both silent for a moment, then Harper answers first.

"It's what soldiers do. Like guard duty. It's so I could protect my mam, if I had to."

In the dark I can hear the huskiness in Harper's voice, the mix of embarrassment and pride. I don't say, "That is so silly, Harper," even though it is. I just say, "Oh."

"Your turn," Harper prods. From his tone of voice I can't tell if he's still mad at me or not. I panic at the thought of telling my whole story in the darkness, without once being able to see his face, to judge his reaction.

"Do you think it's safe to light a candle in here?" I ask. "I mean, that the watchman won't notice . . . ?"

"I guess so," Harper says. "And you know, that's one good thing about the straw being kind of wet and mushy. There's no danger that we'd start a fire."

I sense, rather than see, that he's standing up, rummaging around on a shelf nearby. Then a tiny flame leaps to life at the top of a candle. Glissando moos softly in surprised protest, then seems to fall back to sleep, settling into a position that makes it easy for me to lean against her side. Harper sits down too, his hand cupped around the flame.

"Well?" he says.

The candle doesn't help much. I can't see Harper's freckles very well. I can't see his sticking-out ears. What I can see—his nightshirt—seems odd. Harper isn't a nightshirt type of person. He belongs in the daylight, in pants with ripped knees, with his fishing pole over his shoulder.

I remind myself that this may be my last chance to tell Harper the truth. I gulp.

"I came to apologize," I begin.

"For what?" Harper asks.

Boys! I think.

"For insulting you this morning," I say. "On our way to the pond. When you said you'd protect me and I made fun of you. About your harp."

"Oh. That," Harper says, and I can hear the edge in his voice again.

"And for not waiting for you when it was time to get Dancer and Grease from the pasture," I add. "I knew it just made you madder, but I had my reasons. I did. I'm sorry."

I lower my head, humbly, contritely. And also, so that I don't have to look Harper straight in the eye.

"That's all?" Harper says. "You woke me up in the middle of the night just to tell me that?"

I could say yes, I realize. I could let Harper think I was just conscience-stricken and a little crazy, and now that I've sought forgiveness, I could trot right back to my bed and sleep peacefully the rest of the night. But I think of the dark path home, of the effort I made coming down here, of the danger lying in wait for me. I don't want to lie to Harper anymore.

"No," I say.

"Listen, Eels," Harper says, with a harsh laugh. "People have been making fun of me and my harp all my life. I'm used to it."

"But *I* haven't," I say. "Have I ever said so much as one word to—"

"You did this morning," he says sulkily.

"And that was the only time, right? I'm sorry. Like I said, I had my reasons." I draw in a shaky breath. "That's what I came to tell you. My reasons."

"Okay." Harper shrugs. "What are they?"

I shift positions, turning to face him. I'm still practically reclining on the cow, which isn't exactly the best location for announcing, "I'm the true princess." I decide to start with background.

"Remember, years ago, how the king and queen were murdered?" I say. My voice shakes a little bit. I always feel a little bit weird about this part of my story. "Murdered" is such a brutal word. But calling my parents "the king and queen" makes them sound remote and distant, like all my other long-dead royal ancestors. I don't have a single memory of my parents, so I don't really miss them. My earliest memories are of Nanny and Sir Stephen—Nanny and Sir Stephen and Harper.

I swallow hard.

"And remember how the assassins couldn't find the baby princess? So she was saved from being murdered too?"

"Yeah, sure," Harper says. "Princess Desmia."

"No," I say. "Not Princess Desmia."

I wait, because there's a chance that Harper might jump up and say, *Aha! I knew it all along! It was you, wasn't it? You're the real princess, right? I could tell—it's so obvious!* Because I know I'm supposed to be in hiding, but shouldn't there be something about me that's so completely royal and regal and, well, special that people could figure out everything if they tried very hard?

Harper just sits there with a blank, slightly confused expression on his face.

"Desmia's a fake," I say. "A decoy. They just tell people she's the princess so the real princess will be safe. In case the assassins come back."

Now Harper's eyes narrow into a concerned squint.

"Uh, Eels?" he says. "You should be real careful about who you say that to. I mean, not that I would tell on you, but I think that's, uh, treason or something. You're not allowed to say anything bad about the princess."

I realize I've forgotten to swear Harper to secrecy, to make him promise that he won't ever tell anybody else what I'm telling him. I guess I don't have to. I already know I can trust him.

"Harper, listen. I know this might be a little . . . surprising. But I'm telling you the truth. Desmia isn't the true princess. I am."

Harper's expression doesn't change. He still looks concerned and confused. He blinks a few times, befuddled. Then his face clears. He groans and slaps his hand against his forehead.

"Eelsy! I can't believe it! My mam put you up to this,

didn't she? Don't tell me you're going to start nagging me to go to that music competition too. All that talk about how those people in the capital are no better than us . . . I have to admit, this one's pretty creative. You could be a princess as easily as Princess Desmia, and I could be the royal harpist as easily as . . . as my father went off to war and became cannon fodder." His voice sounds strangled.

"Harper—"

"I didn't think you were on her side, though. Good one, turning my own friend against me." He laughs, bitterly. "But it's not going to work. Hear that?" He throws his head back like he's planning to scream at the top of his lungs, loud enough for his mother to hear him inside the cottage. "It's not—"

For the second time tonight, I cram my hand over his mouth, cutting off his scream before it starts.

"Stop it!" I command him. "This doesn't have anything to do with your mother or any music competition. This is the truth. I'm the real princess."

Harper's eyes grow to huge shadowed disks. He looks stunned enough that I think I'm safe pulling my hand back.

He shakes his head.

"Eelsy, this is crazy. How could I ever believe that?"

I blink back sudden tears. I didn't expect this question.

"I'm your friend," I say. "I wouldn't lie to you."

"But you do play tricks on me sometimes," he says suspiciously.

"Hey! You play more tricks on me than I play on you! Remember that time you gave me that candy made out of onions?"

"Yeah, but you're the one who put starch in your hair, to make it stick out straight, and told me you'd been struck by lightning."

I'd been particularly proud of that prank, but I'd almost ruined it because I couldn't stop giggling.

"Well," I admit, "if you'd been smart enough to ask, 'Cecilia, is that the honest truth, swear to God, cross your heart, hope to die?' I would have confessed."

Harper runs his hand through his hair, making it look even messier than usual.

"Eelsy, you're sitting in manure! Princesses don't sit in manure!"

"They do if they're in hiding, pretending to be peasants," I say. My voice cracks on the word "pretending." "Being a princess isn't just about sitting in a castle looking pretty."

Harper squints at me.

"Cecilia, is this the honest truth, swear to God, cross your heart, hope to die?"

"Yes," I whisper. "Except I'm hoping *not* to die, and that's why I was so scared this morning that I was mean to you, and I really am in danger, and I really do need someone to protect me, and if we were in the same cottage, I would be glad if you were sleeping beside the door, making sure we were safe . . ."

Harper looks down and gulps so hard that I can see his Adam's apple bob up and down. (When did Harper get grown-up enough that his Adam's apple sticks out?)

"I don't understand," he says. "If you're the princess, why would they hide you here?"

"It's out of the way," I say. "They thought it'd be safe. No one would recognize me."

Our village is so remote that no one would come here who's ever been face to face with royalty. No one would ever see me and say, "My goodness, that child is the spitting image of our poor deceased queen." (Am I? This is something Sir Stephen won't discuss with me.) I've seen my grandfather's and great-grandfather's profiles on coins, and I've studied the coins and compared them to my own image in the pond. But the coins show my grandfather and great-grandfather as old men, with beards and grizzled eyebrows and sagging jowls. And I'm just as happy not to look like that.

Harper seems to be considering my story with great seriousness. His eyes narrow again.

"But if you were just a baby . . ." He tilts his head suspiciously. "Did they change your name? And Desmia's? So they didn't have to say, 'Oops, sorry everyone, the princess's name is actually Desmia, not Cecilia. Don't pay any attention to this little switch, it doesn't mean a thing—'"

"I hadn't been christened yet, when my parents were murdered," I said, my voice dropping to a whisper. "Remember, it's the custom with the royal family that they don't announce a baby's name until the christening day."

This is a part of the story that's always bothered me. I ache a little every time I think about the fact that my parents never got to hold me up in front of the entire kingdom and God himself and announce, "This is our dear, dear child, our baby Cecilia, whom we love beyond endurance. . . ." Sir Stephen says I was barely seen publicly at all before the murderers came. So that saved me from having to live my life under a complete alias, the impostor taking even my name. But somehow, even though I never would have remembered the moment myself, I wish that my parents had lived long enough for my christening ceremony, long enough to show me off to the world, to claim me as their own.

"But where did Desmia come from?" Harper said. "You can't just pick up a spare baby in the marketplace—'Hey, just need a loaner for a while. We'll bring her back when we're done.'" He makes a disgusted face.

"Desmia was just an ordinary orphan. She had no family, no one to care what happened to her," I say softly. Maybe it's the word "orphan," but I can't look straight at Harper while I say this.

"So because she's an orphan and nobody cared, it's okay to just let her die?" Harper asks in a harsh voice.

I glance up at him in surprise.

"No, no, Sir Stephen never said she'd die," I say.

"Sir Stephen—that's the guy who always comes to visit your nanny?"

"He's visiting me, not Nanny. He teaches me about being royal. He's a knight."

"A knight, huh? And he's really told you that Desmia won't die?"

"Well, no," I admit slowly. "He hasn't said that she won't die. But he's never said that she will. There are guards and everything in the castle. I'm sure they're trying to keep her as safe as possible." I feel like my tongue is getting all knotted up, trying to explain. I can tell that it's the middle of the night and I've had no sleep, because I'm having trouble thinking clearly. I resort to using the same explanation Sir Stephen has always used with me. "When . . . when the dark forces come back, they'll be revealed if they even try to attack Desmia, and then they'll be vanquished. And then I can take my throne, and Desmia can go . . . live her own life."

Harper has one eyebrow raised.

"So the castle guards can protect Desmia, but they wouldn't be able to protect you? They can make sure that she's not killed, but they can't make the same promise about you if you were living in the castle with that royal princess life you're supposed to have?"

There's a bitter twist to his words that I don't quite understand. Then I get it. I see that Harper, who's had barely any education except harp lessons, is trying to trap me. This is like the logic proofs Sir Stephen has only begun to teach me: If A, then B; if B, then C; If A, then . . .

"I think," I say starchily, "that it's a matter of odds." Sir

Stephen has taught me about odds and probability, too. "The *odds* are that Desmia will be safe—that I might have been safe too—in the castle, living openly as the princess. But no one wants to take any chances with my life, since I'm the last in the royal line, my parents' only heir."

"But it's okay to take chances with another girl's life?" Harper asks. "Someone who doesn't even have a stake in the outcome? If she dies in your place—oh well, too bad. She was only an orphan, anyhow."

I start to remind Harper that Desmia's getting a much better life out of all of this—the silk dresses, the satin sheets, the sumptuous feasts—everything that ought to have been mine. Then I see the glint in his eye. It's not fury he's working from. It's pain.

"This is about your father, isn't it?" I say. "Your father, who died for another man's cause . . ."

Harper is nodding, violently.

"My father died for the *king's* cause. If you're the princess, my father died because *your* father sent him off to war!"

I gape at Harper in the candlelight. I have honestly never put that together before. In the village people talk about the king and the war and everything else about the outside world like it's all so distant and far away. When I picture my father the king, I imagine a stately man in royal robes hugging close his beloved child (me). I have never once pictured him sending soldiers off to war, off to certain death.

But I know he did that. I don't actually know if he ever hugged me.

"I—I'm sorry," I stammer. "I never . . . never thought about that."

Harper kicks at the matted straw.

"Then I guess that's proof," he says bitterly. "You really are the princess. Or something royal. Royalty only think about themselves, about keeping power and building the royal treasury. They don't think a thing about ordinary people. They don't care if we live or die."

"Harper, you know I'm not like that," I protest.

I reach toward him without thinking. I'm not sure if I'm intending to hug him or pat his arm comfortingly or grab his shoulders and give him a good shake—or maybe even punch him. But he pulls back away from me, dodging my hands. He ends up on the other side of the cow, staring at me resentfully.

"How could you?" he asks. "How could you let another girl take all the risks for you? How could you let someone die in your place?"

"I told you, Desmia's not going to die!" I say, but I choke on the words. This is something else I've always managed to gloss over. Or wanted to gloss over. Why else would I have spent so much time imagining the ceremony I'd have to thank her? "Anyhow, I didn't arrange this. I was just a baby when they brought me here. I didn't have a choice. I'm not responsible for Desmia's life."

"What good is it to be princess, then?" Harper asks. "If you don't have any control over anyone's fate? Even your own?"

"I *will*," I say. "When I come out of hiding . . ." But even as I say these words, I doubt them. When I come out of hiding, I'll have royal advisers. All the men who have been running the kingdom since my father died will just keep running it. "Well," I add, "if I could, I'd end the war. And then wouldn't you be mad at me? Because you've always wanted to be a soldier going off to war?"

Harper stares at me from the other side of the cow.

"I want to be a soldier because it's *something* to do. Taking action. Better to do that—to do something—than spend my whole life playing music I hate, just so I don't die."

I can't see Harper's face very well in the dim, flickering light. But I feel like I'm seeing him with something beyond vision. Harper's been my best friend my whole life, but I've never known this much about him.

"What would you do if you were me, then?" I ask in a ragged voice. "Go tell Desmia she doesn't have to take any more risks for me? Take over as princess?"

"Yes," Harper whispers.

I feel dizzy.

"I really could end the war," I say, suddenly awed at the possibility.

"You could send all the soldiers home to their families," Harper says. "The ones who are still alive, at least. You could open the royal treasury to feed the poor. You could pass any law you want."

"I could outlaw harps!" I say, giggling.

"Why not?" Harper asks, grinning.

Anything seems possible, suddenly, sitting there with Harper and the cow in the Suttons' tiny shed. I feel like all my choices are spinning around my head, glittering like gold. I'm so glad I've told Harper my secret.

And then I remember why I told him.

"My enemies—I think they've already found out where I am," I say. I tell him about Nanny's strange behavior, about the cut in our door latch, about my own fears about the shadow on the path. "Sir Stephen will probably want me to hide somewhere else."

"And then, if your enemies find you there—"

"I'd have to move again," I say.

The possibilities spinning around my head turn dark and dreary. I see a different life for myself: trudging from village to village, a homeless wanderer, always cowering in fear. I could use up my entire life like that. It'd be like Harper spending his whole life taking harp lessons, hating every moment of it.

"Maybe . . . ," I say. "Maybe I should stop hiding."

"What?" Harper says.

"I could do what you said you'd do. If my enemies could find me here, they could find me anywhere. So why not just go back to the castle, tell Desmia thanks for her service, but it's no longer needed; she no longer has to risk her life for me. And then I would just . . . be the princess."

The candle flickers. Harper's jaw drops.

"Wouldn't it be a little more complicated than that?" he asks. "More . . . dangerous?"

"Well, sure, but . . . Harper, I've been studying for this my whole life. I know the Royal Code, the Principles of Governance. I know every single export Suala produces, and the ratio of iron ore to rock in the Gondogian mines. I'm ready!" My words ring with confidence. I am surprised at myself. I sit up straighter, no longer leaning on the cow. I inhale deeply, and it feels like the first free breath of my life.

I expect Harper to argue with me, to try to talk me into being practical, into being safe. But he's sitting up straighter too, his face a mask of determination.

"I'm going with you," he says.

8

We make our plans with amazing speed. Maybe we're afraid that if we don't go right away, we'll chicken out. Maybe we've both been waiting so long to leave the village, to begin our real lives, that we can't stand to stay here a second longer than we have to. We talk at the same time, our words overlapping: Harper volunteers to bring leftover bread and an old canteen for water while I jump in to offer dried jerky from Nanny's pantry. But we're in complete agreement about everything, until I say, "And you should bring your harp, as our cover story along the way."

"What?" Harper explodes. "No—I am not taking the harp! That's what I'm running away from!"

"I'm not saying you have to play it. Or practice or anything. But people will wonder about two children out on their own. If you have the harp, we can tell everyone that you're going to the capital to find work. And we can say I'm your sister or something, coming along to help out . . ."

"We might as well say I'm going to that stupid music competition," Harper grumbles.

"Perfect!" I say. "That's what you can put in your note to your mam."

"My note?" Harper sounds incredulous.

"Well, yeah, you weren't going to just run off and not tell your mother anything, were you?"

I see by his face that he had intended to run off and not tell his mother anything.

"Eelsy—Cecilia—my mother wants to go to that music competition with me," he says. "She wants to sit there in the audience and listen to me play better than anyone else. She wants to be there when they put the gold medal around my neck, when the director of the castle musicians walks over and begs me to work for him. Except—none of that would ever happen. I'm not better than everyone else. When I play in public, my hands get all sweaty and my fingers slip and I forget to count time. . . . I'm not even good enough to be the village musician, and there's no competition here except Herk the tailor playing his cowbells!"

"Then write that she makes you nervous and that this is something that you have to do for yourself," I say impatiently.

I'm surprised that Harper stops arguing. A few moments later we blow out the candle and creep out of the shed, each of us giving Glissando/Grease a good-bye pat. I wait by the door of Harper's cottage while he tiptoes in and changes clothes and gathers up his things. I don't see the note he leaves for his mother, but when he emerges through the doorway, he's got his harp strapped across his back.

"You're going to have to carry it some of the time too," he growls at me. "It's heavy. Danged harp!"

"No problem," I mutter.

We escape the village without running into the watchman again, although I think I hear a faint echo of his voice from near the village store: "Four o'clock of the morning. All's well. All's well. . . ."

I shiver and wrap Nanny's shawl tighter around my shoulder. All isn't well. We've got a dark path ahead of us, the beginning of a journey full of unknowns. For all I know, the path just between the village and Nanny's house is lined with enemies. Maybe I won't even make it that far. Maybe I won't even get to tell her good-bye.

A lump grows in my throat, and I realize that, for all my ideas about what to tell Harper's mam, I haven't thought of anything to write to Nanny. If I tell her where I'm really going, she'll send Sir Stephen after me. She's spent the last fourteen years of her life taking care of me, keeping me safe. How can I tell her that I don't care about being safe anymore? That I'd rather sit on a throne and wear silks and satins than stay with her?

Dear Nanny, I compose in my head. *I believe that my enemies are closing in on us. I don't want to endanger you, so I am leaving. . . .*

That sounds so noble and high-minded that I'm proud of myself. I didn't know I had that in me. Maybe once I come out of hiding, I will be a better person. I will go down in history as Cecilia the Good. Generations from now people will talk about how kind and gentle I was, how saintly.

Harper stops in front of me so suddenly that my face slams into his harp, the wires digging into my skin.

"Ow!" I complain loudly. "Double dragon drat, Harper, give me some warning next time. Now I'm going to have bruises in stripes all over my face."

"Shh!" Harper says. "Listen!"

Above the racket of the crickets and other noisy night insects, there's a swell of sound coming from ahead of us, a keening. It's even eerier than the village watchman's "All's well . . ." It's sadder, too, because even though the sound is far away and I can't make out any words, it's clearly the wailing of someone who does not believe that anything's well, someone whose world has just fallen to pieces.

Then the wailing gets closer, and I can make out a word: "Ce-ciii-liiia . . ."

"It's Nanny!" I hiss at Harper, and take off running. "Maybe she's hurt!"

I promptly trip on a rock in the path and tumble to the ground. *More bruises to go with the wire marks,* I think. But I spring up right away, calling out, "Nanny! Over here!"

Harper pulls me back.

"Hush!" he cries. "What if she's the bait in some trap? You need to be quiet!"

I jerk away from him.

"Nanny! I'm coming!" I yell.

Now I can see the glow of a lamp up ahead on the path. I sprint forward, toward the glow. I can see it's just Nanny, by herself, out searching in the dark. As soon as I draw near, she all but leaps at me, wrapping me in a hug.

"Cecilia, child—I thought I'd lost you," she murmurs into my hair. "I thought—"

"I just had to go tell Harper something," I tell her.

Harper catches up with us just then. I'm amazed to see that he was clever enough to hide his harp and knapsack before stepping into the light. Nanny draws him into a hug too.

"And you were kind enough to walk Cecilia home," she marvels. "I'm so grateful."

Harper's eyes goggle out at me. Both of us now have our heads smashed in against Nanny's shoulders, the lamp clutched between us. Nanny gives no sign that she's ever going to let go. Harper starts making faces at me, his expression clearly asking, *What do we do now?*

I push away from the hug.

"Nanny, I'm fine; everything's fine. I didn't mean to worry you."

"No, no—I think you saved us both," she says dazedly.

"What?"

Nanny releases Harper from her hug and straightens her skirt. She smoothes back her hair.

"I woke up, and you were gone," she says. "I thought maybe you'd just stepped out to the privy, but I went to check, to see . . ." She says this matter-of-factly, as if I would expect her to be so paranoid. "It's a ways from the cottage, you know. . . ."

I wait, because it's obvious that she has more to tell me than the distance to the privy.

"I was almost there when I heard the muffled hoofbeats," she says. She shoots a glance at Harper, as if she's hesitant to tell this story in front of him. Then her eyes well up with tears and she clutches my hand and the words just burst out, as if she can't stop herself. "They were trying to sneak up on us, being quiet—all these men on horseback. They circled the whole cottage before they made a single noise loud enough to wake anyone. And then they just attacked, screaming and hollering and climbing in through the window and the door. . . . It was like they just expected that door to give way for them. . . ."

The cut door latch, I think. I remember what I suspected before—that someone had cut the latch ahead of time to prepare for a middle-of-the-night attack. To make sure we had no warning, no chance to escape. I shiver, thinking, *If it hadn't been for the wind blowing the door open, and my going to Harper's . . . and then Nanny going out to look for me . . .*

"Oh, Cecilia," Nanny wails, clutching my hand tighter. "I think they wanted to kill us. They had their swords drawn, their knives unsheathed . . ."

Her words dissolve into sobs, but she doesn't loosen the iron grip on my hand.

Harper steps closer, his arms out in a defensive pose.

"Are they still there?" Harper hisses. "Still looking for Cecilia and you're out here screaming her name?"

He's peering around in all directions at once, but there's only darkness around us. He reaches for the lamp—to extinguish it, I think, so we won't be so obvious—but Nanny swings it away from him.

"They're gone, I'm sure of it. I heard them riding away."

"But if someone comes back on foot . . . ," Harper argues.

I can tell Harper is trying to think like a thief or a murderer, like my enemies. I lean over and blow out the lamp. In the sudden darkness Nanny begins sobbing harder.

"We have to get her somewhere—somewhere safe—to calm her down," I tell Harper. "Can we go to your mother's?"

I hope he understands that our little adventure, our trip to the capital, is off. I can't leave Nanny like this, in hysterics. We'll go back to Harper's cottage, and he can destroy his note before his mother sees it, and then, I don't know, Nanny and I will cower in hiding at the Suttons' until Sir Stephen shows up and tells us what to do. I feel such a strange swirl of emotions thinking about this change in plans: relief and regret all mixed up together. What I don't feel is fear. I think I'm too stunned for fear.

But there were horsemen, hunting me. . . .

"No!" Nanny screams. "We can't go to the village—you can't go to the village. You have to leave. You have to get to Sir . . . to Sir . . ." Her voice falters, and I know she's remembered again that she shouldn't reveal secrets in front of Harper.

"Of course. We can go to our good friend who visits so often," I say quickly, because there's not time to explain that Harper already knows everything. Not that I'd want to explain that to Nanny anyhow. "Our friend will keep us safe."

"Yes!" Nanny says, relief in her tone. "I've got money. We'll hire a carriage . . ."

She starts pulling me back toward the cottage. In the dark we slam into tree trunks and get our faces slashed by branches, but Nanny doesn't seem to notice. Harper grabs my arm and follows along, constantly swinging his head right to left, left to right, like a sentry. But what good is a sentry when there's no light to see by?

We reach the cottage and Nanny dashes in. Harper won't let me follow.

"Stay hidden," he whispers, huddling with me behind a tree.

Nanny reappears in seconds.

"They stole all my money!" she wails, the panic escalating in her voice. "They ransacked the entire place—they even took your books!"

This loss reaches me. It's not that I was fond of Latin or geometry or *A Royal Guide to Governance*. But those books were my link to my true identity, my proof that I wasn't just another barefoot peasant girl. I had kind of thought that I would carry them with me when I went to the capital, to show to Desmia. After all, she wouldn't relinquish her throne to just anyone.

"I could sell my harp for you to have money for the carriage," Harper says, calmly.

"There isn't time!" Nanny says. "You don't understand— Cecilia has to leave *now*. She has to get to safety as fast as she can, and I can't walk that far. And I can't send her alone—"

"I can take Cecilia wherever she needs to go," Harper says, and it's almost annoying how polite he's being, how helpful.

Nanny stares at him. In the past few minutes the earliest light of dawn has started to creep through the woods, so I can see the emotions playing across her face: despair, hope, worry, fear, and then resignation.

"Yes," she murmurs. "I suppose that's our only chance."

"And you go stay with Mrs. Sutton, so you'll be safe too," I urge.

We're in a rush then, packing up more food, Nanny writing directions to get to Sir Stephen's. Before I know it, Nanny is wrapping a cloak around my shoulders and hugging me good-bye.

"I can't leave you like this," I whisper into her hair.

"You have to," she whispers back, and this time she pushes me away.

9

We've barely started up the village path—the path away from the village, the path that leads to the cow pasture and then to the world beyond—when I realize that we're walking on fresh hoofprints. I can see the exact imprint of the horseshoes: strange horseshoes, with a crest at each end.

"This—this is the way the horsemen went," I gasp, and clutch Harper's arm in sudden panic. "Harper, we're following them."

"We're not going to catch up with men on horses," Harper says.

"What if they stop and lie in wait for us?"

"How would they know to do that?" he asks. "How would they know that we're behind them?"

But he flicks the hood of my cloak up over my hair, and I notice that he slows a bit, carefully scanning the path ahead every time we come to a bend or a rise.

Once we're past the cow pasture, the path splits. The horseshoe marks continue to the left. The path to the right, which is actually wider, looks innocent and safe. It's bright enough now that I can make out the signs at the crossroads: WEDGEWEDE with an arrow pointing to the left; CORTONA with an arrow to the right.

Sir Stephen lives in the direction of Wedgewede. Regardless of the horseshoe prints, that's the way Nanny told us to go.

Cortona is the capital, where Desmia lives in the fabled Palace of Mirrors.

I come to a halt right in the middle of the path's split.

Harper's so busy looking around—right to left, left to right, examining every bit of the horizon before us—that he doesn't seem to notice that I've stopped. He veers to the right, kicking up a cloud of dust that glows in the dawn light.

"Harper!" I mutter through clenched teeth. "Where are you going?"

"Cortona—isn't that the capital? Where the palace is? Where you wanted to go?"

I squint at him in confusion.

"That was before," I say. "Nanny thinks you're taking me to Sir Stephen. To safety."

Harper's gaze follows the line of hoofprints leading in the direction Nanny wanted us to go, toward Wedgewede and Sir Stephen's.

"Do you really think you'll be safe there?" he asks quietly.

I wince. I can feel my long, sleepless night weighing on me, immobilizing my brain as well as my feet. I want to curl up and sleep for about twelve hours—then maybe I'd be capable of making a decision. Each path leads to a different fate, and I can't see more than about twenty steps into either choice. Harper's question echoes in my ears. Is safety really what I want, anyhow? Safety—or action, power, control, and a chance to treat Desmia honorably? Even staring at that line of hoofprints I still have faith that Sir Stephen could protect me in Wedgewede. He's a knight; he knows everything. Even now Cortona seems like the greater danger, the greater unknown.

And yet, slowly, agonizingly, I force myself to turn and follow Harper.

"When I get to the palace," I tell him, "when I've taken up my rightful place, I'm going to send a message to Sir Stephen and Nanny, to let them know I'm safe *there*."

My voice shakes, saying that. I'm sure Harper can tell that I'm bluffing, that I'm trying to convince myself that safety's still possible. But Harper only nods curtly, his head bumping against the harp on his back. I should probably offer to carry it for him, since I'm the one who insisted on retrieving it from the bushes when we rushed away from Nanny's. But each step forward already takes great effort. My feet drag so badly that I think this path is perhaps made of quicksand—how is it that Sir Stephen left out that little bit of information when I was studying the topography of the countryside?

"Cecilia—you're asleep on your feet," Harper says the next time he looks back at me. "Do you want to stop and rest?"

I shake my head stubbornly. If Harper can keep going, so can I.

We trudge onward, the woodlands along the path smoothing out into acres and acres of waving grasses.

My kingdom, I think, picturing the maps I used to pore over with Sir Stephen, the yellow stains of the grasslands contrasting with the green forests, the gray mountains. Unaccountably, this thought brings tears to my eyes. I'm not sure if it's from exhaustion or patriotism.

When I am princess—no, more than that, when I am queen—I will rule wisely and well, I vow. I will treat my subjects honorably. I will make my kingdom proud of me.

I am already feeling proud of myself for so nobly walking toward the capital, walking toward certain danger rather than possible safety, risking my own life to be sure of saving Desmia's.

"About your parents," Harper says suddenly. "If you don't mind talking about this . . . why did the murderers kill them?"

I pull my gaze back from the waving grasses.

"Our enemies are evil men," I say. It's an easy answer, because this is what Sir Stephen has told me so many, many times.

Harper doesn't look convinced.

"But why?" he asks. "Why are they evil? What did they want so badly that it was worth killing for?"

I have to think about these questions a little harder.

"Power, I guess," I say. "Control. It's"—I swallow a lump in my throat—"it's been common throughout Sualan history for evil, unprincipled men to challenge the monarchy. Kings have been assassinated three times. But good always triumphs in the end."

A troubled look crosses Harper's face.

"Don't take this the wrong way," he says, "but if there was ever some time where the royal family was wrong—maybe just because they made a mistake, maybe because they didn't understand something, maybe because they didn't care— shouldn't there be a way for ordinary people to stand up and say so? Without killing anyone? Hasn't there ever been a bad king who deserved to be . . . sent away?"

I gape at Harper.

"You think my father—my father *and* mother—you think they deserved—" I'm suddenly so indignant I can barely speak.

"No, no, that's not what I'm saying," Harper interrupts quickly. "I don't know much of anything about your parents. Except about the king and the war."

"It's always about the war with you, isn't it?" I glower at Harper. "I'll have you know, my father started a building campaign throughout the kingdom, setting up good roads between every major town. He simplified the legal system, so judges hear their cases more quickly. He hired scribes to keep good records of imports and exports. He, um . . ." I know there are lots of other accomplishments Sir Stephen taught me; I just can't think of all of them right now.

"Okay," Harper says mildly.

I stomp past him anyway. It is easier to walk now that I have fury fueling my pace. But I can't help thinking about the spots in *A Royal History of Suala* where the authors seem to be trying entirely too hard to find something nice to say about a particular monarch. King Dentonian the Third, for example, was most notable for his absolute lack of ear wax. Queen Rexalia is credited with discovering excellent fertilizer for the castle daffodils, because she had a habit of spilling things when she strolled through the gardens. And then there were all those kings with their silly excuses for starting wars. . . .

Not funny, I think. *Not funny at all.*

My pace slows again, and Harper catches up with me.

"I think . . . ," I say slowly. "I think it was something about the war that led to my parents' deaths. I don't know what it was exactly, because Sir Stephen never would tell me. He was always . . . squeamish talking about the murders. I think maybe he was friends with my father. It was too painful for him to discuss." Too painful for me, too, really. I certainly never pressed him for hard answers about my parents.

"Then why do you think the murders were connected to the war?" Harper asks.

"Sir Stephen always got this look on his face anytime anybody said anything about the war. It was like it hurt him just to think about it. And he's a knight and all, but he never once told any war stories."

"Maybe that's just because you're a girl," Harper says, hesitantly, as if he's not quite sure he wants to point out that fact.

"But I'll be queen someday," I remind him. "I'll be ordering people into battle; I'll be deciding whether or not to declare war, whether or not to stop it—shouldn't I know what I'm talking about?"

If Harper gives me an answer, I don't hear it. All I can think about suddenly is the information I *don't* know. Who sent the horsemen to Nanny's cottage? Were they intending to kill us or just scare us? Who else is working with the horsemen? Who else is working with Sir Stephen? Whom will I be able to trust in the castle? How should I reveal my true identity? What should I do once I'm in charge? What can I do about my enemies?

"Cecilia," Harper says. "You're *swaying*. Let's stop for breakfast before you fall on your face."

This time I don't argue. We wade into the grasses on one side of the path, sit down, and are instantly hidden. We gnaw on the stale, crumbly bread that Harper filched from his mother.

"She's really a better cook than this," Harper says. "If we'd just been able to wait until dawn, when she always starts a new batch—"

"It's fine," I say, though I'm not really tasting the bread. I'm barely alert enough to chew.

Harper gives a harsh laugh.

"This isn't exactly typical palace fare," he says.

"I'm not exactly your typical princess," I murmur, but my

eyes are closing on me. I force them open just far enough to see that Harper is gazing at me with an odd expression— squinting his eyes and furrowing his eyebrows and studying my face as though he's never seen me before in his life. He looks . . . what? Doubtful? Awed? Curious? Confused? Worried? My eyes slide shut again, and I slip off to sleep, still trying to understand.

10

When I wake up, the sun is beating down on us from high in the sky. I'm still wearing the heavy felt cloak that protected me from the dawn chill, so my whole body is prickly with sweat. And I'm a little puzzled about why I still have half-chewed bread in my mouth.

"Harper?" I whisper. I sit up dizzily and see that he's asleep by my feet, his body precisely perpendicular to mine. "Now, why would you sleep there?" I mutter. "Do you like the smell of stinky feet?"

Harper's eyelids flutter. I've never seen his eyelids flutter before; I've never seen him with his eyes shut.

"Soldier style," he murmurs, still more than half asleep. "In case of attack . . ."

I think I see his point. If some enemy attacked us, and we had no time to prepare, Harper could strike back instantly in the area facing away from me, and I could strike back in the area facing away from him. Those few extra seconds could save our lives.

Thinking about things like that makes my stomach queasy.

"I slept too long," I complain. "Shouldn't we get back on the road?"

"All right," Harper says, scrambling up. "If you think that's best."

I glance over at him suspiciously, but he doesn't seem to be making fun of me. He offers me a hand to pull me up, and this is strange too. Only yesterday he would have gleefully pushed me into a mud puddle, and today he's trying to help me up from perfectly dry ground? It doesn't matter—I'm already on my feet.

"How many days do you think it will take to get to Cortona?" I ask as we head back to the path.

"Three or four," Harper says. "I know because of the messengers who come out to say who's died in the war. . . ."

I think about what a strange life Harper's had—almost as strange as mine. All the new war widows in the village always go straight to Mrs. Sutton's cottage, where the sobs and wails mix with the mournful harp music. I guess Harper must try to distract himself by talking about other things with the messengers.

"And what do the messengers say about . . . Desmia?" I ask.

Harper gives me a sidelong glance.

"They say every day at noon she comes out onto a balcony in the castle and waves to the crowd below," Harper says. "But that's the only time anyone ever sees her. And she always wears a veil, and the balcony's so far away . . . nobody's really sure what she looks like."

Hmm, I think. *That could help me.* Maybe we could simply trade places—completely swap lives—and the people outside the castle would never have to know.

But do I really want to spend the rest of my life being called Desmia? When I'm ruling so wisely and well, do I want Desmia to get all the credit?

My head starts to ache thinking about the complications.

This will work, I tell myself fiercely.

But as we walk on, no brilliant plans or strategies present themselves to me. Harper is strangely quiet as we walk. He doesn't once ask me to take my turn carrying his harp, and when I finally offer, he just shakes his head and mutters, "Nah, that's okay. I'm used to it."

The first time someone comes toward us on the path—a tinker with an empty cart—Harper and I both stiffen. "Stay behind me," Harper murmurs. I slip into position, keeping my head down, following in Harper's footsteps, so that he's always between me and the tinker. And then the tinker's past us.

"He didn't even look our way," Harper marvels. "Didn't even say hello."

No one else that we pass—a sheepherder, a farmer with a hay wagon, a tailor with a bag of samples—pays any attention to us either. Then we come to another village.

This one has a fence ringing its outskirts.

"Good grief and curdled codswallop—why would they have that?" I ask Harper.

"Protection," he says briefly, and steps up to a guard station by the gate.

"We're just passing through on our way north," he says. "Request permission to enter?"

The guard, a burly man with a gruff face, glares at us.

"Permission denied," he growls. "Couple of pickpockets, I'd wager. You can walk around the outside, you can."

The way he's looking at us, *I want so badly to say, If you knew who I am, you'd let us in! You'd roll out the red carpet! You'd bow! You'd treat us with respect!* I clear my throat and open my mouth. Harper flashes me a worried look.

"What's the name of your village, pray tell?" I ask in my haughtiest voice.

"Spurg," the guard mutters. "Now go. Get out of here. We don't want you in Spurg."

Spurg, I think. *I'll remember that. When I take my throne— when I'm in charge—Spurg is going to be sorry this guard wasn't nicer.*

I follow Harper away from the path with great dignity, holding my spine perfectly straight. Surely that will make the guard see that we're not a couple of pickpockets. But it's hard to maintain a dignified, haughty posture while fighting through brambles and weeds, pressed close against the wooden fence. As soon as we're out of the guard's sight, I give up all pretense of dignity. I swing my arms viciously, shoving past thistles and thorns; I cry out, "Ow! Drat!" and "Harper, do you have to let those branches swing back right into my face?" and "Why do they need a fence when they have all these hawthorn trees right on top of each other?"

The sky is nearly dark when we finally come out on the other side of the village of Spurg.

"We need to find a place to stop for the night, but I want to get as far away from this village as we can," Harper whispers to me as we step onto the blessedly bramble-free path again. "Can you make it another mile or two?"

"Sure," I say, feeling the eyes of another surly guard on us.

We walk and walk, into darkness, into exhaustion.

This is worth it. I'm doing the right thing, I tell myself, just to keep going.

Finally we collapse beside the path, rolling into the grasses again. I would be content to fall asleep wherever I land—I'm that tired—but Harper has to carefully arrange us and our possessions. He positions the harp between us and the path, "so anyone coming toward us will run into it, giving us warning." He tucks our food sack under his clothes, so no squirrels or moles can nose into it in the night. He insists on sleeping at my feet once again, "for safety."

"Safety," I repeat as I cuddle into my cushioning cloak. "Right." But Harper is too far away to hear me. I wish, peevishly, that he didn't know anything about how soldiers sleep, how they protect their fellow soldiers. It would be nicer if I could share the cloak's warmth with him, if we could lie with our faces together, whispering into the night.

Strangely, this thought makes me blush, because I am

describing how husbands and wives sleep. And I'm not asking for *that*. It's just . . . I never really thought before about how being the one and only true princess is really a lonely thing. When I relieve Desmia of her duty, it will be me alone on the throne, alone on the castle balcony waving to the throngs below, alone worrying about when my enemies might attack. . . .

I fall asleep feeling grateful that, at least for now, Harper is with me. I'm not alone.

Yet.

11

We reach Cortona four days later, just before noon. We are much the worse for our travels: our bare feet coated with dust, our faces dirty, our clothes snagged beyond repair by the brambles and thorns beside all the village fences we had to walk along—outside Spurg, Tyra, Donnega, and Kahreo. But nobody's stopped us; nobody's recognized me. (How could they?)

We begin seeing the spires of Cortona from a distance of miles. First we see the spires, then the turrets, then the domes, and finally the sturdy white city walls that somehow seem gracious and airy, rather than mean and inhospitable like all those village fences. The arched gateways that lead into the city are a marvel, as peddlers, dancing girls, goat tenders, and what look to be court officials stream through them.

My stomach lurches with panic.

"Don't you think we should at least wash our faces before we go in?" I ask Harper. He has been so quiet and standoffish the past four days that I resist the urge to clutch his arm while I say this. And really, clutching his arm isn't the kind of thing I would have done back home anyhow. Is it? It's kind of hard to remember who I am and what I'm like, when I'm standing in the shadows of those massive walls, watching the river of humanity flowing through the gates.

I am the true princess. I am the true princess. I am the true princess even if my face is dirty. . . .

I'm working so hard to remember myself, I almost miss Harper's answer.

"Looking like ragamuffins is a pretty good disguise," he says. "Maybe we should go in now, get a feel for the lay of the land, then adjust our appearance accordingly. Is that all right with you?"

Okay, I *know* that's not like Harper, to ask my opinion so deferentially. He must be just as awestruck as I am. I shrug agreement, and we let ourselves be swept through the gates along with everyone else. No one guards the gateways here, but once I get into the city, I see why: On nearly every corner soldiers stand on alert, staring coldly out into the crowd. The soldiers look taller than any of the men back in our village, just as the buildings here tower higher, soaring three, four, even five stories above the ground. And the buildings aren't made of sticks and logs and rotting boards—they're bronzed brick, imperial stone, gleaming stucco, all lined with shining windows.

I'm so busy looking around that when the crowd surges forward, I very nearly lose track of Harper.

He reaches over a goat that's come between us and grabs my hand.

"Don't let go!" he orders.

Harper's hand is dry and warm and soothing, while mine is sweaty with fear. We've never held hands before. I think about what it means in the village when boys and girls only a few years older than Harper and me wander around with their hands clasped together. They're always peering dreamily into each other's eyes, sneaking shy kisses . . . and soon after, there's a wedding.

And then usually the boy gets sent off to war, and that's the end of that.

Harper is *not* peering dreamily into my eyes or making any attempt to kiss me. He's practically pulling my arm out of its socket as the crowd pushes him in one direction and me in the other. I have to leap gracelessly over the goat to avoid being torn limb from limb.

"Slow down!" I call to him.

"—can't—" That's all I hear of Harper's reply, because a large man's belly is shoved against my ear. Then Harper yanks me toward him. *Thanks a lot, Harper—I guess you're counting on the fact that at least my other arm will still work, and all I'll really need it for is to sign royal proclamations. . . .* My body slams against his side; he releases my hand and grabs my waist instead.

"Hold on to the harp," he mutters.

He's taken it from his back and is holding it in front of him.

Together, we use the harp to plow our way through the crowd. I've never really thought much about this, but it is an impressive instrument: skillfully carved willow wood, shiny strings . . . Harper and I look like we belong in a backwoods village—a very poor backwoods village—but the harp looks like it belongs in Cortona, and so people step out of the way for it.

"Look," Harper breathes.

The crowd has pushed us into a wide courtyard. There's an impressive clock tower in the center of the square, with huge clock hands pointed very nearly to noon, and at first I think that's what Harper's referring to. Then I see that just about everyone else in the crowd has turned to the right, to gaze up at . . .

The palace.

I see suddenly why the crowd has fallen silent and stopped pushing and shoving. Several people have even let their jaws drop open. The palace is overwhelming—overwhelmingly large, overwhelmingly beautiful, overwhelmingly grand. It has graceful arches and frilly turrets, and you would think that that would be like putting a lace bonnet on a soldier. But the arches and turrets and other flourishes just make the palace look more majestic, more imposing, more daunting. I realize that my notion of impressive architecture is a one-room cottage without any holes in the roof, but I think *anyone* would be stunned and amazed by this palace.

"She's coming!" "Up there!" The people around us begin shouting and pointing.

I tilt my head back farther, so I can see the balcony that

soars out over the crowd. It seems so high up that I wonder if it's hidden by clouds on less sunny days. Six men in regal black stand at alert on the balcony. They're too far away for me to see their eyes, of course, but just by the way they stand, I can tell that they're constantly scanning the crowd, looking for any possible danger at every moment. Behind them, at the window—or the door? Is a door still a door if it's entirely made of glass?—a figure dressed in palest yellow is stepping out into the sunshine. Maybe it's just because of the gauzy dress and veil she's wearing, but the figure seems unreal, like a spirit in a dream.

"It's the princess . . ."

"Princess Desmia . . ."

"Our beloved princess . . ."

The awed whispers flow through the crowd, as if everyone thinks that speaking out loud would break the spell and Desmia would vanish.

"She's so beautiful," a boy murmurs behind me.

"How can he tell?" I mutter to Harper. "Her whole face is covered with that veil!"

I expect him to join me in sarcasm—kind of like how we always join together to make fun of Herk the tailor and his cowbell concerts. But Harper just looks from Desmia to me and back again without saying a word.

Great. He's apparently fallen under Desmia's spell too.

What? Are you jealous? A little voice in my head taunts me.

I stare at the figure on the balcony as she raises one hand

and gracefully waves it back and forth. It's like watching a willow tree sway in a gentle breeze, the movement so delicate and dainty that it could be set to music. I could never wave like that. Hoisting buckets of water and stacks of firewood isn't very good practice for such tiny motions.

Thanks a lot, Nanny, I think bitterly. *You too, Sir Stephen— what were you thinking? Didn't you know I'd need to wave like that? Couldn't you have slipped in a few lessons in gracefulness along with the geometry?*

Desmia keeps waving. Her veil ruffles in the breeze, and even that doesn't break her concentration or the precise motion of her hand. She's like a perfect china doll.

Really, I think, *I wouldn't want to have to wave like that. Too careful. Too tedious. I'd rather carry water buckets. The people of Suala are just going to have to get used to a princess who waves her arm back and forth wildly. People like exuberance, too, don't they?*

Desmia leans out over the balcony, the bottom of her veil pinned against the railing.

"Blessings," she calls in a faint, bell-like voice. "Blessings upon my subjects."

The crowd cheers. They love their china-doll princess.

Maybe when I take up my rightful position, I'll have to hire Desmia to keep waving from the balcony every day. Just to keep the people happy. But will they still love her so much if she's not the princess? And would that endanger her? If the point of revealing my true identity is to keep Desmia safe, would it be fair to expect her to keep appearing before the public?

And . . . if Desmia's their idea of a princess, will they ever love me?

I'm so dizzy with questions and doubts that I almost miss Desmia's exit. She's backing away from the railing now, gliding back through the glass door. The six guards peer out suspiciously at the crowd for another few moments; then they, too, retreat out of sight. The balcony hovers high above us, completely empty.

Many of the people in the crowd around us let out great sighs—maybe they've been holding their breath ever since their first glimpse of Desmia, and they just now remembered that they need to breathe. Or maybe they're sighing with disappointment because she's gone. Or maybe they're still so filled with awe and disbelief at what they saw that they have to express it somehow. Maybe they'll be sighing for hours—no, years. Decades from now they'll be telling their grandchildren, "And once I went to Cortona and stood in the courtyard by the palace and saw Princess Desmia on her balcony. . . ."

"Cecilia?" Harper whispers. "What do you want to do now?"

Slowly I turn and focus my eyes on my friend. The crowd is thinning out around us now, and people are giving us a wide berth because we look so ragged—and probably because of how we smell, now that I think about it. But to me the sight of Harper's dirty, freckled face is a comfort. Just looking at him shores up my resolve and banishes some of the more unpleasant questions hanging around my mind.

"We need to gather information, remember?" I tell him.

"Well, yeah, but—"

"Come on," I say.

I'm tempted to grab his hand again—just to pull him along, for no other reason, really—but I chicken out. Instead I beckon him forward, toward the palace. The closer we get to it, the more it seems to soar overhead. I think it really must be as tall as the tallest mountain in the kingdom, Mount Valerian, and that's more than fourteen thousand feet high.

The huge doorway leading to the palace is surrounded by double rows of guards. I go and stand directly in front of the nearest guard.

"Excuse me, sir," I say. I clear my throat and try to forget that I'm barefoot, ragged, and filthy. I'll be wearing royal finery soon enough. "What must one do if one wishes to arrange a private audience with the princess?"

He looks down at me. The sides of his moustache begin to twitch.

"By 'one,' you mean yourself?" he asks. "It's you who's wanting an audience with the princess?"

"Yes," I say, making myself stare straight back into his eyes, even though it's really hard to do that, the way he's looking at me.

"Then"—he begins laughing—"there ain't nothing you

can do, because the princess ain't never going to have anything
to do with the likes of you!" His laughter bubbles over, and
spreads, and soon the guards beside him are laughing too.

"Imagine, a beggar thinking she can meet with the
princess!" one whispers to each other.

"Hey, girly!" another one calls. "The princess expects her
visitors to wear shoes!"

I'm thinking that as soon as I reveal my true identity, my
very first official act should be firing these guards.

"Let's go," Harper says, tugging on my arm.

But the guards aren't done making fun of us.

"Hey!" one hollers after us. "If you can play that harp—if
you didn't just steal it—maybe you can get to see the princess
by entering the palace music competition. She's one of the
judges!"

This makes some of the other guards double over with
laughter.

"Imagine! Beggars in the royal music competition!" They
chortle.

"I'll have you know—," I begin.

"Er—thanks for the advice," Harper interrupts. He jerks
on my arm so hard that I'm sure it's dislocated this time. Or
maybe not, because the rest of my body seems to realize that
it has to follow along. He jerks me completely off my feet and
all but drags me away, my shameful bare feet scraping along
the flagstones.

"Stop it!" I hiss. "I can walk on my own!"

"Fine," he says, letting go so quickly that I fall to the ground.

I glare at him and toss my head, because the guards are still watching, laughing so hard they're practically rolling on the ground as well. We're like a comedy show to them, maybe a Punch and Judy routine. With as much dignity as I can muster I stand up, turn around, and walk away. I don't even check to make sure that Harper's following me until we're outside the city walls once more.

"Wait!" he calls. "Where are you going?"

I don't answer. I veer off the road and climb a small rise in the shadow of the walls. Away from the crowd I sink down onto the bare ground. I want to curl up into a little ball and sob my eyes out, but I'm still trying to hold onto a little bit of dignity.

Harper sits down beside me.

"The ragamuffin look is a horrible disguise," he says. "You were right—we should have at least washed our faces."

I shrug.

"At the moment it's all we have," I say, trying my best to keep the humiliation out of my voice.

I tell myself that I shouldn't care about the guards making fun of my bare feet and rags, because that's not who I am. It's only a disguise, and soon everyone in the kingdom will know that I'm the true princess. I'll wear gauzy dresses like Desmia. I'll stand on that balcony, and people will cheer for me even louder than they cheered for her. And when my enemies are vanquished, then I'll come down from the balcony and walk directly through the crowd, shaking hands and patting heads and kissing babies. And if I see anyone in ragged clothes and bare feet—even someone filthier and more ragged than Harper and me—then I will be especially kind to that person. I will invite all the beggars into the palace, and I will feed them the most exquisite foods in the royal larder. I will give them shoes. I will . . .

"What are we going to do now?" Harper asks, as if to remind me that there's the slight matter of revealing my identity before I can take up my role as Lady Largesse.

I peer off into the distance, toward the hordes of people streaming in and out of the city gate.

"I still think Desmia's the first person I should tell," I say. "She's the only one I'm sure I can trust." I think about all the lessons Sir Stephen has given me in the art of negotiation and compromise. *You have to think about what other people truly want. You have to listen to what they're not saying. You have to make them think you care about their interests as much as your own. . . .* In this instance that last part shouldn't be hard, because all I'm trying to do is help Desmia. I don't know anything about her advisers and courtiers and guards; I don't know whose side they're on. But I know Desmia will be very happy to see me, if I can ever get close enough to her to talk.

I tilt my head back. From this vantage point I can see the very peak of the turret that rises above the balcony where Desmia stood. Maybe if Harper and I got a very, very long rope, and managed to fling one end of it up on the balcony in the middle of the night, and then . . .

I dismiss this possibility as completely insane.

"There's got to be some way to get in to see her," I say.

"The guards had a suggestion," Harper says sulkily. He's tugging at the blades of grass at his feet; he pulls so hard that an entire tuft comes up in his hand, scattering clumps of dirt onto his harp.

He doesn't bother brushing it away.

"You mean the music competition?" I ask. "That only gets you in, not me. And Harper, if you hate it so much, I can't ask you to do that."

Harper shakes his head.

"Do you believe in fate?" he asks. "Do you think that God made each of us for a certain purpose, and no matter what *we* want, we have to do it? Even if we try to run away, even if we try to make some other choice, he shoves us back onto the path he wants for us?"

"I don't know," I say, because I really haven't thought much about fate before. None of the books Sir Stephen gave me were titled *A Royal's Guide to Fate*. I always kind of thought being royal meant I'd get to make lots of choices. Once I came out of hiding, anyway.

"I mean, look at us," Harper rants. "You're the true princess, I'm the harp player—and there's no way we can be anything else, we have to fulfill our destinies." He kicks at the wooden frame of his harp. "I might as well have this thing nailed to my hands!"

"It'd be kind of hard to play, then," I tease. He doesn't laugh. I sigh. "Look, Harper, once I'm on my throne, I'll pass a royal decree that says you never have to play the harp again. I'll make you, I don't know, Lord High Chancellor of Fishing Ponds. You can spend the rest of your life fishing. Or whatever else you want."

Harper snorts, and stands up. He picks up his harp and begins striding down the hill.

"Where are you going?" I ask.

"I'm going to play on the street corners in Cortona and hope there are enough fools willing to toss me enough coins so we can buy shoes," he says. "And then I'm going to sign up for the music competition. The Amazing Harper and Cecilia—the one and only two-person harp-playing team!"

12

I follow Harper back into the city. He finds one of the few corners not already occupied by soldiers, squats down, and settles his harp in his lap.

"Harper," I whisper, "do you want me to announce you or anything? I could say, I don't know, maybe, 'The amazing Harper—he looks like a beggar, but he plays like a prince!'"

"*No,*" Harper says, glaring at me. "Don't say anything!" He takes off his cap, tosses it to the ground in front of us. "For collecting money," he says awkwardly.

He launches into one of the lugubrious tunes I've heard many times coming from the Sutton cottage back home. I don't think there are any words to this song, but if there were, they'd be something like, *Dead, dead, just about everyone we love is dead; sorrow is everywhere, and all we can do is cry.*

People are edging away from Harper's corner. One cheerful-looking fellow with a jaunty feather in his hat crosses the street just before he comes to us, and I'm sure it's because of the music.

I tug on Harper's arm, causing him to drag his fingers across several strings at once. The harp gives out a waterfall of sound, a cheerful noise, like even the harp is glad to be done with that song of misery.

"Eels! What are you doing?" Harper hisses.

"Can't you play something peppier?" I ask. "That song makes people want to lie down in the gutter and die, not give you money."

Harper frowns at me.

"My mam says harps are made for slow, sonorous tunes," he says. "She says peppy pieces aren't . . . dignified enough for a harp."

Behind the dirt on his face he looks every bit as miserable as the music he was playing.

"Well, then—aren't there any *happy* slow songs?" I ask. "Can't you play, I don't know . . . a love song? Something to make people feel good?"

"A love song," Harper repeats numbly. He gapes at me. "You want me to play a love song?"

"Well, yeah," I say. "People like love songs. I know you're not in love with anyone or anything, but you could imagine what it's like and pretend, just while you're playing . . ."

"A love song," Harper says again, as if he's never heard of such a thing.

A young woman behind us squeals, and calls out to a

cluster of her friends looking into a millinery's window on the next block, "Ooh—Mabella, Liandra, Suzerina! Come away from those hats and listen! This one's going to play a love song!"

Harper narrows his eyes at me.

"Only if you leave," he says brusquely. "Go find out what shoes cost or something. I'm not playing a love song while you're standing here listening!"

"Fine," I say, glaring back. "I'll be back in three hours."

I haven't really been paying attention, so I'm not sure if the clock tower by the palace last chimed out one o'clock or two o'clock. But I'm not about to ask Harper which it was. Not now. I'll just have to listen closely for the next chiming.

I shove past three giggling women—Mabella, Liandra, and Suzerina, I suppose—already clustering around Harper before he plucks his first note. I don't understand why this bothers me. I don't understand why it suddenly seems like we were having a fight. Unaccountably, tears sting at my eyes, and I brush them away.

Well, thanks a lot for your concern, Mr. Harper Sutton, I think. *I guess you don't think it matters if I go wandering around all by myself, where anybody could attack me. You really don't think I'm anybody important, do you? Even if you don't care about me at all, don't you care for your kingdom? What part of "true princess" don't you understand?*

Angrily, I stomp off down the street. I'm not sure how many blocks I walk before I remember to look for a cobbler's shop. The signs in this area are written in such fancy script that I have to squint to figure out the words hidden in the curlicues. I resort to simply looking in the shop windows. Here are flowers in one window, then dresses, then men's coats, then more dresses, then—aha!—shoes.

I push my way into the shop past a heavy wooden door.

"Yes?" a tidy young man says, as soon as I'm in the shop. "How might I help you?"

He's wearing a linen coat and pants, along with a white shirt so perfectly clean that it must be the first time he's ever worn it. His hair is neatly tied back with a black ribbon, and he's got shiny brass buckles on his shoes. Looking at him I remember every burr tangled in my hair, every patch on my skirt, every clump of dirt on my ankles. I bend my knees, so at least my skirt will cover my bare feet and dirty ankles. My fingers brush the nearest pair of shoes.

"How much do these cost?" I ask.

"Shoes in that style?" he asks. "Fifty gold coins."

I gasp. Maybe I don't have enough confidence in Harper, but I can't imagine that he'll be able to play any love song well enough to earn a hundred gold coins.

"And we have a backlog of requests, so any new orders will take at least three months," he adds. "We're starting to take orders for the winter season right now."

I gasp again. Winter is months and months away.

"Do you know of any shop that's cheaper and faster?" I ask weakly.

I force myself to look up, and I see that this young man has a kind look in his eye. He glances around, as if to make sure no one else is listening, then leans in close and whispers, "Try the poor section of the city. You might be able to find some secondhand shoes that you could walk home in."

I blush, because I didn't know that the city has a rich section and a poor section. (Back home in my village, there's only one section—I guess because everyone's poor there. We don't even have a cobbler.) And I'm embarrassed that, despite my efforts to hide my bare feet, this man has very clearly seen that I need shoes now, that I can't wait another day, let alone months. He probably even noticed exactly how many burrs I have in my hair.

"Th-thank you," I say.

"Five blocks that way, and then turn right," the man says with a wink.

I turn and flee, out the door, down the street, as fast as I can go. The blush spreads across my whole face, much faster than I am running. *How is it,* I wonder, *that he made me feel worse than when the palace guards made fun of me? That man was being nice!* I rethink my plan to give away shoes and feasts when I'm properly on my throne. *I'll need to do something more subtle than charity, something that doesn't make people feel bad for being poor. . . .*

Around me the streets are getting narrower; the windows in the shops are smaller and dirtier. The curlicues and fancy script have disappeared from all the signs; instead of CHARLES J.

STEWART, ESQUIRE, CLOTHIER, these signs are more likely to read BREAD HERE, or CANDLES, POTS, or even the highly descriptive JUNK. Then, a little farther along, the signs don't contain any words, just vaguely scrawled pictures. I stop in front of one of the picture signs, trying to figure out if it's a shoe or a boat. A ragged boy behind me pokes me in the ribs.

"Don't you be thinking about stealing from *him*," he whispers. "That one's a fast runner, and he'll catch you, sure."

"I wasn't thinking about stealing," I say indignantly. "I wouldn't do that!"

My words ring out too loudly in the filthy street. Up and down the block people seem to freeze for a moment: slatterns in doorways, drunkards sitting on the curb, idlers leaned against walls. Then it's as if they've all decided to ignore me, to leave me to my own fate, and they go back to their own slumping, sagging, and despairing. Even the ragged boy shrugs.

"Your loss," he says.

I shiver, and then, to prove I'm not afraid, I push open the door of the shoe—or boat—shop. Even inside I'm at first not sure what it's selling. A row of dark, dingy lumps line a single glass display case.

"Are those shoes?" I ask, pressing my face against the glass.

"Five gold coins apiece," an old man says grumpily from behind the display case. "Take it or leave it."

My eyes are adjusting a bit to the dim shop. I can see well enough now to tell that the shoes are all in tatters. A few look like they were chewed by wild dogs, others like they've been vomited on and never cleaned. Wearing these shoes into the castle would be worse than going barefoot.

"You're kidding," I tell the man. "Five gold pieces for those? That's highway robbery!"

He shrugs, watching me with narrowed eyes.

"Cheapest prices in Cortona," he says. "Like I said, take it or leave it."

I open my mouth—ready to lecture him about taking advantage of poor people, I think. But before I can say anything, I hear screaming outside.

"No! Don't take me! Please!"

I rush to the door to look out. It's the ragged boy who warned me about stealing. He's struggling to free himself from three large, burly men.

"I'm a messenger!" the boy yells. "Without me, my mam and my sisters won't have any money! They'll starve! Don't—take—me—off—to—war!"

"They're taking him to the war?" I mutter. I start to push out the door, ready to scold the burly men. The ragged boy can't be more than eight or ten. He's not old enough to be a soldier. And if his mother and sisters would starve without him—

Suddenly I feel a hand clamp down on my shoulder with an iron grip.

"Stay out of it," the store owner growls. "It's none of your business."

"But if they're taking him off to war—that's not right! He should have a choice!"

I try to tear myself away, but he's holding onto me too tightly, his hands now gripping both of my arms. Outside the door the boy is kicking one of the burly men, but it's like a mouse fighting back against a hawk. The man simply wraps his huge hand around the boy's ankles, and the three of them carry the boy around the corner.

The store owner lets go of my arms.

"I don't know where you're from, girl, but people don't have choices in Cortona," he says bitterly. "They've had press gangs wandering the streets for years—when they ran out of men to send off to war, they started taking the boys. When everyone's dead, maybe they'll stop then."

I was wrong about the words to that miserable song Harper was playing on the street corner. What the store owner just said—those would be the perfect words to that awful song.

Harper . . .

"They take . . . boys just . . . out on their own?" I say in a shaky voice. "Any boy on the street . . . alone?"

"Aye," the man says, shrugging. "They take whoever they want."

Instantly, I shove my shoulder against the door. I fly out of that shop, my feet barely touching the pavement. Everything passes in a blur. The streets broaden, words begin appearing on signs, then curlicues and fancy loops. *It'd be a left turn this time, five blocks back to the fancy cobbler's shop and then—how far to Harper's corner?* I barrel through the crowded streets, ramming into solid, well-fed bodies and women in lovely, frilly dresses, and I don't even stop to apologize. I don't look at any face long enough to focus my eyes; I'm just looking for freckles and dirt. And listening—I'm straining my ears to hear the first strains of harp music, off in the distance.

Nothing.

Maybe Harper's just between songs, taking a break to collect all the gold coins people want to pay him. . . .

I pass a shop window filled with hats, and something tickles my memory. *Ooh—Mabella, Liandra, Suzerina! Come away from those hats and listen! This one's going to play a love song!* This is the millinery shop the three women were looking at when their friend called to them. So Harper will be on the very next corner. He will. He will. He—

Isn't.

Harper is nowhere in sight.

13

"Harper!" I scream, as if my voice has the power to conjure up people from thin air. I wish being the true princess meant having that power. I glance around frantically, because maybe Harper switched corners; maybe he thought he'd make more money on the other side of the street. The other corners are crowded with scurrying strangers. No matter how much I crane my neck or duck down low, I can't catch any glimpse of a familiar freckled face or a carved wooden harp.

"Oh, Harper," I moan. My thoughts come in disjointed, panicky bursts. *Got to get to Desmia NOW. . . . Stop the press gang that must have taken Harper. . . . As the true princess I ought to be able to do that, right? . . . Got to stop them before Harper gets to the battlefield. . . .*

I step out into the street, thinking that might help me see. I gaze far down the block. Maybe whoever took Harper isn't far away; maybe if I can catch them I can just tell them that

I'm the true princess and they're not allowed to carry Harper off to war—I forbid it!

Strong hands grab at me, jerking me back from the street. A flash of black mane whips past my eyes.

"What are you doing?" someone yells. "Didn't you see that horse about to trample you?"

I turn around and focus my eyes on freckles and splotches of dirt and messy, sand-colored hair. It's Harper. I throw my arms around his shoulders and hug him close.

"I thought they'd taken you away—I thought you were gone forever—I thought I'd never find you again . . . ," I babble.

Harper pulls back a little, holding me far enough away that he can see my face. I think he's trying to tell if I've gone totally crazy.

"You really are an idiot," he says, but there's a trace of fondness in his voice that makes it seem like it's not an insult. "You said you'd be back in three hours, and it's barely been two."

I'm a little embarrassed. Three hours? Two? I'd completely forgotten about listening for the clocks and keeping track of time.

"But you were sitting right there playing music," I say. "You didn't tell me you were going anywhere else."

Harper lets go of me. He looks down, kicks at the harp he's holding at his side.

"I wasn't making much money," he says. "So I thought I'd just go sign us up for the competition before you got back.

And then I found out why I wasn't making any money. There are musicians all over the place. All of them playing better than me." He sighs. "I'm a failure at my own fate."

"No, no—I bet it's just a matter of economics," I say comfortingly. "The laws of supply and demand. Because of the music competition, there are probably hundreds of musicians in Cortona, all of them trying to get some last-minute practice. The city's full of music, so nobody wants to pay for it."

Harper shrugs.

"How much money did you make?" I ask.

Harper reaches into his pocket, pulls out a meager collection of coins.

"Pennies," he says.

I don't even bother to count the coins—it's clearly not enough to buy so much as a fraction of a secondhand shoe that's been covered in vomit and chewed by wild dogs.

"Guess I better start playing again," Harper says hopelessly, as he drops the coins back into his pocket. "We got one of the last open slots in the competition. The only times left were at the very beginning or at the very end, weeks away, so . . . we play first thing tomorrow morning."

My heart gives a little jump at this news. If we're in the competition tomorrow, then I'll get to talk to Desmia tomorrow—my true fate, my real life, is only a day away. Everything I've been reading about and studying for and daydreaming over is about to begin.

Then I remember what made me rush to this corner so frantically.

"Harper—it's not safe for you to be out here on the streets," I say. "There are these people who wander around grabbing men and boys and carrying them off to war." I think about how the ragged boy was carried away, and how the well-dressed man in the cobbler's shop didn't seem to be at any risk. "They take away poor men and boys," I add.

"Yeah, I know," Harper says sulkily. "They're called press gangs."

I stare at him in shock.

"You know about the press gangs?"

"The messengers from Cortona, the ones who come out to our village to tell us who's died in the war—they told me about the press gangs." Harper smiles, a little grimly. "At first I thought they were talking about people who roam around carrying flatirons, but it's 'press' because they 'impress' people into the war."

I'm a little stunned that Harper knew something about the kingdom that I, the true princess, was totally ignorant of. Then something else strikes me.

"But, Harper—you knew this, and you—you were still willing to come to Cortona with me? And to sit out here alone, playing music, when at any moment some press gang could—"

"What? You think if you'd been sitting here with me while I was playing love songs, you could have protected me from a press gang? You—big, bad Cecilia?"

The words are teasing, but there's a darker tone in his voice. And I *had* thought that. Almost. It wasn't that I was big, bad Cecilia, but that I was the true princess, and a simple word from me should be able to stop any press gang.

If they believed me.

I'm still gasping at the risks Harper has taken—is taking—for me, without me even knowing it. Harper's sitting down, pulling his harp onto his lap again, resignedly positioning his fingers on the strings.

"Harper, *no*," I say, tugging on his arm, as if I'm strong enough to pick him up. "You can't stay here. We've got to get you out of the city. Just in case a press gang shows up—"

"Cecilia, I *want* to be a soldier, remember?" he says brusquely.

Staring into his eyes I think, *He's lying.* And it's so weird to think that, because Harper's been saying he wants to be a soldier for years, for as long as I can remember. I've always believed him before. Why should I doubt him now?

It's different now. This time he's lying. I am so sure of myself. I just don't understand what's changed.

"It's not like I'm royalty or anything," Harper adds, still in that harsh, unfamiliar voice. "It doesn't matter what happens to me."

I want to say, *Of course it does,* or *Don't you know that you matter to* me? But couldn't he tell that from the way I flung myself at him just a few moments ago?

I don't know how I can feel so sure of myself and so

confused, all at the same time. I draw in a shaky breath.

"If you want to go off and join up and fight in the war tomorrow afternoon or——or the next day . . . if that's what you really want, then that's your choice," I say. I have to struggle to keep my voice steady, because I really don't want Harper to *ever* go off to the war. "It's just, right now——"

"I know, I know. Right now you need me," Harper says, and now he sounds angry. "You need me to earn money for shoes, and you need me to teach you how to play a harp in one evening, and you need me to get you into the competition tomorrow, and——"

"Harper, it's not like that," I say pleadingly.

He just looks at me, and everything in his face says, *Yes, it is. Today you need me. But tomorrow afternoon or the day after tomorrow you'll be a princess in your palace, and you can throw me out in the weeds like all the other peasants. I bet by next week you won't even remember my name.* I stare back at him, and I hope everything in my face says, *Okay, you're half right—— today I need you for very practical things. But I'm still going to need you tomorrow and the day after that and long, long after that, because you're my best friend and always have been and always will be, and Harper, I am terrified of going into that palace. You're the only one who's giving me the courage to do the right thing, so you have to stay with me, you have to help me . . . please don't go off to war. Even if I didn't need you, I wouldn't want you to go off and die in the war.* But I just can't open my mouth and say any of that, because if I do, I'll be throwing myself at him again and blubbering like a little baby.

Between all this looking at each other and trying to say everything with our faces and not moving at all, we're creating a bit of a roadblock. People keep ramming into me. At first I think it's all by accident, but then I hear a woman say, "Beggars should know to get out of the way of their betters!" and then—clearly on purpose—she brings down the heel of her shoe right on my bare foot.

"Ow! Oh!" I start jumping up and down, making more of a scene and—coincidentally—making it even harder for her to get past me.

"Do you *mind*?" she says, in a voice that could turn boiling water to solid ice in an instant. I let her pass, but not before I've gotten a really, really good look at her. Whoever she is, if she ever shows up at the palace, I'm going to have the guards escort her out the door immediately.

"Anyhow," Harper says.

Now it's completely impossible to say any of those things I was thinking. So instead, I say "Harper, you could sit here playing music for the next ten years, and we still wouldn't have enough money for shoes."

Something in his face shuts down, shuts me out.

"Oh," he says. "Then . . . we can't go to the competition."

"Of course we can," I snap. "We'll just have to make our own shoes." I think about the thick cloak I wore from our village. "Do you think we could start a new fashion—shoes made out of felt? That way we just need to buy a needle and thread. And *I'll* do the buying. You can go hide somewhere safe."

I expect Harper to argue with me, but he just shrugs and stands up.

"Whatever you say."

He stands there looking at me for a moment longer then he needs to. For a split second his expression seems transparent again; I could swear I can see him thinking, *I wish* . . .

And then he turns away from me, hiding his face.

"I'll be outside the city," he says. "Where we were before."

"All right," I say. "I'll meet you there as soon as I can."

"Good," he says, and he sounds like the old Harper now, the one who always makes fun of me. "Because you have one night to learn fourteen years' worth of harp lessons."

14

I don't sleep much that night. First there are the harp lessons, and then I sit up late sewing, pushing the cheapest, flimsiest needle in all of Cortona through the thick felt of my former cloak. After the sun goes down, I do this in the dark, so it's hard to know what the "shoes" are going to look like. And I prick my fingers so many times that I'm sure it will be pure agony touching the harp strings in the morning.

You knew this wasn't going to be the easiest way to get to your throne, I tell myself to keep from crying with each stitch. Finally, the shoes are done, and I can lay my head down on the remains of my cloak, stretched out on the ground. But I don't fall asleep right away, like I expect to. We are hiding outside the city, on the other side of a hillock from the city walls. Here the ground is hard and lumpy, and every time I shift position, I discover a new pebble lying beneath my spine.

Really, it's not much worse than most of the places I've

slept the past several nights—and it's not like I was used to
pure luxury at Nanny Gratine's, anyhow. But these pebbles
plague me, each one a reminder of some unpleasant thought.

*Sure, tomorrow I'll be sleeping on a princess's bed instead . . . but
how hard will the rest of my life be, as princess? What kind of
danger will I be in? Will I be able to tell who's on my side and
who's an enemy? Will I be able to trust anyone besides Harper
and then Sir Stephen and Nanny when they come? Will Harper
even stay around, or will he run off and join the army right
away?*

I reach out in the darkness, and my hand brushes Harper's.
Because he's asleep, it's safe to do this: I wrap my fingers
around his palm. Harper fell asleep while I was still sewing,
and I was too exhausted to remember the soldiers-guarding-
each-other T-shaped formation. So he's right there beside me.
And this is how I feel safe, lying here clutching his hand.

The next thing I know, it's morning. The sun is rising over
the city spires, and Harper is leaning over me.

"Cecilia, it's time," he whispers in my ear. "The music
competition—our performance—"

I sit up so quickly I almost clunk my head against Harper's.

"We have to wash our faces," I say. "We have to get
ready. . ."

We rush to a nearby stream. The water on my face wakes
me up, sharpens my mind. I want to ask, *Uh, Harper, when
you woke up, was I holding your hand?* But I don't know what I
would say after that, how I would explain it away. I stick to

the basics: "Harper, wait, you missed a spot of dirt up by your eye. . . . I know we don't have a comb, but maybe if you wet your hair down, you can pat it into place. . . ."

Finally, we're done. When we get back to our hillock, Harper retrieves our food sack from the bush where he hid it while we were washing. I grandly wave him away when he offers me the first chance at it.

"Oh, no, none of that. We'll be feasting at the palace right after we play," I say. "Might as well keep our appetite for all those delicacies."

"You think Desmia will give us a feast?" Harper asks.

"*I* shall order it," I say. Then I giggle, because it's still funny to think about, getting to order people around.

Harper looks down into the sack.

"Mam says it's not good to play on an empty stomach," he says sheepishly, and reaches in to pull out a fig that's only slightly moldy.

I don't tell him that I'm too nervous to eat anything. Even if we had tables before us spread with the finest food in the kingdom—pastries, breads, meats, cheeses, fruits—I'm not sure I could eat a bite.

When Harper's done eating, we walk into the city and back to the courtyard where the guards ridiculed us yesterday. Only a few men stand by the palace doorway now—I guess they're saving most of their troops for later in the day.

"Let me do the talking," Harper mutters as we approach the palace.

I try to stretch up tall, to stand regal and proud before the guards. Harper bows low.

"Esteemed sirs," he says, speaking directly to the cobblestones, as if he's too humble to raise his head. "We are here for the music competition. Harper and Cecilia Sutton. We should be on your list."

The most decorated guard ruffles through papers. His face twitches, as if he's trying hard not to laugh.

"Aye, you're on the list," he says. "Go on in."

He steps aside to let us pass. Harper shoves at the heavy door, and I can hear the head guard explaining to the others, "They always put the worst acts on first, so nobody has to hear them."

"Or see them," somebody else mutters.

My cheeks flame red, and it's all I can do to resist whirling around and scolding, *Just wait until you find out who I really am! You'll be sorry!* To distract myself, I mutter to Harper, "Cecilia Sutton?"

"I didn't think I should use your real name," he mutters back. "You're the one who said we could pretend to be brother and sister. Remember? Back in the cowshed?"

I don't reply, because we're stepping into a grand entranceway now, a huge hallway that towers over us like a cathedral. And practically from the floor level up to that ceiling, which hovers over us like clouds, there are mirrors on every wall—the mirrors that give the palace its name.

My acquaintance with mirrors has been very limited. Our

village store sometimes had looking glasses for sale, and when the storekeeper, Mr. Leaven, wasn't looking, it was possible to crouch down by the shelf holding the glasses and gaze at a tiny portion of my face: one greenish eye at a time, or my lips and just the tip of my nose. For a wider view there was only the pond, which always made me look vague and wavy. (But at least not jowly, like my ancestors.)

So it is incredibly jarring to suddenly see myself and Harper, as we really are, complete and clear, life-size and reflected from every angle. Everywhere I look, I see myself.

It is not a pretty picture.

Oh, my features are all right—I rush to assure myself of that. My nose is straight enough, my eyes are big enough, my chin dips just enough that a generous person might call my face heart-shaped. (And really, when I am on the throne, will not everyone want to be generous in their descriptions of me?) Give me a velvet ribbon to tie back my unruly brown hair, and from the neck up I might even be called pretty.

But I do not have a velvet ribbon for my hair. I don't even have an old, frazzled piece of twine, so my hair hangs down into my face, curls leapfrogging over one another to mar the heart shape.

My eyes travel down from my reflected face, and this is where it really gets embarrassing. Last night Harper and I tried to scrub out the worst of the stained, dirty spots from our clothes. Laundry is difficult enough under the best of circumstances, and trying to wash clothes while wearing

them hardly qualifies as the best of circumstances. I think
we gave up much too quickly, our eyes deceived in the dim
evening light. In this bright, mirrored room, I can see that
our scrubbings only spread the stains. My simple cotton shift
is covered in grass stains and ground-in dirt and dried fig
juice—and those are just the stains I can identify.

Yesterday afternoon, in a fit of what I thought was inspiration,
I used our last pennies to buy two small lengths of sash from
a peddler on the street. They're bright yellow—I suppose I
was thinking of Desmia's paler yellow dress. I thought sashes
would transform my plain dress and Harper's ordinary shirt and
breeches into clothing fit for a palace. His clothes, I thought,
would look like a courtier's; mine like a royal ball gown.

We look ridiculous. I could only afford enough sash to
wrap around our waists, not enough to tie and leave the ends
dangling elegantly. So I had to sew the ends of the sashes
onto the back of my dress and the back of Harper's shirt.
Somehow the splash of color around our waists emphasizes
all the wrong details: the stains, the patches, the unraveling
beginnings of holes, the bunchy clumps of felt on our feet
that I thought would pass as shoes.

"You can't make a silk purse out of a sow's ear," I mutter
to Harper—one of those common sayings in our village that
I never fully understood before.

We're sow's ears, both of us.

Harper looks jolted, and glances at our reflection for
possibly the first time.

"You're the true princess," he whispers back to me.

And that helps. Clothes are only clothes. Sashes and shoes—even badly pinned, poorly sewn, ill-chosen ones— are meaningless compared with the knowledge in my head, the truth I'm about to reveal. I stop hunching over, stop attempting to hide my stained dress.

An infinity of mirrored images keeps flashing at us as we walk the length of the hall, but I train my eyes on the door at the other end. A man is standing there.

"Ye-es?" he says imperiously as we approach.

"We're the first, uh, competitors," Harper says.

The man nods condescendingly.

"Ah," he says. "Wait here."

It's a long wait. I fiddle with the edge of my sash, wanting to tuck it differently, or maybe just rip it off completely. And the shoes! I shall have to tell Desmia that felt shoes were simply the fashion in my village. . . . Maybe Desmia and I have the same size feet, and she'll loan me a pair of real shoes before we go to tell anyone else who I really am. Maybe she'll loan me a dress, too.

"Cecilia?" Harper mumbles. "Remember, you play five C's before the first time you move to the D string. . . ."

I nod, but a moment later I can't remember if he said five C's or four. We worked out a simple song, where he plays the melody and I pluck a string every so often in harmony. I couldn't master true harp-playing, the way he does it— flicking his fingernails against the strings, bringing out a clear bell-like sound—so my technique is more of a strumming.

It doesn't matter, I tell myself. *You only have to play well enough that no one kicks you and Harper out before you have a chance to talk to Desmia.*

"Ready?" the man says.

I guess he went through the doorway and just now came back out—I wasn't paying close enough attention. Now he holds the door open for us.

"You will walk to the center of the stage," he says. "There's a chair if you must use it." He frowns, not in apology for having only one chair, but as if he already regrets offering it to us. "When you are finished, you will bow or"—he looks at me disdainfully—"you will curtsy in front of the judges. And then you will leave through the opposite door." He sniffs. "Good luck," he adds, as though he's certain we will need it.

I sniff back, and toss my head.

"Thank you, good sir," I say, trying to sound every bit as imperious as him.

Then the door shuts behind us. We're in an even larger room now, one that's mercifully a bit dimmer. And as far as I can tell, there are mirrors on only two of the four walls.

"There are stairs up to the stage," Harper hisses at me. "Follow me."

So far my eyes haven't focused well enough to locate Desmia or the other judges. Only when we're standing on the stage, peering out at rows and rows of cushioned, empty seats, do I realize that the judges are seated off to the left, near the door we'll be leaving through.

So I can talk to Desmia on the way out....

"I'll have to take the chair, since I'll be holding the harp," Harper whispers to me.

"Fine," I say.

I stand beside him, and we have a few moments of confusion, figuring out how my arms can stretch around the harp he's holding. I hear someone laughing, and someone else muttering, "This one is billed as a musical act, not a comedy routine. . . ."

Lamps flare to life, and I am blinded glaring out at the judges.

Harper has to arrange my hands, so I'm ready to pluck the right strings.

"Harper and Cecilia Sutton," someone announces.

I lean forward, prepared to play, and I feel something pulling at the back of my dress. In the silence, I even hear the first sound: *ri-ip* . . . I want to clutch the back of my dress, but that would mean taking my carefully placed hands off the harp.

"Now," Harper whispers.

Dazedly, I pluck my first C, thinking, *How much ripped back there? Was it just the sash or a huge swath of the dress?* I'm supposed to wait for Harper to play ten more notes before it's time for me to pluck my second C, but I'm so distracted, trying to listen for another *ri-ip* and watching for the sash to maybe go swinging down toward the floor, that Harper barely makes it through two notes before I pluck my harmony note again.

"Slow down!" Harper hisses at me.

"Speed up!" I hiss back. "My dress just ripped and I'm scared it's going to fall off completely!"

Harper gives me one darting, startled glance and instantly shifts into double time. From there the rest of the song is like a race, Harper flicking frantically at the strings, desperate to catch up with my plucking. Flick, pluck, flick, pluck . . . Finally, I'm done with all the notes that my right hand is supposed to play and I reach around and clutch the back of my dress.

"We can slow down now," I tell Harper, but I don't think he hears me. So then it's me plucking frantically, trying to keep up with him.

Finally, we run out of notes.

Harp music lingers. A properly appreciative crowd, I think, is supposed to wait until the last chiming note fades out of hearing. Our last notes fade into nothingness, and still there's a shocked silence. I squint, trying to see past the bright lights trained on the stage. Harper, beside me, is dipping into a bow.

"You're supposed to bow in front of the judges, right before the door," I whisper.

Jolted, he stands up again. Still there's no applause. We scramble down the stairs and stumble toward the judges. Now I can see that they're staring at us—in awe and amazement,

I hope, not complete disgust. The judges are a collection of distinguished-looking men in dark coats, and one girl in a pale pink dress, with a glistening crown nestled in her dark hair.

Desmia.

Forgetting the music—fiasco or phenomenon, whichever it was—I weave my way toward her. This is my lucky day: She's sitting in the front row. Still clutching the back of my dress, I lower myself into a curtsy. Rising, I scoot forward, so that my face comes up only inches from her right ear.

"I am the true princess," I whisper. "I have come to relieve you of your dangerous duty."

Desmia squints at me for a moment, and at first I think that I have spoken too fast; she seems not to have understood a single word I've said. But then her eyes widen, her rosebud mouth forms into an *O* of surprise.

"Meet me in the antechamber," she whispers back. "I'll be there as soon as I can."

I nod, and then I feel Harper's hand on my back. Bless him—he's clutching the ripped part of my dress together for me, under the pretense of chivalrously guiding me out of the room.

We step through a lavishly padded door into another hallway that's just as mirror-filled as the first one. This hallway has pillars as well, so every other step blocks out my view of the mirrors. It's funny to see how our faces change between steps: At first we both just look stunned, as if we're surprised we've escaped the music competition alive. Harper has sweat dripping off his brow, and his hair is sticking out in all directions. By the next glimpse we both have huge grins on our faces, relief making us giddy. And then, two steps on, anxiety and anticipation have taken over our expressions again. I'm thinking about how Desmia will be coming out to meet us, and what I should say and do then.

I don't know what Harper could possibly be thinking, to look so grim.

"It worked!" I whisper to him. "I told her!"

"Good," he replies in a clipped voice.

"She's meeting us in this hall, I guess," I say. Surely that was what she meant by "antechamber," wasn't it? I crane my neck, looking around, as if I expect to see a huge sign someplace labeling the room. This motion pulls at the back of my dress, and I feel a few more stitches give way.

"Uh, Harper?" I say. "How bad is it back there?" Now I'm trying to look over my shoulder, but I can't see the rip.

Harper bends down, his hands hesitantly touching my waist.

"I think if I just pull off the sash . . . ," he says, and I feel another tearing behind me. He stands to face me, and holds up the mangled, fraying remains of the yellow ribbon I'd been so proud of. "There. You've still got a rip in the dress, but it's not that big. At least now it's not going to get any worse."

"Thanks," I say. "That's a relief."

Harper stuffs the ruined sash in his pocket.

"It doesn't matter," he says roughly. "Soon you'll be

getting a new dress. All the dresses you want. New dresses, new home, new life . . ."

"Sure," I say, and smile at him. But he's looking past me, over my shoulder.

I turn around, and Desmia is right there.

15

Desmia is stepping through the same door from the theater that we used. Her cheeks are flushed just as rosy pink as her dress—*she's excited*, I think. *Thrilled that I've come to rescue her.* Her dark eyes are still wide and startled-looking—*of course. She never expected me to just show up like this.* Even though she's rushing toward us, her skirt sways with a graceful elegance that I could never emulate. The dress worries me anyhow. It's silk, I think, and gleams as much as the mirrors around us, beauty beyond beauty. You'd have to be so careful, wearing a dress like that. Maybe you wouldn't even be able to breathe. *And I didn't do very well even with regular clothes. . . .* I sneak another glance in the mirror, at my ripped dress with its grass stains and dirt smears and fig juice spills. I don't look so ridiculous without the sash, but I still look like a ragamuffin. I look even worse in contrast to Desmia.

But I am the true princess, I remind myself.

"Desmia—," I begin.

"Shh," she shushes me, her finger to her lips. "We can't talk here."

A man I hadn't noticed before comes up behind us, and clears his throat in a way that makes me feel scolded.

"A-hem. Contestants should not be bothering the princess," he says.

The brass buttons on his coat are so large and polished to such a gloss that I can see our reflection in them—mine, Harper's, and beautiful Desmia's.

"You're dismissed, Fulston," Desmia says imperiously. "I shall see these competitors out myself."

"Yes, Your Highness," the man says. "As you wish, Your Majesty."

He bows low and backs away, and I nearly giggle, because that is exactly how servants act in *The Royal Guide to Palace Decorum*, Chapter 3: "It Takes a Village to Run a Palace." He all but fades into the shadows, opening and closing the door back into the theater so quickly and quietly that it's almost as if he was never there.

As soon as he's out of sight, Desmia beckons to us.

"This way," she says.

She slides around behind one of the pillars, gently touches the frame of one of the mirrors, and—amazing!—the mirror swings out like a door. Behind the mirror, stairs ascend into darkness.

"A secret passageway?" Harper whispers, in awe.

I'm awed too. But I'm also thinking that I should have

known about this. With everything else Sir Stephen had me memorize, why didn't he have me study a map of the palace? Knowing about secret passageways in my own home seems a lot more useful to me than knowing the exports of countries three mountain ranges away.

"Where does . . ." Harper starts to ask, but Desmia has her finger pressed against her lips again, silencing him. She gazes anxiously from side to side, then removes a lamp from its ornate holder between the mirrors.

"You can't talk in here at all, understand?" she says. "People can hear everything from the rooms around the passageway, and they're not supposed to know it exists."

My head is bursting with questions. Like, *Why would the princess—or someone pretending to be the princess—have to skulk around in secret passageways in her own palace? Who is she hiding from? What "people" is she so worried about? What would happen if they did hear us?* But I bite my lip and follow her into the darkness.

Desmia moves swiftly up the stairs, and Harper and I have to rush to keep up with her, to keep up with the light. This isn't easy in clumsily sewn felt shoes, since the stone stairs are slippery and uneven. After a few steps and a near stumble I see Harper shrug and pull the shoes from his feet. "I'd make an awful noise, tripping," he whispers apologetically in my ear. "I'll put them back on as soon as we get to the top."

I decide his logic is sound, and so I do the same. I hope Desmia doesn't notice.

She glances back at us every few paces, but it doesn't seem like she's trying to make sure that we're keeping up. Now that we're in this dim, narrow stairway, I can't see her face, can't read her expression at all. But it's starting to feel like she's trying to run away from us. Like she's afraid of us.

I want to act graciously toward Desmia. I have the words of my old playacted ceremony from the cow pasture running through my head: *I, Princess Cecilia Aurora Serindia Marie, do hereby proclaim my gratitude to the commoner Desmia. . . . It is a fortunate ruler who has such loyal subjects. . . .* Dealing with Desmia will be my first deed as the newly revealed true princess; I want everything to go exactly right. But I can't help but feel annoyed that she's being so inconsiderate, keeping the light so far ahead, not even acting like she cares that we're falling behind.

Fine, be that way, I think. *I can run fast too.*

I speed up, paying less attention to the slapping of my bare feet against the stone steps. If I'm too loud, it's not my fault—it's hers. But then Desmia speeds up as well. By the time we finally reach a door that's dozens and dozens of steps above the ground floor, all three of us are panting. Desmia opens the door a crack and peeks cautiously out. Harper and I both try surreptitiously to cram our felt shoes back on our feet, but I've got the second one only halfway on when Desmia shoves the door all the way open, revealing a spacious, airy room, with an entire wall covered in a colorful tapestry, and imposing gilded furniture scattered at tasteful intervals. There's not a soul in sight, so I risk whispering, "Can we talk yet?"

Desmia shakes her head.

"Not until we're somewhere we're sure no one will hear us," she says.

She turns her back on us once more, her hair bouncing gracefully on her shoulders, and she leads us through a labyrinth of rooms. I see a huge, veiled bed just around one corner—off to the left, as we're turning to the right—and it occurs to me that these must be her bedchambers.

No, my *bedchambers,* I remind myself. My head feels woozy; my stomach's gone twitchy with nerves. Everything I've been reading about and dreaming about—it's real! *Take slow, regal breaths,* I think. Just off the top of my head I can remember six times in my country's history when a princess or even a queen toppled delicately into a swoon. But I don't think fainting would be the wisest course of action for me right now.

It would help if I could take slow, regal steps along with my slow, regal breaths, but Desmia is hurrying even faster now.

"Come," she calls back to us, and Harper, at least, races ahead.

We've reached another stone staircase now. This one isn't hidden, but it loops back upon itself so I can't see where it leads. No, wait, now I do—it spirals up into a tower.

"We can talk at the top," Desmia murmurs, from her position on a higher step.

I want a few moments to gawk. I've just come to the first window in the tower wall. Down below I can see the courtyard where Harper and I stood yesterday, watching Desmia. It's so early that only a few people scurry across the stones; from this distance they seem as remote as ants. Beyond the courtyard I can peer down on the roofs of the city and the graceful city walls, and then far out to the rolling hills of the countryside.

"Move along!" a harsh voice cries out. "Bawk!"

I jump so high in my astonishment that I'm lucky I don't fall out the window. I gaze around frantically for the source of the voice. It was so loud, right in my ear, but Harper and Desmia are now far above me, and anyhow neither of them has a voice like that—no one I've ever met has a voice like that. . . . Ah.

Right beside the window, in a little alcove I didn't notice before because I was too amazed by the scenery, there's a wire contraption. If I didn't know any better, I would say it was a sculpture, or maybe some odd, heretofore unknown plant: From a slim metal pole it rises from the floor and bursts, at eye level, into twists and turns of wire that flare out like petals and then all meet again at the top, high above my head.

It's a birdcage.

I know, because I've seen pictures in books. *Which king was it who was known as the Bird King because of his vast aviaries? Somebody the Fifth. Alphonse? No, maybe Aldons, the same one who—*

"Bawk! Move along!"

This time I don't jump, because I see the bird, finally.

I don't know how I missed it before. It's bright green and bright yellow and bright red, and swinging on a little stick on chains in the middle of the cage. Even though I've read about talking parrots, even though I saw the bird's beak move when I heard the words, this still seems too incredible to believe.

"Cecilia?" It's Harper, calling out to me from above. Worried.

"Coming," I call back softly. Then I dare to add, "Did you see the talking bird?"

"Three of them, so far," Harper says, and I can hear the grin in his voice.

I rush on up the stairs—twisting, turning—and he's right. There's one alcove after another, each one with a more elaborate birdcage containing a more brilliantly colored bird.

"Bawk! Watch it!" one cries.

"Bawk! Be careful!" calls another.

Every few steps there's a new bird. We've set them off— or their brothers and sisters' calls have set them off—because they're all squawking now. I can't make out individual words anymore; it's just one huge cacophony of screeching and shrieking and squealing.

Was *this* why Desmia thought nobody could hear us up here? Did she think to wonder about whether we'd be able to hear each other?

She's looking back at us, Harper and me. She's still a few steps ahead, almost around the bend in the spiral stairs.

"Hurry," she says.

At least that's what I think she says. I'm mostly just reading her lips.

We rush up around another few turns, and the squawks and screeches die down behind us. The stairway is narrowing; there's no more room for birdcages.

And then I turn a corner, and the floor is flat ahead of me—we've reached the end of the stairs. Through a wooden door I see a row of windows letting in glorious sunlight after the dimness of the past stretch of stairs.

"Desmia?" I say, because she seems to have disappeared.

"After you," she says. She's standing over by the edge of the door—an area that seems shadowed in contrast to the sunlit room beyond. She lifts her hand, gracefully indicating that Harper and I should step into the room first.

I think about this. Everything I've learned from Sir Stephen suddenly seems jumbled in my mind. What's the rule—does royalty always enter a room first? Or last? Is Desmia honoring me, acknowledging my true identity? Or has she forgotten that now she won't have to pretend anymore, claiming royal privileges she doesn't deserve?

Harper, not one to be plagued with etiquette questions, simply steps into the room. I glance at Desmia to see if she approves or disapproves—if, maybe, she would be annoyed that Harper's gone ahead of me, breaking the rules. But Desmia's face, in the shadows, is a mask I can't interpret.

I step into the room too. I want to race over to the window and peer out, to see how much farther away the ground seems, how much smaller the people look, now that we're at the top of the tower. But I remind myself of my royal role. I have duties and obligations now. This is what I was born to, what I was raised for, what I walked so far to do. I turn back toward Desmia, my old playacting words on my tongue, ready to be spoken for real: *I hereby proclaim my gratitude* . . .

Perhaps I should save those words until Desmia is kneeling before me?

Desmia is not kneeling. Desmia is not getting ready to kneel. Desmia is slamming the door behind us, turning a key in a lock, sliding a bar across the door.

Desmia is on the other side of the door.

I freeze. My mind can't seem to grasp what's just happened.

Desmia puts her face against a tiny window——a tiny window crisscrossed by smaller bars.

"You are *not* the true princess," she snarls through the bars. "I am."

16

"No!"

I fling myself at the door, shoving against it. The bar and the lock hold firm. I wrap my hands around the window bars and jerk on them, uselessly.

"Desmia, you don't understand," I say. "I came to *save* you! Didn't anybody ever tell you the truth?"

She's backing away from the door, toward the stairs. She lifts her head, regally, looking down her nose at me.

"They told me to beware of pretenders to the throne," she says. "They told me that I have enemies, that I must always be on guard—"

"No, no, that's not the truth," I say, shoving against the door again. It doesn't budge. "I mean, there are enemies, yes, but you and me, we're on the same side. They're enemies to us both. *You* are the pretender, but you're doing it to help me, the true princess, and—"

"Who's wearing silk?" she asks, her words practically a hiss. "Who's wearing rags?"

"Desmia, this is ridiculous," I say. I try to think if Sir Stephen taught me anything about how to handle subordinates who are insubordinate, but all my royal textbooks were sketchy when it came to talking about sedition. I don't think "Off with their heads!" would go over very well right now.

I try a more diplomatic approach.

"Go ask your royal adviser, or the leader of the knights, or someone who would remember my parents, the king and queen," I say. "Surely someone can tell you the truth. Someone can tell you that your life is in danger as long as you're pretending to be the princess, that it's in your best interest to—"

"Are you threatening me?" Desmia gasps.

"No, no, it's not like that. You're not in danger from me. I'm here to rescue you, to relieve you of—"

But Desmia is gone. She's already whirled around, dashed down the stairs. I can hear the birds again, far below: "Watch it! Be careful! Bawk!"

"Desmia, wait!" I scream. "Come back! I am the true princess! I'm not lying to you! I *am* the princess!"

I go a little crazy, I think, because suddenly I'm battering my shoulder against the door and shaking the bars and clawing my fingernails at the crack between the wooden door and the stone wall. And the whole time I'm screaming out, "I am the true princess! I am. Listen to me! I'm the princess!"

Then I feel a hand on my shoulder. Harper's. I've forgotten that he's here with me, that he's locked in too.

"I'm the princess!" I sob to him. Somehow my shoulder is down near the bottom of the door now, my face only inches from the floor. I've sagged down to the hard stones, practically rock bottom. "I am!" I whimper.

"Eelsy," Harper says, leaning over me. "What if you're not?"

17

I can only stare at Harper. My cheek hits some-thing hard—the stone floor. I've completely collapsed now. I am prostrate on the floor.

"You . . . you think I'm lying?" I whimper. "Then why did you come with me? Why did you act like you thought I was telling the truth?"

Harper's looming above me. I can hardly bear to look up at him. The tears in my eyes blur him into somebody else. Somebody who doesn't believe me. Somebody who'd rather believe a stranger in a silk dress.

"I don't think you're lying," he says impatiently. "Not on purpose, anyway. I think you've been lied to."

"Lied *to*?" I repeat. I'm having trouble understanding. My mind is creaky and stupid and numb. Then I grasp his meaning. "You think Sir Stephen and Nanny Gratine . . . oh, no, Harper, they weren't lying to me. They wouldn't. They were telling the truth."

In my mind's eye I can see Nanny's kindly wrinkled face, Sir Stephen's piercingly honest blue eyes. I can't imagine not trusting them. I can't let any doubts creep into my mind.

"What if someone lied to them?" Harper challenges. "Or what if somebody lied to whoever told them? Or—"

"Harper, I am the true princess!" I wail again, trying to drown out his treacherous words. It has to be true, because it can't not be true, because it is true, because . . . if I'm not the true princess, who am I?

Nobody, a voice whispers in my head. I can hear Nanny's bitter words from years ago echoing in my mind: *Just an ordinary orphan child . . . plenty of orphans in the kingdom nowadays . . .* That was my cover story, my pretense.

But what if the pretense is actually the truth?

It can't be. It can't be, it can't be, it . . .

A high keening hovers over us. The wails are coming from my own mouth. I flail about, sobbing, pounding my hands against the floor, against the door. I feel a burst of pain in one hand, and Harper gathers my hands together, holding them tight so I can't hurt myself again.

"Hush," he says. "I don't see as how it matters now, anyhow."

"What?" I say, shocked into some semblance of reason again. I stop struggling and sit up. Harper lets go of my hands.

"Either way, we're locked away in this tower," he says, leaning back on his heels, slumping against the wall.

"But, if I—I mean . . . ," I can't come up with a complete

sentence. "Treason," I say. I finally put it all together. "Desmia locking me up is treason."

Harper winces.

"And locking me up is . . . what? Perfectly all right?" he asks. "Because there's no chance that I would be royal."

The bitterness in his voice is hard to take.

"No, Harper, that's ridiculous," I say. My mind is clearing a little. Clearing enough that I can think, *If Desmia were the real princess, she would have reason to lock up Harper and me. We would be the ones committing treason. . . .*

I shiver. I can't stand that thought, can't stand the look on Harper's face, can't stand the fact that I'm locked in this tower. And all of a sudden I'm ashamed of myself for collapsing and wailing and throwing a fit. I'm the princess, but Harper's the one who's responding to this crisis with aplomb and fortitude. To compensate, I stand up and walk toward the window. I will come up with a plan.

"Maybe if we make a rope . . . ," I say.

"With what?" Harper asks. That's a good question. This tower room is absolutely bare: stones and mortar and nothing else. Its sole amenity is a small hole inside the wall, which could probably be used as a privy. No help there. And Harper and I carried nothing into this room except the harp and the clothes on our back. Even if we strip down to bare skin and tie my dress and his shirt and pants together (and the already ripped fabric miraculously holds), that would only carry us down a yard or two. And—I peer out the window—the ground looks miles away.

"Maybe if we yell for help?" I say.

"He-e-lp!" Harper screams, in his loudest voice. "Up here! Somebody save us!"

The words whip away in the wind. Nobody down on the ground looks up. It's too far away. The only thing Harper's screams have accomplished is to rile up the birds again.

"Bawk! Careful! Bawk! Watch it!"

I wait until their squawks die down.

"Maybe we could just climb down, holding onto the stones of the tower . . . ," I suggest.

Harper doesn't even bother answering that. He doesn't have to. I can look out and see how few handholds we would have. I can calculate how quickly our hands or feet would slip and we'd go plunging to our deaths. I lean out as far as I dare. Now I can see the balcony where Desmia stood the day before, and even that is far below us. Yesterday it seemed impossibly high, practically in the clouds.

I draw my head back in through the window.

"Maybe Desmia will come to her senses and come back for us," I say.

Harper doesn't answer that, either, but I can see by his face what he's thinking: *Don't count on it.*

"I'm sorry, Harper," I whisper.

He looks away from me, staring out into empty sky.

"You didn't even have breakfast," he says.

I shrug. Breakfast is the least of my worries right now. Or, no—maybe it should be my biggest worry. I see what Harper means. If Desmia doesn't come back, and we can't escape, I will soon be thinking of nothing but breakfast. Breakfast, dinner, supper—any kind of food. I think about the food sack we left outside the city walls, with its remnants of rotting figs and molding crumbs—the food that I so grandly refused because I thought I would soon be ordering a feast. I remember how carefully Nanny packed that sack for us, her hands lingering over the burlap as if she were wrapping up her love and care, not just oat cakes and jerky.

Something like a sob catches in the back of my throat.

"Nanny thought she was sending me off to safety," I say.

Harper sinks to the floor, his back against the unrelenting stone walls.

"This is all my fault," he says. "You wanted to go to Wedgewede like you were supposed to, but I started off toward Cortona. I said, 'Isn't that the capital? Isn't that where the palace is? Where you wanted to go?' like I was making fun of you for being afraid. . . ."

"No, it's my fault," I say. "I should have known that Desmia . . . that she . . . I should have known we'd be playing chess."

Harper doesn't tell me that this makes no sense, so I don't have to explain. But I know that I've failed another one of Sir Stephen's chess lessons. "You can't expect your opponents to think the same way you do," he always told me. "You have to study their moves, look for the pattern of their thoughts, their strategy, their desires. . . ." But I didn't know that Desmia was my opponent. I studied nothing about her, except for her waving style and her taste in dresses.

Harper is staring at the door.

"Wish we had some gunpowder," he says. "Toss a little bit on the hinges, and—pow!—we could blow that door to bits."

"You'd know how to do that?" I ask, a little awed. There's a lot I didn't know about Harper, either.

Harper looks down.

"No," he admits. He gives a harsh laugh and kicks at his harp. "I don't know why Mam never let me learn anything useful."

"You are a good harpist," I say.

Harper shrugs. It doesn't matter now.

"I know the top thirty exports of Suala, in order," I say. "I know the dates of every war we've fought in the past three hundred years. I know the order of courses at a royal feast, and which silverware to use for which course. Why didn't I know that Desmia wouldn't listen to me? Why didn't I know she'd lock us up?"

"Because," Harper says, "you don't think that way. You wouldn't be that kind of princess."

It's not much comfort, but that's probably the nicest thing Harper has ever said to me.

18

Eventually I fall asleep. There's nothing else to do, and at least when I'm asleep I can forget the twisting in my stomach, its utter emptiness. When I wake up, the sun is high in the sky, its rays streaming in through the windows. And I can hear music—harp music?—like nothing I've ever heard before. The song is soft but fast, the notes zooming around each other like bees dancing over a meadow of flowers. It's wild and joyous and unbelievably beautiful.

I bolt upright.

"Harper!" I exclaim. "You're playing music? On purpose? By choice? When your mam's not even here to make you practice?"

Harper gives the strings one last strum to finish with a cascade of sound, like every bee is racing away happy and full of nectar. He grins sheepishly.

"Oh, Mam would hate this," he says. "She'd say it was irreverent—a fine instrument like the harp must be played with respect, you know." He's caught the drag of his mother's voice, the way grief weighs down every word. Then he sounds like himself again: "It's just, you were asleep, and I was getting sick of thinking the same things over and over again, 'How are we going to escape? No, that won't work . . . that won't work. . . . How are we going to escape?' And then I started wondering about how we played this morning, about whether I could play a whole song that fast, on purpose, all by myself, and then . . . well, I'm sorry if I woke you up."

"You didn't wake me up," I say. "The sun did. But Harper, that song, it was . . . incredible. It was perfect. It was the best music I've ever heard anyone play."

I'm expecting Harper to laugh at me, to shove the harp away, maybe to shove me away too. But he just sits there, hugging the harp to his chest.

"Really?" he says.

"Absolutely," I say. "If . . ." I have to swallow a lump in my throat to go on. "It doesn't look like this is ever going to happen now, but if I ever do get to sit on my throne, I'm sorry, I couldn't outlaw harps. I couldn't make you Lord High Chancellor of Fishing Ponds. I'd have to have you as my royal harpist, playing like that!"

Harper's grin fades. He carefully puts the harp on the ground and stands up. He stares out the window.

"I don't think I could play like that if it was someone forcing me to, ordering me around," he says. "It wouldn't be fun, then."

I've ruined things again.

"Okay, okay!" I say. "I didn't mean it like that! You can still be Lord High Minister of Fishing Ponds. It's just, whenever you felt like playing, I'd want—I mean—it'd be really nice if you let me listen!"

Harper pushes his hair back, erasing all evidence of the careful patting-down he gave it this morning.

"You don't have to be the princess on the throne for that," he says softly. "I'll play more later. It . . . it makes me forget where we are."

I'm glad he seems to have forgiven me. But I didn't want to be reminded that we're locked in the tower. I'm stiff from sleeping on the hard stone floor, and my stomach feels emptier than ever. And now my throat is beginning to ache too, because it's so dry. I don't know how I can be so high up in the sky and yet still feel like I'm swallowing dust.

"Harper," I say. "What are we going to do?"

He lifts his hands, palms outstretched—a helpless, hopeless gesture.

"What can we do?" he says.

Just then, there's a thud behind us. I whirl around and see a rope dangling down from the barred window in the wooden door. I rush over and grab the knotted end of the rope—it was the knot hitting the door that made the noise.

"Hey!" I yell. "Wait!"

I've reasoned things out—for the rope to hit the door like that, someone had to have tossed the rope in. I peer out between the bars; I'm just in time to see a figure in a pale dress disappear around the curve of the spiral stairs.

"Desmia?" I call cautiously. I'm not sure it's Desmia. It could have been a maid or a serving girl. "Someone?" I add. "Please, come back! Please——"

But my call has roused the birds again, and I'm treated to another round of "Bawk! Careful!" "Bawk! Watch out!"—— words I should have paid attention to the first time around. The birds are so loud I can't listen for the footsteps retreating down the stairs.

"Bawk! I am the true princess!" one of the birds screeches.

"What?" I cry.

"Bawk! True princess! True princess! Bawk!"

I'm outraged.

"Stop it!" I command. "Shut up, you stupid bird!"

"Bawk! True princess!'

Harper is standing at the door beside me now, and, heartlessly, he's laughing. I whirl on him.

"How dare you laugh at that!"

"Don't you get it?" Harper says, between snorts and giggles. "The bird learned that from you—you said it so often. 'True princess, I'm the true princess,'" he imitates.

"True princess," the bird agrees from just below us on the spiral stairs. "Bawk."

"Well, it's not funny," I say huffily. I frown, forcing the corners of my mouth down. Anytime Harper laughs, it's really, really hard not to laugh with him. And I can see how, if this had happened to one of my stuffy, long-dead royal ancestors, I would have laughed just as much as I laughed at Queen Rexalia's amazing fertilizer discoveries. But this is happening to me.

"Anyway," I say, "how can you laugh when we're trapped in here and we're going to starve to death? Or no, we'll probably die of thirst first. Yeah, that's hilarious."

Harper laughs harder.

"You don't see very well, do you?" he says. "We're not going to starve."

"What do you mean? Of course we are." I almost sound smug, like that's what I want if it'll prove Harper wrong. But then I look down, my eyes following the path of the rope from the knot in my hand, over the rim of the barred window, down toward the stone floor on the other side of the door. Maybe the rope's long enough to . . . no, it stops before it even reaches the floor. But it stops because it's tied to the handle of a basket out there on the other side of the door. And in the basket I can see a jug, a long loaf of bread, a wheel of cheese, a cluster of grapes, and apples, pears, peaches, and berries.

"I knew there'd be a feast in the castle!" I tell Harper.

"The 'true princess' bird must have ordered it!" he counters.

We're giddy hauling the basket up, hand over hand, so we can reach in for the bread and cheese and fruit. The jug proves to be too fat to bring in between the bars, so we take turns reaching out to tilt it back, letting the other person gulp down the sweet, cold lemonade as if from a fountain. We toss grapes in the air and catch them in our mouths; we let the juice from the peaches dribble down our chins. In our glee we almost forget that we're still trapped, behind bars. At least we have food. At least Desmia's not going to let us starve.

At least we know now that she's not that kind of princess.

19

Harper and I fall into an odd pattern over the next few days. We live for the sound of someone approaching on the stairs—we're constantly listening for footsteps and birdcalls. But somehow the birds are always quiet until after our food appears; we never make it to the door in time to catch more than a glimpse of our food deliverer dashing away from us. Eventually I suggest that we take turns at guard duty, watching beside the door so that at the first sign of someone bringing food we can begin pleading our case: *Oh, please, listen to us. We mean no one any harm. We were trying to do the right thing, coming here. . . .*

No one shows up for an entire day. We are hungry and thirsty and tired, and when we hear the clock tower far below us chiming midnight, we give up. In the morning the basket is waiting outside our door, full of food again, and there's a note in elegant handwriting tucked between two apples:

Do not watch for me. I cannot bring your food if you are watching.

The note is not signed.

"Couldn't she have given us a few more details?" I ask, studying the note. "Reasons? Explanations? Maybe some indication of when she's going to let us out?"

Harper shoots me a sidelong glance.

"I think maybe that was all she wanted to say." He takes a bite of an apple, the skin crunching against his teeth. "Can you tell from the writing if it's Desmia or someone else who wrote the note?"

"How should I know?"

"Would a princess leave a big blot of ink like that?" He points to the tail of the *g* in "watching," where, indeed, too much ink has pooled.

I think about my own struggles with ink blots.

"Quill pens aren't that easy to use," I say. "You'd have to be a professional scribe, practically, not to leave any blots at all."

"Well," Harper says, patting my shoulder, "we know something, then. She didn't hire out the writing of this note to the castle scribe."

He tosses me an apple, but I don't lift it to my mouth.

"What if she's the only one who knows we're here?" I ask slowly. "What if she's keeping us secret?"

"Why would she?" Harper asks. "If she's going to have us executed for treason, don't you think she'd lop off our heads in front of everyone and be done with it?"

I don't know how he can keep such a light tone in his voice, talking about that, like it's all a joke.

"We are not treasonous!" I yell out, between the bars of the window, just in case someone—Desmia?—is listening. "We don't deserve to be executed! We deserve to be set free!" I stop short of adding, *I deserve to be wearing your crown!*

"How many people do you know who get what they deserve out of life?" Harper asks.

I bite into my apple then, and shrug, pretending my mouth's too full to answer.

But later on, after we're full and Harper has wandered over to pluck at his harp, I'm still thinking about his question. Harper has an intense look on his face I've never seen before; he's totally engrossed in the way his fingers speed across the strings. He looks . . . happy. Is Harper finally getting what he deserves from his music, after all those years of hated harp lessons? Doesn't he deserve to have the whole world know how incredibly he can play, instead of being locked up in a tower?

Did Nanny deserve to have me disobey her? Did Sir Stephen deserve to have me run away, after all his efforts to keep me safe?

I decide that thinking about what people deserve is a stupid way of looking at the world. But I can't stop myself.

Don't I deserve to rule as princess, after all the time I spent studying and preparing? After all my courage in coming here? I don't deserve to be locked in a tower! I don't deserve to be mocked by a parrot!

But . . . what does Desmia deserve?

I'm thinking about Desmia differently now. The way she creeps up here to deliver our food—like she's afraid of us, even though we're locked away—that makes me view everything else I know about her differently too. I don't know why, but I am sure that she's the one delivering the food. And I'm pretty sure, somehow, that she hasn't told anyone else that we're here. Otherwise I think there'd be curious maids wandering up here to look at us, to laugh at the sight of a princess in rags. Or there'd be advisers and ministers and judges, full of opinions about what Desmia should do to me—or what I should do to her.

Perhaps Desmia, with her pale yellow silks and pale pink satins, her delicate, dainty waves, is not just well-mannered and adorably doll-like. Perhaps she is also timid and unsure. Perhaps she doesn't trust her advisers and ministers and judges. Perhaps she doesn't even trust her maids.

I think about how Desmia darted into the secret passageway, about how she was so desperate to make sure that we wouldn't be heard. I think about how she ran ahead of us. She was afraid. I'm sure of it.

But what is she afraid of? Is it something that I should be afraid of too?

Harper has his music to keep him busy. I have no books, no quill pens, no pots to scrub, no eggs to gather, no cow to fetch from the meadow. I have nothing to do but think and wonder.

As the days pass, I do more and more of my thinking and wondering while looking out on the courtyard, far below the tower. I especially can't stop myself from watching during Desmia's noon waving show each day. It is truly frightening to lean out far enough to see Desmia on her balcony. And, anyhow, her routine is as unvarying as the paleness of her dresses. So usually I just lean out once to see the color of her dress—pale peach one day, pale lavender the next—and then focus my attention on the crowd below. I'm too far away to see individual faces, but I can pick up on patterns. I'm sure that the group of people in top hats and tails must be contestants in the music contest. I think that the cluster of women in matching skirts and aprons must be milkmaids from the same village, all on the outing of a lifetime to see Cortona and Princess Desmia. I wonder at a cluster of men in a foreign military uniform—not the spiffy blue and gold of the Sualan army, but a dignified gray with scarlet trim. They stand in a huddle throughout Desmia's waving and then seem to be escorted into the castle immediately afterward. Their plumed hats make them easy to spot. Then I realize that they're actually surrounding a small delegation of officials without plumes, without uniforms, but nattily dressed, in fabrics that shimmer in the sun.

I can't quite see well enough—I can't quite tell—but . . . is one of those officials a girl?

I watch for days, but no one from that unusual group returns.

I'm so intent on watching for the soldiers or officials to come back that I almost miss noticing two women who come into the courtyard late one afternoon a few days later. They are easily overlooked, just an old woman in a peasant kerchief leaning on a younger woman's arm as they hobble across the stones. But there's something familiar in the way the old woman stops and stands and looks around every so often, something familiar about how the younger woman seems so weighed down, even when she's standing alone.

I know who they are.

"Harper!" I screech. "I see Nanny and your mam!"

"What? Where?" Harper drops his harp and jumps up to look out the window beside me. "Mam! It's me! I'm up here!"

I wave my arms—not daintily, like Desmia, but extravagantly, desperately, stretching out so far that I rip the armpit of my dress, matching the rip at the back.

"Nanny! Oh, please, Nanny! Come and save me!"

They don't look up.

A man in a cloak appears behind the two women, his gait arthritic but sprightly.

"Sir Stephen!" I holler. "Get us out of here! Tell Desmia the truth! No—tell the palace officials. . . ."

The wind whips my words back at me. Below me the birds, at least, hear us and begin screeching their usual mocking chorus: "Bawk! Watch out!" "Bawk! Be careful!" "Bawk! I'm the true princess!" But even their squawks and squeals don't carry down to the courtyard. No one tilts back their head to gaze in our direction.

"Oh, please! Oh, please! Nanny! Can't you hear me? Sir Stephen?"

I am sobbing now, every bit as hysterical as I was that first day.

"Please!" I scream.

"Eelsy," Harper says softly, pulling me back in through the window so I don't fall. "They can't hear us. They're leaving now."

And they are. I watch as they turn around and hobble out of sight, around the corner of a row of shops.

"No!" I wail, heartbroken.

"Shh," Harper mumbles. "It's okay."

He's pulling me close to his chest, comfortingly. This is a new thing—who knew Harper could be so tender? But I don't feel like being comforted right now. I push back against him, breaking his grasp on my shoulders.

"How can you be so calm?" I fume. "Don't you even care that they're leaving us? Don't you want to be rescued?"

Harper looks at me. His sandy hair still sticks up, and his freckles have only faded a little during our time trapped inside, in this tower. But he looks older somehow. Older even than he did a few weeks ago, when we set off from our village.

"I think you've always expected more from your life than I do," he says, finally.

"What do you mean? That it's okay just to give up? Why

did you bother shouting at all if you knew they couldn't hear?" I demand. I am so mad at Harper—mad at him, mad at Nanny, mad at Sir Stephen, mad at Harper's mam. . . . Why didn't a single one of them look up even once? Why couldn't a single one of them listen harder?

"Look, I want to be rescued just as much as you do," Harper says sharply. "But . . ." He swallows hard. "What if them trying to rescue us just puts them in danger, too?"

I gasp and step back, my knees weak. I have to put my hand out and hold on to the stone wall to keep from falling down. I'm suddenly dizzy, a delayed reaction to Harper's having to pull me back from the window, when I was in danger of tumbling down to the ground. No—I correct myself—it's not that danger I'm dizzy from. I'm dizzy because Harper's right. If his mam and Nanny and Sir Stephen had heard us, it might have been like we were luring them to their deaths. They would have done anything they could to rescue us. They would have been foolhardy. They would have taken risks. They love us that much.

"You're right," I whisper. "I didn't think."

Hours later, after we've eaten our evening meal and it's gotten dark and Harper has slipped off into sleep, my heart still pounds unnaturally fast every time I think about Nanny and Sir Stephen and Harper's mam in the courtyard. I try to convince myself that it wasn't them, that my eyes were playing tricks on me. Because if they're here in Cortona, they are looking for us. If they aren't in danger now, they will be soon.

"Please," I whisper. I'm talking to God now. I'm pleading for my safety, and Harper's, and Harper's mam's, and Nanny's, and Sir Stephen's. And maybe even Desmia's, too, even though she's the one who's imprisoned us.

I've barely even begun my prayer when I hear footsteps. And then there's the soft glow of a lantern shining in through the bars, making long stripes of shadow and light across the tower floor. This has never happened before. I poke Harper in the ribs, whisper, "Wake up!" and then spring toward the door. Talk about prayers being answered.

"Harper, we're being rescued!" I hiss. "We are! We are!"

I press my face up against the bars, watching for Sir Stephen's regal frame to round the last curve of the spiral stairs, or maybe Nanny's hunched-over hobble, or even Harper's mam, stepping briskly for once.

And then the figure holding the lantern aloft rounds the corner, and I take a step back from the door.

20

It's a girl I've never seen before. Even in the dim lantern light I can tell that she's not a maid. She's too jaw-droppingly beautiful, too beautifully dressed. And just from the way she walks and stands, it seems like she's her own person, like she's not used to taking orders from other people. Still, I can tell she's not a minister or an adviser or a judge, either, because, well, she's a girl.

"Hello," she says cautiously. Then she turns partway around and addresses someone behind her on the steps, out of my view. "Desmia, they're not screaming or shouting or anything. It's safe to come out."

If I scrunch over to the side, I can see just the tip of Desmia's nose and the peak of her crown as she inches forward.

"But . . . the smell," Desmia whispers.

The first girl sighs, and flashes me an apologetic glance.

"You know," she says, "you lock someone up in a tower for a while without any soap or water, that's bound to happen. Especially at the height of summer."

Is it the height of summer now? I wonder. Exactly how long has Desmia kept us locked up? Two weeks? More?

I turn my head to the side and sniff my armpit surreptitiously. I guess I do smell bad. I remember suddenly how awful my stained, ripped dress looked even before Desmia trapped us in the tower.

"Please," I say, being careful not to scream or shout or do anything else that might scare off Desmia and this girl. "I don't know what Desmia told you about us, but—"

"Wait," the girl says, holding up her hand to stop me. "I'm sure you're dying to tell me your side of the story. I'll listen, I promise. But before you start, you should probably know who you're telling it to. I'm Ella Brown."

She moves our food basket and jug of lemonade to the side and then reaches her hand in through the bars to politely shake first my hand, then Harper's. It's almost as if we've just encountered each other at a fancy ball, rather than on opposite sides of prison bars.

"Are you—are you a princess too?" Harper stammers. I look over at him, and his eyes are wide and awestruck. I did mention that this Ella Brown is beautiful, didn't I? That's an understatement. She looks the way I always wanted to look when I used to peer into the pond, trying to see if I looked like my royal ancestors. She's got thick blond hair that sweeps halfway down her back, and blue eyes that sparkle with intelligence, and white, even teeth. And even though she's wearing a fairly simple dress—dark green cotton, in contrast to Desmia's pale, pale blue satin—it shows off her figure amazingly.

"Don't forget to blink," I mutter to Harper.

Ella laughs.

"I am definitely not a princess," she says. "I tried it for a little while—believe me, it wasn't my style."

"Oh," Harper says, and he sounds so disappointed that I want to jab him in the ribs with my elbow. How come he had such trouble believing that I was a princess, but now can't accept that this Ella isn't one?

Ella looks over at me, and I don't know, maybe it's just an optical illusion in the dim light, but it seems like she's rolling her eyes at me, making fun of Harper a little. It's as if she's saying, *Why can't people see that there's a lot more to a girl than what she looks like?*

But maybe I just want to believe that Ella's thinking that, considering what I look like right now.

"Anyhow," Ella says, "you should probably know that I'm not Sualan. I'm from Fridesia."

Harper and I both gasp at that. Fridesia is the country we're at war with right now, the country we've been at war with forever, it seems. The country Harper's father died fighting.

Ella is our enemy.

Boldly, Harper steps forward, clutches the bars in the door, and glares at Desmia.

"So you imprison us, loyal Sualan citizens, and yet allow *her* to freely roam the castle?" he asks.

"I—I—," Desmia stammers, all but hiding behind Ella.

Ella holds up her hand, as if trying to soothe Harper's anger.

"Now, now," she says. "I am here on a mission of peace. I bear you no ill will, no enmity. I'm part of a delegation attempting to negotiate an end to the war."

I almost blurt out, *Hey! No fair! That's what I was going to do as princess!* But, amazingly, Desmia steps out from behind Ella and speaks.

"It's because of Ella's fiancé," she says. "He's the head of the delegation. He's been here for months. And Ella"— Desmia glances at the other girl, admiringly—"she missed him so much she came to help."

I remember the cluster of foreign gray military uniforms I saw a few days ago, my suspicion that there'd been a girl in their midst. I'd probably seen Ella arriving. I glance back at Ella, and her eyes have gone dreamy.

Oh, I think, *that one is in love.* To travel so far into enemy territory—she'd need courage as well as devotion. My journey was nothing compared with hers.

I understand the wistful tone in Desmia's voice. This is romantic.

Ella seems to shake herself out of the dreaminess.

"So I was talking to Desmia at dinner tonight," Ella says. "And she told me she faced an, ah, *dilemma*, apart from the war—"

"She's trapped us here unfairly!" I accuse. "She doesn't know the truth, and I guess she's afraid to ask anyone—"

At the same time Harper's trying to explain, "We've done nothing wrong! It's a misunderstanding! We just—"

"Please! One at a time!" Ella begs. "I'll listen to everything you say, but take turns!"

We do. Harper lets me talk first, but he keeps adding commentary: "Think of it from Cecilia's viewpoint," he pleads. "She's grown up always being told she was the true princess, so of course that's what she believes. . . ." And, "Really, we mean no harm to Desmia. . . ." And then, "To tell the truth, I personally don't care if Cecilia ever gets to sit on the throne; it's just, she's my friend, and—"

"Some kind of friend you are!" I mutter. He's ruined my whole story. I'm so mad that if Ella and Desmia stepped away for a minute, I'd punch him.

Ella tilts her head, looking from Harper to me.

"Why do you want to be princess?" she asks.

"It's not about what I *want*," I say. "I *am* the princess. It's my . . . my fate. My destiny. Sir Stephen and the other knights were so brave in saving me after my parents were killed. I . . ." I look down. "I owe them. I owe my country."

"But you didn't do what Sir Stephen wanted you to do," Ella says gently.

"Because I *can* think for myself," I say. I glare at Harper. My fury gives me courage. "Sir Stephen and Nanny still want to protect me, like a little child. I was scared coming to Cortona. I've been terrified since Desmia locked us in this tower. But what good is it to be the princess if I don't ever do anything about it? If I care more about staying safe than about helping my kingdom? Suala doesn't need a princess who's just a doll that waves!"

Harper gasps beside me.

"She doesn't mean that," he says. "Not the way it sounds."

"Yes, I do!" I say.

Harper turns three shades paler. He peers around behind Desmia, as if he's expecting to see an executioner lurking in the shadows, waiting his turn.

Truly, I don't want to be *that* kind of princess—the kind that gets executed. But I don't regret anything that I've said. I've never felt so much like the true princess as I do right now, standing up for myself.

"Hmm," Ella says. "This is all very interesting."

Her voice is so mild that I'm sure there's no executioner waiting for us. But then she turns to Desmia.

"Desmia," she says. "Would you like to explain your side of the story now?"

Desmia shakes her head. "I think they should see for themselves," she says in a small voice. "So they'll believe me."

"You want them to see what you showed me?" Ella asks doubtfully. "Wouldn't it be safer just to—"

"No," Desmia says.

Ella frowns.

"How do you plan to accomplish this?" Ella asks.

"We'll tie them up," Desmia says. "Wrists and ankles. And use gags and blindfolds, maybe, until we get there?"

"You expect them to walk down those secret stairways with blindfolds over their eyes and ropes around their ankles?" Ella asks in disbelief. "I thought you said you *didn't* want to kill them."

I shoot Harper a gloating look, as if to say, *See? Even if you'd let me tell my story the way I wanted to, she wasn't planning to kill us!*

"Then just bind their wrists and gag their mouths until we're there?" Desmia revises herself.

"You don't think we could trust them?" Ella asks. "Without tying them up at all?"

Desmia shakes her head. I can't say I blame her.

Ella shrugs and turns back to Harper and me.

"We're taking you to the castle dungeon," she says. "Through the secret passageways—Desmia said you used those before. I know you have little reason to trust me or Desmia, but it's dangerous for all four of us if anyone hears us. I promise you, we do not intend to leave you in the dungeon. I know about dungeons—I would never do that to anyone."

The way she says that, I believe her. But how could this beautiful girl ever have been in a dungeon? I'm tempted to ask her about her story—how does someone "try" being a princess for a while and then give it up? But then a new thought seizes me.

"You're taking us to the dungeons. . . . You haven't captured Sir Stephen, have you?" I ask, suddenly horrified. "Or Nanny? Please, please, don't hurt them, don't—"

I'm prepared to beg harder for their lives than I would for my own. But Ella reaches through the bars and grabs my hands—I guess I'm flailing them about—and orders, "Stop! It's not anyone you know! It's—"

"Shh." Desmia stops her. "We're showing them, remember?"

Things happen fast after that. I want to signal Harper, to work out some sort of arrangement, passing information with a glance: *Once they open this door, you take out Desmia and I'll overpower Ella and then we'll run for help. We'll wake up the whole castle if we have to!*

But I can't catch Harper's eye, and I'm not going to run away and leave him behind. And anyway, I am curious about what Desmia wants to show us in the dungeon. Besides, Desmia insists on tying our wrists together before she unlocks the door—we have to stick our hands out between the bars, and then lean our heads against the door for the gags.

"I'll take the boy, first," she tells Ella. "You take Cecilia."

In spite of myself I have to admit that that's a clever strategy. Surely Harper knows that he can't scream and rouse the whole castle, because then Ella could just throw me back in the tower—or maybe out the tower window. And I can't do anything to attract attention, because that would put Harper in danger too.

Several minutes after Desmia has disappeared around the corner of the stairway with Harper, Ella says, "All right, I think it's our turn. Let's hope I don't get lost."

We've only gone a few steps before I think of another question.

"Why didn't we hear the birds?" I try to ask. But because of the gag it comes out, "I innunt ee ear uh urz?"

"What?" Ella says. Then she seems to comprehend. "Oh, you're asking about the birds? I understand they're usually pretty loud. That's why Desmia covered their cages."

I see that we are passing the first cage, which is, indeed, covered with a white sheet. And above the cage I notice a complicated pulley system connected to a long rope, which must have made it possible for Desmia to lower the cloth from afar. That way, I guess, she wouldn't rile up the birds while she was trying to silence them. Now I want to ask Ella, "How do the pulleys work?" and "Covering them makes them be quiet? Really?" This time it's not worth the effort. But I'm thinking. If Desmia could control when the birds squawked and when they didn't, then maybe she sneaked up to the tower many times, to eavesdrop on us. . . . Above my head I notice a round mirror—mirrors even up here!—but this one is angled so that it shows the door Harper and I were locked behind. So *that's* how Desmia could see when we were watching for her and when we weren't; that's how she made sure we never knew when she was bringing the food.

Sir Stephen would be proud: I am putting things together, working on my powers of observation. But I can't picture Desmia rigging up the pulleys and the cages and the mirror, and I don't know who else would have done that. And I still don't understand *why* Desmia locked us in the tower, or why she's come for us now. If she really believed we were guilty of treason, she would have screamed for help that first day I talked to her, at the music competition. She would have called her guards; she probably would have had us killed.

I am holding on to some sliver of hope, because she didn't do any of that. She's come for me not with guards, but with another girl.

I'm lost in thought as we wind our way down the spiral staircase and through Desmia's private quarters (which should be *mine*, I remind myself stubbornly). But as soon as we begin descending the secret stairway, I have to focus completely on putting down one foot after another without slipping down the dark, narrow stairs. I'm still wearing my felt shoes; it'd be too embarrassing to take them off and go barefoot in front of this girl who looks so much like a princess.

"Curses upon the diabolical Sualan who built this," Ella is muttering to herself. "But what was I expecting? Why should Sualan palace intrigue be any less Byzantine than Fridesian palace intrigue?"

She starts to slip, and I catch the back of her dress steadying her as well as I can with bound hands. The lantern weaves out dangerously, splashing oil on the stairs.

Ella turns to me with round, frightened eyes.

"Thank you," she whispers. "I think you may have just saved my life." She peers far down to the bottom of the steps, where she would have landed. "That's the last thing Jed needs, to have me disappear and die. The rest of the delegation would say it proves the Sualans can't be trusted . . . and it'd be all my fault, because of my own clumsiness!"

She seems to be mostly just talking to herself, but I file

this information away: *So the peace negotiations aren't going well; this Jed she's in love with is at odds with the rest of the delegation. . . .*

"Watch out," Ella whispers, stepping past the spot of lantern oil on the stairs. "As if the steps weren't slick enough already!"

We make the rest of our descent with great caution. The muscles in my legs ache from having to step so carefully, down so many stairs. I'm not sure—I wasn't counting that first day, and I don't count now—but it seems that we have climbed down many, many more stairs than we climbed up before. I'm almost surprised when they finally come to an end. We push out through a stone door, and Desmia and Harper are waiting for us in a narrow, filthy corridor. There seems to be a river of sludge running beneath our feet—sludge which soaks into my felt shoes. I've walked in mud before, in manure, but this is much worse.

"Hurry," Desmia says. "While the jailer's still asleep."

"She put a potion in his drink," Ella whispers to me.

We begin tiptoeing down the corridor, past walls stained with . . . well, I don't really want to think about what they're stained with. Blood? Vomit? Excrement? Whatever it is, it looks like it's been accumulating for ages, possibly since the time of King Saldorn the First, even though Sir Stephen taught me nothing about Saldorn the First's dungeons. For that matter Sir Stephen taught me nothing about anyone's dungeons; in Sir Stephen's version of Sualan history, dungeons don't exist. But there's no denying the reality of the scene around me: the sludge soaking into my shoes, the grimy cobwebs dragging against my face, the choking stench that threatens to cut off my every breath. I begin to gag, and I'm not sure if it's from the stench or just from imagining how Sualan royalty—my ancestors—must have used this dungeon.

"Take small breaths," Ella advises. "Until you get used to the smell."

I hold my breath instead, drawing in air only when I absolutely have to.

Desmia is watching Harper and me.

"See, I was being kind," she says. "Putting you in the tower."

I know what she means—the tower is luxury accommodations, compared with this—but I still want to retort, through the gag, *Why did you have to imprison us at all?* I decide I don't have enough air in my lungs for that.

We pass a small room where a man is slumped over a desk. Ella gently tugs his door shut. Several paces farther along, the corridor widens. I can see flickering torches propped in crude wire sconces on the wall, and rows of bars that stretch from the floor to the ceiling, sectioning off one prison cell after another.

Desmia holds her hand up to stop us. Then she steps forward, into the center of the corridor.

"Which of you is the true princess?" she calls, her voice low but strong.

The response is instantaneous. In every cell I can see, a girl rushes to the door and shouts, "I am!" Tall, lanky girls; short, squat girls; girls with curly brown hair; girls with straight blond hair; every variety of girl from the entire kingdom, it seems, all calling out, "I am!"

"No, me!"

"You lie! I'm the true princess!"

"It's me! I told you, it's me!"

"Please! Somebody listen! I'm telling the truth!"

That's all I hear before I sink to the floor in a dead faint.

21

When I wake up, I am lying on a soft bed, my head cushioned in feather pillows, my body tucked safely under airy quilts. I take a tentative breath and draw in the sweet odor of roses, lilies, lavender.

Finally! I think. *This is where I belong!*

Then I remember the horror of all those girls in the dungeon, all claiming the title I thought was mine, the privileges I thought I deserved.

"Noooo," I moan.

My face is wet with tears, though I don't remember starting to cry. I begin turning my head side to side against the pillows, my moans getting stronger: "Nooo . . . nooo . . ."

Someone lifts my hand and clutches tightly. I open my eyes—it's Harper.

"Oh, Eelsy," he says, and it's like he's apologizing to me, grieving with me for everything I always believed about myself.

Everything I can never believe again.

It could still be true, I think. *Desmia could be lying; all those girls could be wrong. . . .*

But I am just thinking that out of habit. I know that I really have nothing to cling to anymore but Harper's hand. I hold on with all my strength.

"Explain," I whisper. "Please."

Harper looks back over his shoulder.

"Princess Desmia?" he calls.

Desmia tiptoes toward the bed, a wraithlike figure in her pale gown.

"This is your bed," I realize suddenly. "I shouldn't be here, getting muck on your quilts, probably."

I struggle to sit up. If I'm not the true princess, I want no privilege I don't deserve, no luxury I have no right to. I still have my pride. I won't lay claim to anything that shouldn't be mine.

Desmia touches my shoulder.

"It's all right," she says shyly. Then, with a sense of mischief I didn't know she possessed, she adds, "Your shoes already got those quilts so filthy they'll never come clean anyhow."

And then she smiles at me, which removes any sting from the words.

I smile back, feebly.

"I don't understand," I say. I'm not talking about quilts or mucky shoes.

Desmia's eyes meet mine, and it's like looking into a mirror, seeing the troubled puzzlement I feel reflected in her gaze.

"I don't either," she admits with a sigh.

"Ella?" I whisper.

The other girl sits down on the edge of the bed.

"Don't look at me," she says. "It's your kingdom." She shakes her head. "I didn't think any palace could be more messed up than Fridesia's!"

"Ours is," Desmia whispers.

"How . . . ?" I start to ask, then decide that's not the right question. "Why . . . ? I mean, who . . . ?"

I give up.

"It might help if you tell them what you do know," Ella suggests gently to Desmia.

Desmia twists her hands together. She doesn't sit down.

"What I told you before . . . I wasn't lying," she says. "They've always told me there was a pretender to the throne, who wanted to kill me and take over."

"Wait a minute—who's 'they'? Who told you this?" I ask.

Desmia shrugs.

"Everyone. All the palace officials. All my advisers. My governess. My nanny when I was little."

Desmia doesn't say "nanny" the way I say "Nanny." She wrinkles up her nose and grimaces, like the word itself leaves a bad taste in her mouth. Instead of my warm, cozy Nanny Gratine, I picture a prune-faced woman who'd beat a child for sneezing. That's how Desmia makes her sound.

"The danger from the pretender to the throne is the reason I've never been allowed to go out of the palace," Desmia adds.

It takes a minute for that to sink in. Harper reacts before I do.

"Never?" He explodes. I can see by his face that he's having trouble imagining life without ever fishing or running through mud puddles or playing leapfrog and chase and tackle. "That's worse than harp lessons!"

"Well," Desmia says, "a few years ago they started letting me go out on the balcony once a day, but I don't count that. That was just because there were rumors in Cortona that I didn't even exist, that I'd died with my parents, or been kidnapped, or . . . I don't know, never been born at all."

"Those are odd rumors," Ella says.

"But what else would people think, when no one outside the palace had ever seen me?" Desmia asks. Unexpectedly, she giggles. "You should have seen my advisers measuring the distance from the balcony to the ground, making sure that no one could shoot an arrow at me, or throw a knife or hurl a sword. . . . They argued for days about whether it was safe for me to take three steps into the fresh air or if it would be better to have me wave from behind glass!"

I like that Desmia is laughing at this. But I think about how she always stands so stiffly on the balcony, how minimally she moves her hand.

"You're terrified whenever you're out there, aren't you?" I ask.

She doesn't answer.

After a few moments pass, Harper says, "This pretender

everyone always told you about—why did she want to hurt you? What did she hope to gain?"

"Power," Desmia says softly. "Control."

I can't look at her while she's saying that. I want to protest, *That wasn't what I wanted! I wanted to be a good princess! Better than you!* But wasn't that wanting control too?

I shift to another question.

"So you started arresting girls?" I ask, and I can't keep the harshness out of my voice. "Anyone who seemed like she might want to be princess?" I'm forgetting that all the girls in the dungeon didn't just want to be the princess; they claimed that they were the princess. They seemed to believe it. Just like I always have. "Didn't you think they might just be crazy? Or"—I swallow a huge lump in my throat, force the word out—"misinformed?"

Harper squeezes my hand, as if he understands how hard it is for me to say that.

"*I* didn't arrest anybody!" Desmia protests. "I didn't put anyone in that dungeon!"

"Well, then, you had your people do it," I say, and there's an ugly, bitter twist to my tone. "That's how your kind of royalty works."

Desmia blinks. Is she blinking back tears? *How strange,* I think.

"I didn't even know they were there," she protests in a strangled voice. "Until—" She breaks off and glances toward Ella.

"You thought it was safe to tell me," Ella says encouragingly.

"Until I found the secret stairs and started hiding there, eavesdropping on my advisers," Desmia finishes. She stares down at the floor, as if it's now her turn to be ashamed to meet our eyes.

"So, then," I say cautiously, since Desmia suddenly seems so fragile again, "did you ask anybody about those girls? Anybody you trusted?" I'm thinking about Nanny and Sir Stephen, how many questions I asked them, how much I always trusted them. The lump is back in my throat. *What good was it to trust them if all their answers were false?* I wonder. But I can't bear to think about that right now. I focus on Desmia again. "What did the people you trusted say?"

"There isn't anybody I trust," Desmia says. She lifts her head, peering almost fiercely at Ella and Harper and me. "There wasn't."

"Nobody?" Harper asks in a choked voice. He's looking at me, and I know he's thinking about how I came to him in the night and whispered my secrets to him in a cowshed. Despite everything that's gone wrong since then, I'm not sorry that I shared what I thought was the truth.

Desmia winces.

"If you knew the people in this palace, you'd understand," she says ruefully. "Lord Throckmorton, Lord Suprien, Lord Tyfolieu . . ." Her face twists more with each name she recites.

"Not the nicest of people," Ella agrees. "I've barely been here a week, and already I've taken a hearty dislike to pretty much everyone but Desmia." She smiles at the other girl, but the grimness in her eyes cancels out the cheering effect. "They are definitely the type who'd lock girls in a dungeon for no good reason."

I shake my head, still baffled.

"But there's got to be *some* reason," I say. "Some explanation. That's a lot of effort to go to, to hunt down and imprison all those girls." Just thinking about the girls in the dungeon makes me want to faint again. My memory is so vivid and nightmarish: the sludge flowing beneath my feet, the stench threatening to overwhelm me, the eager faces pressed against the bars, all the girls calling out, "I'm the true princess!" "No, I am!" But I fight down the faintness and force myself to think coolly and logically. Just like Sir Stephen trained me. *Look for the facts,* I remind myself. "How many girls are there?" I ask, pretending a calm I don't feel. "Ten? Fifteen?"

"Eleven," Desmia says.

Eleven. That means that I bring the number of girls claiming Desmia's throne to an even dozen. Or an unlucky thirteen, if you count Desmia herself as having no more claim than the rest of us.

"Have you talked to them?" I ask Desmia.

"*I* did," Ella says. "They all tell very similar stories: They were hidden away because of the danger, but educated so they'd be ready to take the throne when the danger passed. I don't know Sualan geography terribly well, but it sounds like they were all raised in remote villages, scattered throughout the kingdom, and everyone in their villages was under the impression they were just ordinary girls."

Childishly, I want to scream out, *No! It can't be! That's my story! Mine alone!* But I bite down hard, holding the words back. I press my lips together with agonizing force.

Harper squeezes my hand again.

Ella tilts her head to the side, thoughtfully.

"Of course, that's a lot of effort to go to, to hide all those girls, to educate them, to concoct cover stories. . . . Did the people who hid all of them away know about the other girls in hiding? Did your Sir Stephen know Sir Roget, who hid Lucia in Gondervail? Or Sir Alderon who hid Fidelia in Tsurit?"

I shrug, because I am still gritting my teeth as tightly as I can. I'm afraid of what I might say if I let myself open my mouth. *My story!* I still want to scream. *Only mine! I am unique! I am special! I am the one and only true princess!*

"And," Ella continues, "I'm thinking that there must be at least two competing sides here, that the people who hid the girls in the first place probably aren't the same ones who put them in the dungeon. . . ."

It seems that Desmia and Harper and I are just going to let Ella, this Fridesian, figure everything out. We Sualans are just lumps, just blobs. Useless. We can't think for ourselves. We don't want to. We're too afraid of where such thoughts lead.

Then Desmia whispers, "I think I know why the girls were brought to the castle. To the dungeons."

We all turn to her, and she wilts a little under the attention.
She takes a step back.

"Why?" Ella asks gently.

"To control me," Desmia whispers. She is twisting her
hands again. I think about differences: Harper is holding my
hand so steadily, but Desmia has no hand to hold but her
own. She brings both hands up to her face and covers her
mouth—it looks like she's trying as hard as I am to hold back
her words. They break out anyway.

"Lord Throckmorton, Lord Suprien, Lord Tyfolieu," she
says, spitting out the names as she drops her hands to her chin.
"My advisers . . . they don't talk about the 'pretender to the
throne' so much anymore. Or about how they want to keep
me safe. They talk about how, really, one girl is pretty much
the same as another, and really, no one outside the castle's
ever seen me except at a distance of hundreds of feet, and
at that I'm always covered by a veil. And how, really, except
for them, the only people *in* the castle who've seen me up
close are servants, and servants are so easily dismissed, their
testimony so easily discredited. . . ."

Desmia is whispering again, her voice barely sounding
at all. But the other three of us are so silent, we hear every
word.

Harper's jaw drops.

"These guys," he says incredulously. "They've *told* you they
want to replace you?"

"Not in so many words," Desmia says.

"You have to understand," Ella explains. "These Sualan officials, they're not the types where you could hand them a rose and ask what color it is and they'd say, 'It's red.' They'd say"—she puts on a tone of supercilious pomposity—"'That tint is one of great distinction, one of the fine shades found only in our great land—we're sure that blossoms in Fridesia are so far inferior that we'd have to shield our eyes from a horror such as viewing what passes for beauty in your land. And since you are our enemies, you should find symbolism in the fact that this bloom has the same hue as the blood shed on the battlefield by all who choose to oppose us, all who, inevitably, lose. . . .'"

Desmia giggles.

"You're making them sound too nice," she says. "Too humble."

I close my eyes weakly, thinking about how I could have been captured so easily at Nanny's hut, or at Sir Stephen's if we'd followed the trail of hoofprints. Or how if Harper and I had managed to escape from the castle tower that first day, we would have run straight to the palace officials, probably to these very lords. Then those men might have thrown me in the dungeon with the other girls. Or, if Desmia's theory is correct, the lords just might have replaced Desmia with me right away. And I would have happily gone along with that plan. How long would it have taken me to understand what those men were really like?

A long time, a tiny voice in my head tells me. *You would have just thought that you'd gotten what you wanted. What you deserved.*

"Wait a minute," I challenge Desmia. "You were judging the music competition. People saw you then. You've met with the Fridesian peace delegation."

"Nobody cares about the Fridesians," Desmia says. She shoots an apologetic glance at Ella. "Sorry," she whispers. Then she turns back to me. "And at the music competition I was in the shadows. Nobody looked at me but you. What I did that day . . ." She looks down, then looks back up with blazing eyes. "I surprised myself. It felt like I was almost . . . fighting back. When you came to me and told me you were the true princess, I couldn't let you be locked in the dungeon with all the other girls. I couldn't let Lord Throckmorton have his victory of capturing all twelve girls—from what I overheard, I think there are just twelve of you."

I wince at that—*No, I want to correct her, there's only one of me*—but I let it go.

"Because I think when he has all twelve," Desmia continues, "I think then he'll feel safe setting all his plans in motion. Maybe then he won't care if he just kills us all."

I notice how Desmia says "us," grouping herself with the girls in the dungeon, too. I forgive her.

"So I locked you away in the tower, keeping you safe," she says. "But I didn't know what else to do, because I didn't think you'd believe anything I told you. And there was just one of me, and two of you, and you can't know what it's like, always living in terror, feeling so powerless. . . ."

"I do," Ella says softly. She reaches over and gives Desmia's hand a squeeze.

"But—but—," Harper breaks in, trying to get his ideas out so quickly that he actually sputters. "You're the *princess*! You're the one wearing the crown! Can't you do whatever you want to with the girls in the dungeon? With those lords who want to control you?"

"'Royals must be firm and decisive in their words and actions,'" I quote. "As it says in *A Royal's Guide to Dealing with Subordinates*. 'The royal who hesitates to wield his power entices his lessers to wield it against him.'"

Desmia snorts, an ugly sound.

"Don't you see?" she asks. "I have no power. I'm just a figurehead. An endangered one. How did you put it?" She narrows her eyes at me. "I'm just a doll that waves."

We are staring each other down. I break the gaze first, shifting my stare to the stone wall.

"But the true princess is the supreme ruler of Suala," I say in a ragged voice. "A single word from her can stay an execution or stop a battle. Or . . . start one. From the loftiest palace official to the lowliest shepherdess, everyone in the kingdom is subject to her judgment, her jurisdiction, her rule. She is Suala!" I'm not sure if I'm quoting now, or if these are words embedded in my soul so long ago I might as well be stripping off my own flesh, laying it in front of Desmia as a sacrifice. The true princess should be able to inspire that sort of devotion.

"I'm nobody," Desmia counters. "Nothing. A pawn."

Ella looks sadly from Desmia to me.

"It's that way in Fridesia, too," she says gently. "Princesses are more commodity than ruler. I have never heard of any kingdom where a princess gets to use her power."

Somehow this seems cruelest of all—that the position I've risked my life for is worth nothing. I turn and bury my face in Desmia's pillows—the soft, deceptive pillows, the empty trappings of power. I sob, and it seems that the others can do nothing but listen.

Then someone is gripping my shoulders, shaking me.

"Okay, okay, Eelsy, stop it!" Harper begs. "Don't you think I've already heard enough crying to last me a lifetime?"

I'm shocked enough that I stop sobbing for a moment. The next sob that comes out half turns into a giggle.

Harper shoves at my shoulder, forcing me to turn over and look at him.

"I knew you for fourteen years before I knew you were a princess—supposedly a princess—and I never thought you were the type to just give up," he says roughly. "You were never afraid to climb the tallest trees in the woods. You were never afraid to put your hand into a full bucket of night crawlers. You were never afraid to swim in the pond, even though you were a sight coming out, covered in leeches. So why are you afraid of some uppity guys with stupid fancy names?"

"Because, because . . ." I sniff. It is hard to completely turn off sobs so quickly.

Harper pokes me in the shoulder.

"So maybe you're not a princess," he says. He turns and points at Desmia. "And maybe you're not a princess with any power." He turns his gaze on Ella. "And you say you're not a princess either." He claps his hands on his own chest. "And God knows, I'm nothing but the son of a dead soldier, who was nothing but cannon fodder. And I don't have anything to defend any of you with except a harp. But—but—don't you see? There are four of us, and no one else knows that Cecilia and I are here. And no one knows that any of us know anything. And no one knows that you"—he's spun around to point at Ella again—"are on our side. And we know that Sir Stephen and Nanny and my own mother are here in Cortona, and they'd help us too, if we could get word to them. So I don't know about the rest of you, but I am not just going to roll over and play dead until the time comes that they actually kill us!"

"I wasn't playing dead," I say stiffly. "I was crying."

"Baby," Harper jeers.

"I am not!" I protest. I scramble up and actually shove Harper, to get him back for all his trying to push me around. "Just because I actually have feelings—I should be allowed—"

"You had days and days and days in the tower to get over yourself," Harper says. "So you're not a princess. So what? Aren't you done yet with all that caterwauling?"

"I—I—"

Desmia steps between us.

"'*Our* side'?" she quotes numbly. "You said 'our side'? Like we're all in this together? On the same team?"

"Well, yeah," Harper says, squinting at her. "Aren't we?"

"You mean, because you're scared of Lord Throckmorton and his cohorts?" Desmia asks. "As in 'The enemy of my enemy is my friend'? And then if—this is crazy!—if we succeeded in vanquishing him, she'd still want the crown?" She is pointing at me, her eyes narrowed to accusing slits.

I am still mad at Harper. I don't like the way Desmia is glaring at me. It would be rather satisfying to just pitch myself down to the ground and beat my fists and kick my feet, to throw a good, long, royal tantrum. But, for all that Sir Stephen must have been wrong about me being the true princess, I still have everything that he taught me rattling around in my head. *You know how to handle this,* that annoying little voice cheers in my head. *Think. Ten Ways to Turn Potential Enemies Into Friends. Twelve Ways to Cement an Ally's Loyalty. Five Ways to . . .*

I see that the finger Desmia has pointed at me is shaking. I see that the corners of her mouth are quivering. I see that she's having trouble holding her glare, and has to squeeze her eyes tighter and tighter together to keep the fierceness in her gaze. I think about how frightening it must be to have absolutely no one to trust. I think about how she's already begun to fight back against her advisers. A little.

"I won't lie to you," I say, and somehow my voice comes out sounding dignified and calm. Almost royal. "I don't know who deserves to wear the crown. It may be you. It may be me. It may be one of those girls down there in the dungeon.

But I think all of us deserve to know the truth. I think Suala deserves to know the truth. I can't promise you what I'll feel like when we solve all the mysteries. But I can tell you—I can swear to this—I'll do whatever's best for my kingdom."

Desmia's eyes widen, the menace slipping out of her stare.

"That's good enough for me," she says. She smiles at me, hesitantly. Then the smile turns wistful. "But what can we possibly do?"

Ella steps up into our little circle.

"A lot, actually," she says. "I have some ideas."

She drapes her arms around us—one arm on Desmia's shoulder, one on mine—and the four of us begin to plan.

22

I squat on the hard stone step, my ear pressed against a chink in a stone wall. This is my role in our little plot: eavesdropping on the palace officials. It makes sense that this is my job—I am the one who must stay hidden, and there's no better hiding place than the secret stairways. Ella and Desmia have to appear at state dinners and such (you know, the entire kingdom would probably fall to pieces if Desmia didn't appear on the balcony at noon each day) and we agreed that Harper is the best person to try to sneak out of the palace to look for Sir Stephen and Nanny and Harper's mam.

In truth I was eager for this assignment. I wanted to hear everything the advisers had to say. It's not that I don't believe Desmia—it's not that I don't trust her. It's just . . . well, maybe it just comes down to Point Nine of the Guidelines for Wise Rulers: "Trust, but verify." I can remember being baffled by that one, when I used to huddle over my books back in Nanny's cottage. But now I do want to hold up what

I hear from Lord Throckmorton's room against what Desmia told me about life in the palace, against what Sir Stephen told me about how the palace power structure is supposed to work.

Someone is coming into Lord Throckmorton's office. The chink I have my ear against is at floor level, so I hear footsteps particularly well.

"Sign here, sir."

There's a rubbing sound, undoubtedly from a quill pen traveling across parchment. Then a growl: "Dismissed."

I sigh soundlessly. I *was* eager for this assignment, but that was hours ago. So far, that "Sign here" / "Dismissed" conversation is about the most significant one I've heard. And now my legs are cramped and my back is stiff from not moving, and—you wouldn't think this was possible—even my voice box aches from not speaking to anyone in so long. I plan what I will tell Harper about this tedium when I see him again: "It was like all the worst parts of fishing without any of the fun. Or the tasty fish."

Or, no—I will not complain to Harper again. I remember what he said last night in Desmia's room: *You had days and days and days in the tower to get over yourself. . . . Aren't you done yet with all that caterwauling?* I know what he thinks. He thinks I'm a spoiled whiner, a selfish brat. I can imagine what else he might have wanted to say: *You know, I've known all my life that I wasn't royalty, that I wasn't anyone important, and you don't see me crying about it. . . .*

"You don't know how it feels," I whisper, and I actually dare to make the s sound audible. If Lord Throckmorton hears me, on the other side of the wall, he's going to believe the palace is infested with snakes.

No footsteps tromp over toward me, so I think I'm safe. I go back to imagining how I could explain this to Harper. All I can think of is the beef that Nanny used to buy from the village butcher for special occasions. She could only afford the gristliest, toughest cuts of meat, so when she got it home she'd pound it with a spiked mallet, beating it for hours sometimes, until it was soft enough to chew.

I feel as though someone's used that mallet on my heart. I feel as though I've been cut open and bloodied and beaten limp. I feel like if I think about this much more, I will start screaming and wailing again, and I will be discovered here in the secret stairway, and . . .

Footsteps sound on the other side of the stone wall again. I hear a door creaking shut.

"No one suspects, do they?" This is Lord Throckmorton's growl.

Suspects? Suspects what? I wonder. I press my ear harder against the chink in the wall.

"Well, sir"—it's another man's voice, higher pitched with anxiety—"surely the jailer must realize—"

"No, dimwit, no one who *matters*."

"Well, there's your answer, then. No one matters but the people in this room, do they?"

There's a cackling laugh in response. Lord Throckmorton doesn't seem like a cackler—is there a third person in the room?

I turn my head and try to peek through the chink in the stone, but I see nothing but the brown wood of a table or desk leg. Then a heavy black boot kicks against the wall, covering over my chink. Even though the stone wall is at least a foot thick, I react as though I've been kicked in the eye. I reel back, smashing my head against the opposite wall of the stairway, the jagged stone tearing into my scalp. It takes all my willpower not to cry out. I press my hand against the wound, which is already sticky with blood, and dizzily force myself back to the chink. If Lord Throckmorton knows I'm here—if he kicked the wall on purpose—I need to be prepared to run. Desmia showed me several entrances and exits from the secret stairway: Should I scurry back to her room, even though it's still two flights up? Or should I try for the door in the hallway behind the theater where the music competition is, amazingly, still going on?

I press my eye back against the hole in the wall. The boot has swung away again. Ah. Lord Throckmorton's desk is right beside the wall, and he only happened to scrape his boot forward. I'm safe. I turn my ear to the chink again.

"—find the last one?" Lord Throckmorton is asking.

"It appears that she knows we are looking. She's vanished."

Are they talking about me? I press my ear so tightly against the chink in the wall that I think I'm going to have permanent indentations in my head from the stone. Still, I'm afraid I've missed something, because the next thing I hear is, "Yes, and someone must have warned Sir Stephen, because he left right after we searched his house."

"Idiots!" This is definitely Lord Throckmorton's growl again. "Should have captured him right away and been done with it!"

"They're using him as bait, sir, following him, watching who he talks to, where he goes. . . ."

I jerk back again, but this time I manage to avoid bashing my head against the wall. I barely notice. If Lord Throckmorton's men are using Sir Stephen as bait, I know who they're going to catch.

Harper.

23

It suddenly seems as though there is no air in the secret stairway. I scramble up anyhow. I can run without breathing, if I have to. And I have to. For I can't stay here listening to their plotting—I can't. I have to go find Harper, to warn him, to keep him safe.

I rush down the stairs, my desire for haste warring with the need to be quiet, the need to keep from slipping and plunging to the ground. Desmia gave me a new pair of shoes last night, and they're not as slick as my now-discarded filthy felt. But they're a little big, and my feet slide forward and back inside them, like unmoored boats. I force myself to watch my step and concentrate on the directions Desmia gave me to that ground-floor door, the one in the hallway behind the theater.

Turn left at the corner of the stairs where there's a red ribbon tied on the post—yes, there it is. Then go down two flights and turn right. . . . But was it left then right or right then left? Was it two flights or three? I can't remember. I'm too panicked.

If I thought my heart was flayed open before, learning that everything I'd always believed was a lie, learning that I'm just one of twelve girls making unfounded claims . . . well, I was wrong. That was nothing. *This* is what it feels like to have my heart pounded into a pulp, to feel utterly crushed. Harper is in danger, and it's all because of me.

I remember how I rushed back to find Harper on the street corner after I saw the boy kidnapped by the press gang and carried off to war. I'd been worried about Harper then, but that was only the possibility of danger. This is worse. This is all but certain.

Oh, Harper. There are things I should have said to you—not just my secrets about being a princess. . . .

The stairs below me are completely dark. I'm carrying a lantern, but its dim light seems so easily devoured by the inky blackness around me. I feel like I've been descending these stairs forever. Surely I've climbed down more than two flights since the post with the red ribbon. Haven't I? The stairway veers, dropping into a jagged dip to the right. I don't remember that from before. Wouldn't I have noticed? I crouch down, holding the lantern close to the steps. Ahead of me the uneven stairs jerk right and left, forming a zigzag path down into the darkness. My heart sinks. This is totally unfamiliar.

Nothing to do but turn back, I tell myself.

I race up again, taking steps two at a time. I feel something wet on my cheek and touch it—*oh, yeah,* I think vaguely. *Blood from my wound.* It doesn't matter now. I turn at the landing, but I can't find the post with the red ribbon anymore. The next time I see stairs going down, I take them. These, too, seem to descend endlessly.

Fine. These probably go to the dungeon. I'll go out the door there and just climb up the regular stairs. If anyone sees me I'll bluff my way out. I'll think of something. I have to.

I almost cry with relief when I see the outline of a stone door ahead of me, at the bottom of the stairs. I shove against it, but it doesn't budge. *Oops, no—pull!* It takes all my strength to tug the door open a crack. *A little more . . .* Finally, the doorway is wide enough that I can slip through.

This is not the same dungeon that I was in before. The stench is worse, the filth is worse, and the curtains of clammy cobwebs are so thick against my face that I'm forced to breathe with my hand over my nose. Also, it's not just sludge beneath my feet here—it's torrents of sludge, a river of sludge, maybe all of Cortona's sewage mixed with the refuse from every slaughterhouse in the kingdom.

Wonderful, I think. *Another pair of shoes ruined.*

With a trembling arm I lift the lantern high, trying to see a way out.

I gasp.

In front of me and slightly to the left an executioner's pike leans against the wall, alongside a rack and a row of thumbscrews and a blade hanging from the ceiling over a stone table strewn with ropes. Sir Stephen never taught me about any of those things, but I heard stories in the village.

You pull a man's fingernails out, oh yeah, he'll start talking. He'll tell you anything you want to know. . . .

The way the rack works, see, you turn the crank and then the body stretches—bet you didn't know a body could stretch that much, huh? Well, it can't, not really, not without dying. Eventually . . .

Those were stories I closed my ears to, stories I didn't want to hear. Even Harper didn't like those stories. But I heard enough that I know what this place is.

I've found the palace torture chamber.

I turn to the right because I can't bear to look anymore, not when I have to decide whether to go back up the secret stairway or force myself to continue through this chamber of horrors, looking for another way out. My arm is shaking so badly now that I can barely hold on to the lantern. I swing the light out in a wide arc.

And that's when I see the eleven men hanging on the wall.

24

At first I think they are dead. How can they not be, when their bodies are so skeletal? They are old men, shrunken down to bone and beards, their arms pulled to either side by solid chain, their legs tugged toward the ground by cuffs around their ankles. They look like they've been crucified.

Then one of them lifts his head and speaks.

"Oh, miss," he creaks. "I pray thee, have a kindness—what can you tell us of the princess? Is she safe?"

"D-Desmia?" I stammer.

"No," he says weakly, "not her. She is but a fake. Know you of the true princess?"

I think that it must take great effort for him to form those words, to move his ancient jaw. But he's not asking for food or water or release. He's asking about the true princess.

"What is the true princess's name?" I ask cautiously.

In spite of everything that's happened, everything that I've seen and heard, I am still longing for all eleven men to chime in together: "Cecilia!"

They do not say this.

"If you knowest not her name, perhaps I'd best not say," the first man mumbles.

The man beside him whispers, "Oh, come now, this is a mere girl, not Throckmorton. . . ."

"How else will we ever know?" another adds.

And a bold man on the end throws his head back and calls out, "Lucia! Her name is Lucia!"

At once the other men turn on him.

"Roget, how can you say that? What good are jokes, now?"

"Roget, who knows how much time we have before Throckmorton returns . . . ?"

"It's Fidelia, miss," one man says while the others argue.

"Fidelia? You jest! The true princess is Sophia!"

"Aramina!"

"Porfinia!"

"Ganelia!"

While the skeletal men spit out names and argue, I notice for the first time that a twelfth set of chains and ankle cuffs hangs at the far end of the wall. *A twelfth set waiting for a twelfth man,* I think. *Waiting for Sir Stephen.*

"You were all knights," I say. "Knights who became tutors . . ."

"Well, *I* became the true princess's tutor," the one the others have been calling Roget replies. *Sir Roget,* I think, remembering Ella asking me, *Did your Sir Stephen know Sir Roget, who hid Lucia in Gondervail? Or Sir Alderon who hid Fidelia in Tsurit?*

"How dare you say that! I was her tutor," another man corrects him.

"No, I was!"

"No, me!"

I don't count, but I'm sure I hear eleven claims and counterclaims. I close my eyes, weakly.

"Why?" I whisper.

The men fall silent. I open my eyes, and they are all staring at me.

"Why did all of you lie?" I ask. "Telling those girls, each one of them, 'You are the one and only true princess,' when it wasn't true?"

"I promise you, miss, I did not lie," Sir Roget says. "On my honor as a knight, I swear—"

His oath is drowned out by ten other knights also swearing, "I did not lie, I promise."

I can't figure this out. They all seem to be telling the truth—or they all seem to *think* they are telling the truth, which is perhaps an important difference. I can't even understand how all of them could have been hanging there for God knows how long without having thought to compare stories.

"But Sir Stephen always told me . . . ," I begin, and stop. I still want to believe Sir Stephen. I still want to believe—no!

I know!—that he and Nanny are trustworthy. I remember Harper's theory that maybe Sir Stephen thought he was telling the truth, but someone had lied to him. *So many lies and possible lies,* I think. *How can I ever find the truth?* A lump is growing in my throat because I miss Sir Stephen so much—Sir Stephen and all his certainty. . . . My eyes turn again toward the twelfth set of chains and cuffs. I force my gaze away.

"Sir Stephen?" Sir Roget says eagerly. "You know of Sir Stephen? He is our only hope now. Is he well? Is he preparing a plan of attack?"

My head is spinning. These knights know about Sir Stephen, so he must know about them—does he know they all claim to have tutored the true princess? Does he know they're all here in the torture chamber? Does he know about the chains and cuffs waiting for him?

I shake my head impatiently, trying to clear it.

"A friend of mine is on his way to find Sir Stephen," I say. "But Lord Throckmorton . . ." I don't have time to explain. I don't have time to straighten out their stories, either, not when Harper could be stepping into Lord Throckmorton's trap at this very moment. "I have to go. Is there another exit from this room?"

The knights are silent, as if reluctant to let me leave. Then the oldest-looking one, the one who spoke first, croaks, "They brought us down the stairs over there." He points to the right.

I turn in that direction, then stop and turn back. I peer again at the eleven knights reduced to near skeletons, chained in a torture chamber. Eleven knights who asked nothing for themselves, but only wanted to know the fate of eleven girls. Eleven knights who seem truly admirable, loyal, and honest—but surely must be lying. I whirl around and grab the executioner's pike. I step toward Sir Roget and lift the pike high above my head. It's heavy, but I don't waver.

"Miss!" he exclaims. Still, he does not beg or plead. He lowers his head, nobly.

I bring the pike down squarely on the chains that confine his right wrist. The chains fall away with a satisfying clunk. I do the same with the chains on his left and, more delicately, with the cuffs about his ankles. When he tumbles to the ground, I hand him the pike.

"Free the others," I tell him. "The girls you ask about are in the dungeon. There is a way to find it if you go up those stairs." I point to the door I came through. "I can't begin to tell you how to get there. But when you find the girls, go to the highest point in the castle—there's a tower there where you'll be safe. I think Desmia will help you, and Ella . . . I'll meet you there if I can."

I take off running without looking back.

25

The stairs are nearby, but then I have to climb and climb and climb. . . . I am dizzy by the time I reach the top, and so stupid with exhaustion that the door utterly confounds me. It's solid wood and seems sealed tight, undoubtedly locked from the other side. I find myself wishing I'd kept the executioner's pike—I have such a lovely picture in my mind of myself slashing the door down to splinters. I think about backtracking and retrieving the pike from the knights, but that's so far away.

Think, I command myself. *Maybe something Sir Stephen taught you would be useful?* Not palace manners, not Latin, not geography, not rhetoric—maybe geometry? *The door is a rectangle,* I think, ever so brilliantly. *Bounded on the left by hinges, and . . .*

Hinges. I reach down and pry out the pin of the bottom hinge. By the time I'm done, my fingers are as bloody as my head, but when I shove against it, the door creaks out a little.

I pull the pin from the next hinge up, and then the one above that, and by battering my shoulder against the door I make enough of an opening to squeeze out.

I don't even check to see where the door leads—I'm just lucky I don't arrive in a room full of soldiers. Instead, I'm outside the palace, in a dark alley strewn with garbage and rats.

"Harper, you had better appreciate this," I mutter, because there is nowhere to put my feet without stepping on a rat's body.

Some of the rats are evidently dead, because they don't move when I step on them.

It's a good thing I'm not really a princess, after all, I think, *what with having to walk on rat carcasses.* But, annoyingly, one of Sir Stephen's maxims immediately springs to mind: *"A royal caught in unpleasant circumstances does not panic, but remembers the value of distracting oneself. Humming a patriotic song is always helpful."*

The only music I can think of are the tunes Harper plays. Tears blur my eyes—and really that's a good thing, because then I can't see the rats I'm walking through.

The alley curves and shifts, and then, as if there's an invisible fence somewhere, the rats disappear from underfoot. Respectable shops appear around me now, along with respectable townspeople, who stare and gape and yet somehow manage to pretend that they are not staring and gaping.

Oh, yeah, I think. *My head is bleeding, my hands are bleeding, my shoes are covered in sludge. . . .*

I consider smiling and uttering a polite, *And how are you this fine day?* but no one will meet my eye. Regardless, I need all my concentration for forcing my feet forward.

Where am I going, anyhow? Why didn't I ask Harper exactly where he planned to go to look for Sir Stephen and Nanny and his mam?

The alley—now just an ordinary street—curves again and spits me out into a vast sunlit square. No, not a square: It's the courtyard in front of the palace. And it must be noon, because the courtyard is packed wall-to-wall with people all staring toward at Desmia's balcony.

I sway, nearly overcome with dizziness and despair. How could I possibly have thought that I could find Harper in all the crowds of Cortona? Why hadn't I thought to beg the knights from the torture chamber to come with me? They were rickety skeletons, near death, but there would be *someone* to help me, so it wouldn't be just me alone, desperately searching an entire city for a single boy.

And then, across the crowd, I spy Ella.

I can see her only because she is being lifted onto a sort of viewing platform in the center of the courtyard. She is wearing a dainty rose-colored dress that gleams in the sunlight, its glow almost matching the marvel of her golden hair. Though she wears no crown, she looks every bit a princess; several in the crowd are staring at her rather than Desmia's balcony. Dimly, I remember her part in our plans: Under the guise of simply wanting to know more about our delightful kingdom she was going to ask for a tour of Cortona, so she could gauge the mood of the countryside and find out whether Suala's subjects were more loyal to Desmia or Lord Throckmorton.

What a stupid plan, I think. But then some of Sir Stephen's chess training kicks in, and it's like I can step back and see an overview, all of us like pieces on a chessboard. Ella's plan— our plan, the one all four of us put together last night—was not stupid. It was simply cautious, a plan perfectly suited to a foreigner who doesn't want to ruin her fiancé's peace mission and a princess who already feels like her life is in danger and a girl who no longer knows who she is and a boy who . . . Well, I can't think of Harper's reason for caution; that's probably why he'd agreed to do the most dangerous task. Still, last night we were like chess players deciding to push a few pawns forward so we could figure out our opponents' mindset and strategy. We thought the game was just beginning. We thought we had time.

We didn't know about the half-dead knights in the torture chamber and the trap laid around Sir Stephen and . . . I feel the color drain from my face. There are probably other dangers out there that I still don't know about, because I ran away from my listening post.

I had to, I tell myself fiercely. *The time for caution is past.*

I begin struggling through the throngs of people toward Ella. The crowd does not exactly part for me the way I saw it part for her. I have to shove, elbow, pinch, poke, and—once, when everything else fails—threaten to smear my bloody hands on a nasty woman's dress. By the time I reach Ella's viewing platform, Desmia must be done waving up on her balcony, because the crowd is reluctantly beginning to turn away.

Guards circle Ella's platform. I hear the woman sitting next to her—a stiff, matronly type in an ugly, eggplant-colored dress—say, "I've arranged a carriage to pick us up now, because you *surely* don't want to associate with any of the riffraff in the streets."

I plant myself directly in front of Ella's platform, in plain sight. I want Ella's help looking for Harper; I want to tell her about what I overheard and how I found the knights in the torture chamber. I'd love it if she could figure out how each one of the knights could be so certain that *he* was the one who'd tutored the true princess. But I can't tell her anything when so many other people are within earshot.

The matron sitting beside Ella catches a glimpse of me and sniffs in horror.

"My—my smelling salts," she gasps.

Do I really look that bad? Sure, my shoes and legs are a bit muddy, and my hair's probably a mess, with the blood and all. But Ella and Desmia did make sure that I got a new dress last night—a plain one pulled from the maids' supply, because any of their clothes would have been too conspicuous on me, but still, it's clean and unripped and . . . I peer down, indignant, and see that the formerly clean dress is now smeared with mud and blood and adorned with filthy strings of cobwebs. And I guess I must have ripped a couple of the seams when

I was wielding the pike on Sir Roget's chains, or pulling out the door hinges, or running across the rats.

Okay, so I look terrible. So what? Wait a minute—can I use that?

"Please, miss," I say, addressing Ella. "I am but a poor ragamuffin child, but I wanted to talk to you. I can tell you that even Sualans like myself understand how lucky we are to live here. Suala is a glorious land, and Desmia is a wonderful princess."

Ella's eyes bug out when she sees me.

"Listen to that," the matron beside Ella says, having evidently decided she doesn't have to faint. She simpers. "Even our beggars here in Suala have perfect grammar and diction. And appropriate gratitude."

"Please, miss," I say, trying again, staring at Ella. "If I could just tell you my story privately . . ."

Ella casts her eyes hesitantly toward the matron, and down toward the guards.

"Er—," she says.

The matron clutches Ella's arm.

"Oh, no!" she exclaims. "We would never allow such a thing with a visiting dignitary. That one would lure you into a dark alley and beat you senseless, she would!"

I'm thinking that I would like to lure this matron into the rat-infested alley I just left, just to see if she herself can maintain perfect grammar, diction, and gratitude under such trying circumstances.

Ella clears her throat.

"I would have thought this beggar might be located elsewhere," she says, grimacing slightly. Almost imperceptibly she twitches her head toward the palace and wrinkles her brow curiously.

Code language and facial expressions, I think. *That's all we're going to be able to use.*

"Are you implying that our beggars are too forward?" the matron asks, offense creeping into her voice. "What do you do in Fridesia, cage them up so they're out of sight?"

Ella turns toward the matron.

"Oh, no," she says, forcing her eyes into a wide expression of mock guilelessness. "In Fridesia we have so many beggars that one can barely walk two paces without having to step over a ragamuffin like this one. I've been admiring the fact that Suala's indigents are so rare as to be practically nonexistent."

She glances my way, as if to ask, *Am I laying it on too thick?*

I frown, because this could take forever.

"Believe me," I say, "I was exactly where I belonged, earlier this morning. But then"—*How can I say this?*—"I, uh, had good cause to come this way. I, um, wanted to sing Suala's praises to you, but . . ." Suddenly, I'm inspired. "How can I sing without a harp? And *Harper?*"

I'm proud of myself for being able to ask so directly, without giving anything away.

"There was a fine harper at the palace," Ella says, her face as serene as if she's doing no more than musing on all the pleasant music she's heard since arriving in Suala.

I glance at the matron, who doesn't look suspicious yet.

"Is the harper still there?" I ask, and somehow I can't keep the urgency out of my voice. You'd think that I would be good at pretending after all my years of practice, but I sound so worried that even people on the other side of the platform turn and stare at me with great concern.

"Aye, at the music competition——," Ella begins, which makes me wonder if she understands what I'm trying to say at all. The matron beside her interrupts before I have a chance to clarify.

"That's enough! Beggar, begone!" she orders. "We'll not have you troubling our visitor with your nonsense."

"Oh, please," I say. I think to humbly bow my head. "I have to——"

Ella gasps before I can say another word.

"You have to get treatment for that gash on your head!" she exclaims. "How is it that you're even conscious?"

The matron gasps too.

"That's blood?" she shrieks, horrified. "Not just dirt?"

She faints dead away, her body crumpling onto the platform.

Ella stands up and taps one of her guards on the shoulder.

"You, carry Lady Throckmorton back into the palace. Make sure you keep her in a dark room for at least an hour, do you hear me?" She turns to another guard. "And you, make sure there's a needle and thread and candle waiting in my quarters. And you"—she's addressing a third guard now—"carry this child into the palace so I can take a good look at her injury."

"You, miss?" the guard says doubtfully, even as the other two scramble to obey. "*You'll* take a look at it?"

"Yes." Ella's reply is firm. She may not be a princess, but even Sir Stephen would be impressed with her tone of command.

Not that I plan to obey her.

"I am not going to the palace!" I say, stamping my foot. "Not when the *harper* is outside."

"Didn't you hear me? The *harper* is in the palace, watching the music competition," Ella practically shouts back at me. We are barely pretending now, but I hear a man nearby whisper, "Those are some serious music lovers."

"The harper is watching for a most unusual act," Ella adds. "Two ladies and a gentleman . . ."

I reel backward, woozy in my despair. Why can't Ella understand? What do I care about acts in the music competition? Two ladies and a gentleman? So what?

Oh. Two ladies and a gentleman: Nanny, Harper's mam, and Sir Stephen.

"Take me to the palace, then," I whisper, and the guard scoops me up in his arms.

26

I don't like being carried. For one thing, the guard holds me at arm's length, as if he's terrified that touching me will give him fleas or some other vermin. This makes me feel like I'm constantly in danger of being dropped. For another thing, as long as the guard's holding me, I can't say anything to Ella.

She's walking at a dignified pace behind us, surrounded by a cortège of the other guards. I can hear her proclaiming loudly, "Sualans are so merciful, that they would allow a beggar child to be treated for her wounds at the palace. Desmia truly is a munificent princess. . . ."

Is she out of her mind? I wonder. *Calling attention to how weird this is?* But then, over the guard's shoulder Ella winks at me, and I remember another one of Sir Stephen's maxims: *"Praise people in advance for doing what you want them to do, even if you don't truly expect them to do it, and sometimes they'll surprise you."* I can't remember if that's from Ten Guidelines for Forcing

Subordinates to Rise to the Occasion or Twelve Rules for
Controlling a Dicey Situation, but in this case, it seems to be
working. We're almost at the palace.

Everything goes dark, but that's only because we've
stepped from the bright sunlight into the dimness of the
palace entryway. This is a different entrance from the one
Harper and I used for the music competition, and when my
eyes adjust, I am thunderstruck by the gilt that seems to
cover every square inch of the ceiling, the mirrors that hang
from every wall, and the throngs of elegantly dressed people
standing around chatting.

*And yet down in the basement there were knights being
tortured,* I think, and that helps keep me from being quite
so dazed.

"We shall take her to my quarters," Ella whispers to the
guard, and then goes back to loudly praising Suala's mercy
and Desmia's compassion for the poor.

Maybe I black out for a few minutes, because I don't
really keep track of all the stairways the guard ascends, all
the corridors he walks through. He's not making much
effort to be gentle with me, so I have to squeeze my eyes
shut and grit my teeth to keep from screaming from the
pain of being jostled. My head truly throbs now, in a way
I hadn't noticed when I was climbing stairs and walking
through sludge and rats.

"Almost there," Ella whispers.

We enter a doorway surrounded by more uniformed

men, and then the guard unceremoniously dumps me on the floor.

"Ahhh," I moan.

"You're dismissed," Ella says sharply to the guard. "You can wait outside with the others."

As soon as he's out the door, I scramble up, ignoring my throbbing head.

"Thanks, Ella, for bringing me back into the palace. I've got to go find Harper and warn him—"

I weave to the side. Ella grabs me by the shoulders, either to steady me or stop me.

"You're not going anywhere until I clean that wound, and I'm pretty sure you'll need stitches—how in the world did you do this?" she asks. Now that there's no one else listening, her voice is full of fear and concern. "Did—did someone attack you?"

I shake my head, which isn't such a smart move. Now it *really* hurts.

Gently, Ella helps me back down to the floor. She lifts a shallow bowl of water down beside us and begins dabbing at my wound with a wet cloth.

"I was just clumsy, that's all," I manage to say. It's a strain to talk, but I have to tell her about Harper. "Don't worry about me. It's Harper . . . I heard Lord Throckmorton say that they're following Sir Stephen, and watching him, and using him as bait in a trap, and if Harper goes to talk to him, then they'll catch him, too. . . ."

I start to struggle away from Ella again. I'm not really sure, but I think I'm trying to crawl toward the door.

Ella puts the cloth down and holds me firmly in place. She leans her face toward mine, as if she's not sure that I'll be able to listen otherwise.

"Look," she says, "Harper is fine. Understand? I saw him right before I left the palace. He told me he'd seen his mother and Nanny and Sir Stephen come in through the entrance for the music contestants, and he asked someone, and they said that that act would go on at two. So Harper's just waiting in the competition theater—there's a huge audience there now, so he blends in. He won't try to talk to Sir Stephen or anyone else until after they perform, and we've got plenty of time left to get word to him before that. So he's *safe*. Safer than you with this gash in the back of your head and . . ." For the first time she seems to fully take in the rest of my appearance: the muck covering my shoes and ankles, the cobwebs trailing from my hair and dress, the bloody cuts on my hands. "*Where* have you been?"

"I got lost in the secret stairways and had to go out through the palace torture chamber, which is even nastier than the palace dungeon. And, oh, I had to walk through some rats, and . . ." Vaguely, I remember that I need to tell her about the knights and ask her opinion of what they told me. But I'm still worried about Harper. "Are you sure we can't just run down to the theater and warn Harper? Then, I promise, you can do whatever you want to my head."

Ella keeps one hand on my shoulder, steadying me, but she picks up her cloth and begins scrubbing away my blood again.

"This will go a lot faster if I don't have to argue with you the whole time," she says. She frowns. "Did you happen to notice the guards outside my doorway?"

"Uh, yeah," I say.

"And did you see that there were some in gray Fridesian uniforms and some in blue Sualan uniforms?"

"If you say so," I mumble. But I'm not really thinking about the guards. It's hard to think at all when she seems to be digging that cloth deep into my brain.

"And so didn't it occur to you that that means I have soldiers from both sides watching me, and keeping track of my whereabouts, and reporting back to someone about everything I do?"

She puts the cloth down for a second, and I can think a little more clearly.

"Okay, I get it that you don't want the Sualan soldiers telling Lord Throckmorton anything," I say. "But—your own men? Are you worried that they'll tell Jed?"

This bothers me, somehow. Last night, when I saw her eyes light up at the mention of her fiancé, I'd wanted to believe that their relationship was the perfect, true romance, just like in a fairy tale.

Her fiancé having spies watching her doesn't seem very fairy-tale-ish. Or romantic. In fact it sounds horrid.

"Oh, no, it's not Jed I'm worried about," Ella says, picking up the cloth again. "I already told him about you and Desmia and Harper and the alleged princesses in the dungeon. It's the rest of the peace delegation I'm worried about. This is such a delicate process, and really, I think Jed is the only one who believes peace is possible. . . ."

I remember again that I need to tell Ella that I now know more about the alleged princesses in the dungeon and their knight-tutors. And to tell her that right this very minute the knights might be rescuing the princesses from the dungeon. But it's just a dim thought. I don't quite have the presence of mind to explain, not with all that pain. My thoughts skitter back to Jed and Ella, and I think about what it would be like to have a fiancé, whose needs you'd always have to consider. And I think about how Ella, in many ways, is even more restricted in the palace than I am.

"All right," Ella says, with one last dab of the cloth. "Now the wound is clean, at least. But I do think you need a couple of stitches."

She stands up and goes to a table near her bed. I've barely looked around—her room is not nearly as grand as Desmia's. The fireplace is even smaller than the one in Nanny's cottage.

Then I stop evaluating the décor, because Ella is coming toward me with a needle.

"Um, Ella?" I say. "I appreciate you wanting to take care of me and all, but don't you think you should have a doctor do this?"

"I'll warrant I've sewn up more wounds in the past year than the palace doctor," Ella says, a little stiffly, as if she's offended. "And splinted more broken bones, and treated more fevers . . ."

I stare at her, wondering if this is her idea of a joke.

She sighs.

"I know, it's hard to believe when I'm dressed like this"—she waves her arms, indicating the glowing rose-colored dress, the perfectly coiffed golden curls—"but I've been working the past year as the medical officer in a refugee camp near the worst battlefield of the Sualan War. And *that's* why I agree so strongly with Jed that it's time to end the war. I'm planning to train to be a doctor when the war is over, but I promise you, I already know quite enough to sew a few stitches in your head."

I'm quiet for a few minutes, absorbing this. I've never in my life met anyone like Ella.

"I never thought I'd be anything but a princess," I say in a small voice. "And then queen, of course . . ."

"But even as princess or queen, you wouldn't have just sat on the throne all day doing nothing, right?" Ella says, as she scoots behind me, and I brace for more pain. "I heard you say Suala didn't need just a doll that waves. Even without being a princess, can't you still do a lot?"

"I'm still thinking about that," I mutter.

Ella takes the first stitch, and it's not too bad, just a gentle tugging at my scalp.

"Would I sound too much like Lady Throckmorton if I told you that Fridesian medical practices are far ahead of Sualan medical practices?" she asks jokingly.

"Lady Throckmorton—is she Lord Throckmorton's wife?"

"Oh, yes," Ella says. "And she's just as haughty and self-centered and unpleasant as her husband."

I grimace, but that seems to pull at the skin at the back of my head.

"She's the one who was on the platform with you, right?" I ask, mostly so I don't have to think about the pain and the needle touching my skin. "*She's* the one they were going to have show you around Cortona?"

"Scary, huh?" Ella says. "We're just lucky Lady Throckmorton turned out to be a fainter. She never would have let me bring you here. I hope the guards really do make her stay in her room for an hour."

"Will that give us enough time to warn Harper?" I ask.

Ella pats my back.

"Yes, yes, we have plenty of time to get to your precious Harper!" I can't see her face, but I have the feeling she's rolling her eyes.

"I just want to make sure," I say, feeling a little insulted.

Ella giggles.

"I do understand," she says. "Believe me, I'd be the same way if it were Jed."

"Jed's your fiancé. Harper's just my friend," I say.

"Just a friend, huh?" Ella teases. "And that's why he carried you all the way from the dungeon to Desmia's room last night? That's why you walked through sewage and rats for him today?"

I hadn't thought to wonder about who carried me to Desmia's room. I blush.

"Wouldn't you do those things for a friend?" I ask.

Ella seems to be considering this. For a few seconds I don't feel the tug of any more stitches.

"Before I came to Suala, I really only had one other friend besides Jed," Ella says wistfully. "And she was the one who did kind, brave things for me. That's why I've thought . . . maybe it should be my turn now. With you and Desmia . . ."

I hear the snip of scissors behind me. Ella wraps a swath of clean cloth about my head, covering my injury. "There. You're all done. Normally I'd tell a patient with a head wound to rest quietly, but under the circumstances, if I made you rest, you'd probably pop your stitches worrying about Harper. So. How do you propose we go about getting down there to warn him?"

I'm trying to come up with a good answer, when suddenly I see some of the stones near the fireplace seem to jump out. Then they jerk back. I'm wondering if there is something to all of Ella's "head wound" talk, after all—am I hallucinating?

Ella leaps up immediately and rushes over to the wall. She's tugging on the stones, which are apparently part of a door. They come away entirely from the rest of the wall. And then—though I know this isn't actually possible—it really does seem as though twenty-two people tumble out onto the floor of Ella's room all at once.

Eleven knights.

And eleven would-be princesses.

27

"Oh, yeah," I say weakly to Ella. "I knew there was something else I wanted to tell you . . ."

I'm not sure she's listening. She's standing over the jumble of ancient knights and alleged princesses, clutching her face in dumbfounded astonishment.

"Uh—uh," she gasps. It seems she's lost the power to form a coherent word.

"I forgot to tell you," I say. "The knights were in the torture chamber. I set them free. And then they must have rescued the girls from the dungeon."

"You set them free," Ella repeats in disbelief. She gulps and turns toward me, her hands slipping down toward her jaw. The incredulity on her face seems to be melting away into panic. "Did you think about what Lord Throckmorton and his cronies will do? When they find out their prisoners are missing?"

I don't admit that I didn't think that far ahead. I want

to tell her how wrong we were, thinking we had time for caution and stealth. If my thoughts weren't so scrambled, I could give her all my chess analogies, explaining how we can't fool around with opening gambits while our opponents are ready for endgame. But all I say to defend myself is, "Look at those knights. They were dying. I had to set them free."

Ella glances at the knights piled up at her feet. Out of the dark torture chamber they look even more fragile, even more skeletal, even closer to death. The light seems to shine straight through their skin. It's like looking at baby birds fallen from their nests.

"You're right," she agrees faintly. "You had to." Then she winces, fear and panic shooting across her expression. "But this changes everything! It means—"

"Fair lady," the knight on top of the pile says, his deep voice incredibly resonant for one who looks so feeble. "Allow me to introduce myself. I'm Sir Anthony. We have nothing but gratitude to you and your associate. We knew when we heard your voices from behind the walls that this would be a safe place to come when we were so weary—"

"Shh!" Ella hisses, casting anxious glances toward the door out into the castle hall. I know she's thinking of the guards just the other side of the thin wooden panel and how difficult it would be to explain away the rumble of such a deep voice. "If anyone discovers that I'm hosting rebel knights in my chambers, then, then . . ." Her face turns three shades paler and she breaks off, as if the consequences are too dire to put to voice.

One of the would-be princesses gingerly begins trying to untangle herself from the jumble of other girls and knights. Because her leg is caught under one person's head and another person's torso, she has to jerk back hard, jarring against Ella's bedside table.

I see what's about to happen, but I'm not quick enough to stop it. The table plunges forward, crashing into the washbowl Ella had placed on the floor. The resulting clatter sounds like a thunderclap.

Immediately, Ella dashes across the room to the door to the hallway. She presses her hands firmly against the wood.

"Lady Ella! Let us in!" A guard's voice rings out from beyond the door. "Are you all right?"

"No, no, don't come in!" Ella holds the door shut. "I—I'm indisposed!"

"But that noise—"

"Oh, I just bumped against my washbowl. Clumsy me!"

"Are you sure that beggar girl didn't—"

"No, no, she's fallen fast asleep—I think it's probably best to let her sleep it off. So please, don't disturb us again!"

The whole time she's shouting back and forth with the guard, Ella's making frantic faces at me and gesturing wildly. This would be comical if she didn't also look so terrified. Finally she steps cautiously away from the door, still holding her hands near it, and watching for a long moment to see if the guard is going to disobey and shove his way into the room regardless. When nothing happens, Ella rushes back toward me.

"We've got to get these knights and girls out of here!" she whispers in my ear. "I think it's best if you get them back into the secret stairway and take them up to Desmia's room. I'll put some lumpy pillows in the bed to make it look like you're sleeping, and——"

"What about warning Harper?" I protest.

Ella purses her lips.

"I haven't forgotten him!" she mutters. "I'll go down and talk to him, and then tell Desmia exactly what's going on, and then we'll all come up to straighten this out as soon as we can . . . to plan our next step . . ."

She's already scurrying past me, grabbing pillows and stuffing them down under the blankets on her bed.

I want to protest that I should be the one to go save Harper, but Ella's plan really does make more sense. Anyhow, I should be responsible for all the knights and girls, since it's my fault they're roaming through the palace so freely. I stand up, weaving slightly and wincing from the pain. I peer down at the old, feeble men and young, terrified-looking girls, who have all been frozen in place ever since the one girl knocked over the table.

"Well," I say, trying to sound as cheerful and optimistic as I can, in a whisper, "anyone remember the Five Principles of How to Make Yourself Go On Trying Even When You Believe You've Got No Chance?"

28

Just the thought of stepping back into the secret stairways feels nightmarish. I don't know the directions for getting from Ella's room to Desmia's secretly. So, I calculate gloomily, we could easily be lost for the rest of the day, retracing the same steps thousands of times. This would be bad enough if it were just me, but with knights who are fresh from the torture chamber and girls who look rather faint themselves with their dungeon pallor—who's going to end up carrying whom?

To my surprise, as everyone's squeezing back into the hidden staircase, one of the girls whispers to me, "If you don't have a map, I could draw you one."

I stare at her in astonishment.

"You know these stairs?" I ask. "You've used them to go to Desmia's room before?"

"Oh, no." She shakes her head, her russet-colored hair flaring out behind her. "But I looked at the castle very carefully when they were bringing me in to the dungeon. And then you look out those windows"—she points to the high, narrow windows in Ella's room—"and you can see the tower you said we were supposed to go to. I've calculated the gradient of the stairs we already climbed, and the general pattern of the stairways, and I remember how my tutor, Sir Brookings, always described the dimensions of the castle. So, if I drew a map, it wouldn't necessarily be perfect, but it would be a very, very educated guess."

I'm still gaping at her.

"You must have been really good at geometry," I finally say.

"It was my favorite subject," she says simply. "That and architecture, of course, once we started into that."

"I didn't get any architecture training," I grumble.

I'm not sure if any of the girls have figured out that I'm one of them. Given that I still look like the worst kind of ragamuffin, it probably sounds ridiculous that I'd expect to know architecture. But the girl just shrugs apologetically.

"Sir Brookings loves geometry and architecture— anything like that—so once I showed an aptitude, he began focusing almost exclusively on his favorite subjects," she says. "But he didn't teach me much at all about manners and etiquette, which reminds me . . ." She awkwardly sticks out her hand to shake. "I'm Ganelia."

"Cecilia," I say in response, taking her hand firmly, even though a curtsy would have been more appropriate. Sir Stephen always said to adapt to others' customs rather than make them feel awkward.

The girl rewards me with a grin.

"Since you seem to know the way better than I do, why don't you take the lead?" I ask.

"Oh, I'm no good at leadership," Ganelia quails. "That would be Lucia, or Rosemary, or Sophia."

She thinks she's the true princess but claims she's no good at leadership? This makes no sense, but I don't have time to ask any questions.

"Fine," I say. "I'll lead the way, but you can be the one telling me where to go."

We step behind the wall—the last two to do so—and I give Ella a desperate final wave and grimace. She repays me by scrunching up her face sympathetically and lifting her hands, and it almost feels like she's whispered back, *Don't worry. Harper will be okay. And so will the rest of us.*

Ganelia and I—and all the others—have to be silent in the secret stairway, but Ganelia is very good about tapping my hand and pointing whenever we have to go in a new direction. Almost before I know it, we're facing the faint outlines of a door in the stone wall. I press my eye against the crack between the door and the wall and can just barely make out a familiar tapestry full of extravagant reds and golds and greens.

"Desmia's room!" I dare to whisper gleefully. Then I shove my way in.

I'm intending to scout out the scene first, to make sure there aren't any maids or guards or advisers hanging about. I figure I can make up a story to explain my presence much more easily than I can explain twenty-two others. But the girls behind me are pushing forward, and whispering in great distress, "Sir Denton has fainted!" and "Please! Sir Casper needs some air!"

Just then I see Desmia rounding the corner from the other section of her chambers.

"Are you alone?" I gasp at her.

Desmia gives me one look—a strange, startled, desperate look. Then she strides over to the fireplace and grabs the black wrought-iron poker.

"Brigands attacked you in the secret stairs?" she asks, holding the poker high over her head, her arms trembling as much as her voice. "Where are they?"

I've forgotten about the stupid white bandage swathed around my head.

"No, no, nobody attacked me. It's just—it's a long story."

Desmia lowers the poker. She was willing to defend me? I marvel. *Desmia was?* But I don't have time to thank her, because the girls and knights are pushing their way out behind me.

"Sir Roget must have food!" one of the girls is crying. "Else he'll surely die!"

"And Sir Thomas!"

"And Sir Anthony!"

I'm guessing these girls must be Lucia, Rosemary, and Sophia, given the way they're trying to take charge.

"Desmia, they're right," I say. "I found these knights in

the torture chamber below the dungeons, and I *had* to set them free or they would have died, and then they rescued the girls, and . . . They're so tired they still might die. You've got to help."

Desmia freezes, but only for a second.

"Put as many as you can on the bed. The rest can lie down on the rug," she says. "I'll be right back."

The other girls and I half carry all the knights into the other room while Desmia disappears around the opposite wall.

"No, no, you must leave *now*," I hear her saying. "You *don't* need to finish dusting. But run straight to the kitchen and tell the cooks the princess is very, very hungry and can't wait for dinner, so they must send up a huge tray of food, as if for a feast. . . . And yes, guards out, too—no one must be allowed in here except to deliver that tray. . . ."

Then I hear the sound of a door being shut hard.

Good for you, Desmia! I think.

"Please, Sir Thomas, breathe! Keep breathing!" One of the girls I think might be Rosemary or Sophia or Lucia is wailing beside the most fragile-looking knight. His chest is still rising and falling beneath his thin shirt, but it's such a faint movement, barely visible.

"Food is coming!" I say helplessly. "And drink!"

I remember that we don't necessarily have to wait for the tray Desmia ordered. Harper and I still had a little bit of bread and fruit left in the tower, and there might still be a few swallows of lemonade left in the jug. I take off running for the

tower stairs. The birds squawk at me—"Bawk! Be careful!"
"Bawk! Watch out!" "Bawk! True princess!"—but I ignore
them completely. As soon as I reach the tower, I snatch the
handle of the jug. We left the food back by the tower window,
I remember, right beside the harp. . . . I speed through the
door—strangely, the harp is gone, but a half loaf of bread
and a small apple are still there. I scoop them up and take off
running back down the stairs.

I'm panting for air and my head is whirling when I get
back to the bedchambers, but at least Sir Thomas is still taking
his shallow breaths.

"Lift his head!" I command Rosemary or Sophia or Lucia
or whoever the girl is who's quietly sobbing with her face
pressed against Sir Thomas's chest.

The girl obeys, and I pour a trickle of lemonade into Sir
Thomas's mouth.

"That is . . . heavenly," the old man croaks. He turns his
face toward the girl, peering at her through tear-glazed eyes.
"Rosemary, even if I . . . expire, know that you *are* the true
princess. The queen herself placed you in my arms as she lay
dying. She didn't want to give you up, but she knew I would
keep you safe. . . ."

What? I think. Something like jealousy shoots through me.
Sir Stephen never told *me* such a specific detail.

"I promised her I would keep that secret—I would keep
you secret—but since I'm dying now too . . . ," Sir Thomas
whispers. "You remember where we hid your proof?"

Proof? I think. *Proof? How is it that this Rosemary has proof and I don't?*

"My silver chalice," Rosemary whispers, kneeling before her knight, bowing her head to speak directly into his ear. She has tears glinting in her hazel eyes too. "The one you brought with me from the palace when I was but a tiny babe . . ."

I have to look away from this tender scene. I want to shout at the other girls, Hello? *Are you listening to this?* But my eyes immediately fall on the next grief-stricken girl crying at the side of an ancient knight, and she's also murmuring, "Yes, I know where my proof is hidden. . . ." And then I pay attention to all the voices in the room, and it's like listening to echoes:

"The queen herself laid you in my arms. . . ."

"The dying queen kissed you before she gave you to me. . . ."

"The queen herself handed you to me. . . ."

And then I hear the murmured listing of royal objects, of "proof":

"The royal bowl . . ."

"The royal pendant . . ."

"The royal portrait . . ."

I'm thinking I must be the only girl in the kingdom who *doesn't* have a royal artifact, who hasn't been told that the dying queen placed her directly into her knight's arms. I can't help it: My heart pounds with jealousy and grief. I struggle to remember the logic Sir Stephen tried to teach me: If the other girls have proof, does that automatically mean that I have proof too—proof that I'm not who I always thought I was?

No, I think. *Because only one girl's "proof" could be true. If at least ten of the girls have fake proof, couldn't all eleven just as easily be wrong?*

"Please, miss," a girl begs, "Sir Ryland is thirsty, too. . . ."

And then I don't have time to think about logic, because I'm too busy holding the jug up to one set of parched lips after another; I'm dividing up hunks of bread, doling out one crumb at a time so everyone gets a share. After a few moments I realize Desmia is by my side helping, too, and I shoot her a silent glance of gratitude. She looks . . . stronger now, more sure of herself. For all that she's still wearing a pale dress (the faintest shade of pearl gray today), she doesn't look so much like she'd fade away at the first sign of trouble.

How is it that she didn't get her own knight? I wonder. *She has plenty of proof—the palace, the silks and satins, the balcony and the adoring crowd every day at noon . . . but does she have no one to tell her how the queen loved her, how the queen's dying wish was that Desmia be safe?*

It is too much to think about when my head is still throbbing and my heart is still pounding too hard and I'm trying to divide one apple eleven ways. And when there's still a part of me yearning after Harper, hoping against hope that Ella got to him in time, and that she can take care of Nanny and Sir Stephen and Harper's mam, too. It is hard work worrying about so many people all at once—it was easier when all I really cared about was myself.

What must it be like to worry about an entire kingdom? I wonder.

I am so lost in my thoughts that at first I don't hear the tromping of footsteps, the shouts coming from the hallway outside Desmia's chambers. But then I hear the door swing open, and Desmia screaming out, "No! I said no one was to come in!"

The footsteps don't stop.

29

I see Harper first, his face pale and strained beneath his freckles. His mother is clutching his shoulders anxiously, the way I imagine the dying queen must have clutched her true child. Sir Stephen and Nanny and Ella are right behind them, Ella alternating between holding up the old woman and holding up the old man. And surrounding them, surrounding all these people I care about, is what seems to be an entire phalanx of soldiers, their swords drawn, the points of the swords aimed at my friends.

A man steps out from behind this cluster of soldiers and prisoners. An ermine robe with jeweled buttons hangs from his substantial frame; even without a crown he looks like a king. He has such an air of command that I want to ask Sir Stephen, *Is that what you meant when you always talked about taking control of a room with a single motion?*

"Princess Desmia," the man says severely.

I suppress a shiver, because I recognize the voice: This is

Lord Throckmorton. I study the hard look in his dark eyes, the cruel set of his mouth, the haughty lift of his head.

He knows he has us, I think. *He believes he's already won. He's gloating.*

"Yes?" Desmia says in such a tiny voice that she seems to be shrinking away before my eyes, her face as gray as her dress.

"I see you have company," Lord Throckmorton says, cocking one eyebrow at the collection of knights and girls crowded into the room. A heartless smile plays on his lips. "This might be of interest to them as well . . ." He waves his arm with studied carelessness toward Harper and the others huddled between the soldiers. "We caught these conspirators plotting to overthrow you."

He makes it sound like it doesn't matter if he tells Desmia this or not, like their fate's already been decided.

"We were not plotting to overthrow Desmia!" Ella protests. "I—I was merely wishing them luck in the music competition. These are musicians! See the harp?"

I notice that Harper is clutching his harp to his chest in much the same way that his mother is clutching him. In a flash I understand why the harp was missing when I went to get the jug and bread from the tower.

Harper didn't want to wait until after his mam, Nanny, and Sir Stephen played in the music competition. He must have taken the harp to bluff his way into the competitors' room. . . .

The nearest soldier jostles Ella with his sword. I see a thin line of blood appear on her sleeve. Lord Throckmorton takes one step toward Harper and yanks the harp from his arms. He tosses the harp to the side.

"Perhaps now you can see them for what they really are," Lord Throckmorton growls. "As I was saying, these are conspirators. What could we expect? This one"——he jabs Ella on her arm, right where she's already been cut by the sword——"this one is a Fridesian. Our enemy. We shall have to take the whole delegation into custody, to be examined. We shall have all the conspirators executed, beginning now with these five. Give the order."

I look at Desmia. Everyone's eyes are on her, and I wonder if everyone else's mind is racing like mine is. *He could have had them executed on his own, without even telling her——why does he want her to give the order? Oh . . . he wants to prove that he controls her; he wants their blood on her hands; he thinks she is too weak to resist. . . .* Desmia's face has turned completely white now. She is slumped against the wall, as if she can no longer even hold herself up. *She is too weak to resist,* I think.

"Desmia!" I hiss. "You're the princess! These men"——I wave my arm toward the soldiers, the guards——"they're sworn to protect you, to follow your every command! This is your decision! Not his!"

Lord Throckmorton does not even look at me. I am beneath his notice, with my stained, ripped dress, my muddy feet, my bandaged head. I am no one.

"Give the order!" Lord Throckmorton tells Desmia again. "Command your men to execute these traitors!"

Desmia looks at me. She shoots a glance over her shoulder at the feeble knights propped up by the crying girls.

"No," she says.

Lord Throckmorton blinks. But in a second he has his composure back.

"So," he says mockingly, "the princess is too stupid to understand what's best for her, what's best for her kingdom. She is only a pretty face, after all. Only a figurehead. Only a child. As her adviser it falls to me to make the important decisions. And I say"—now he is looking only at the soldiers, as if Desmia has proved herself to be beneath his notice as well—"the traitors must be executed."

I gasp—is he allowed to insult Desmia like that? To ignore her, and order the soldiers to ignore her, too? And she won't even argue?

But Desmia is stepping forward; evidently she no longer needs the wall for support. She's found her spine.

"Yes," she says, "traitors deserve to be executed."

My heart plunges. *How could she?* I begin glancing around frantically for a weapon—I can't let Harper go without a fight. *Anyone who tries to kill Harper or Sir Stephen or Nanny is going to have to kill me first,* I vow. *And Ella! This is not fair to Ella. . . .*

But Desmia is still talking.

"It's just that . . ." Her voice squeaks a little. She pauses to steady it. "These people are not traitors. They are loyal Sualan citizens, and one Fridesian friend." She puts a slight emphasis on the word "friend." Ella nods, and that seems to give Desmia even more courage. She peers directly at the man who appears to be the captain of the royal guard, a man old enough to be her father, with graying hair at his temples.

"You need to arrest the true conspirators," Desmia says. She's standing up very straight now. "Arrest this man, Lord Throckmorton, for the murder of my parents, the king and queen, fourteen years ago."

30

For a long moment no one seems to know what to do. None of the soldiers dash forward to replace Lord Throckmorton's ermine robe with chains and cuffs. But none of them run their swords through my friends, either. They just freeze, as still and uncertain as everyone else.

Then Lord Throckmorton grabs Desmia by the shoulders. I am close enough to hear what he whispers in her ear: "Fool!" He slides his arm around her neck, manhandling her. Silencing her.

"The princess knows not of what she speaks," he says. "She was only a baby then—how could she know? How dare she accuse me, her loyal adviser . . ." He stares down at her, narrowing his eyes. "Perhaps she is not even the true princess, after all."

The captain of the royal guard lowers his sword, then lifts it again in a slightly different direction. It's no longer pointed at my friends. Now it's pointed at Lord Throckmorton.

"Were I you, I would consider my words very carefully before making such an allegation," the captain says. Behind him all the other soldiers seem to be hanging on to his every word. He clears his throat and continues. "As I recall, *Lord* Throckmorton, your claim to power, your claim to becoming the princess's adviser fourteen years ago, was that child herself. Did you not come to the royal guard holding the baby, telling us that the queen herself placed her in your arms for safekeeping—that the queen herself, as she lay dying, said she trusted only you to raise her child, to rule the kingdom until this child was grown?"

Good grief, I think. *Not that story again.* Still, all those years of poring over literary texts with Sir Stephen keeps me from dismissing it instantly. *Notice how Lord Throckmorton's story is just a little bit different from all the others,* I hear in my mind, like an echo of Sir Stephen's teachings. *Notice how rescuing a baby helped Lord Throckmorton—helped him immensely—while it sent all the knights into exile. . . .*

"Ah, yes," Lord Throckmorton says, as though he is not discomfited in the least by the soldier's veiled accusation. "But perhaps I was tricked. Perhaps the queen herself was tricked, in her dying moments. . . . One baby looks much the same as another, does she not? Evidence has come to my attention recently that discredits Desmia's claim completely, and points to another girl as the actual princess—Suala's *true* princess. . . ."

Eleven girlish voices call out at once behind me, "Yes, me! I'm the true princess!" joined by deeper, raspier, more ancient voices: "Yes, it's Princess Rosemary!" "Sophia!" "Porfinia!" "Ganelia!" "Fidelia!" "Lydia!" . . .

I do not listen or look to see if Sir Stephen is also shouting, shouting out his support for me. I do not yell, myself. I am watching Desmia's face, which has turned a frightening shade of purple. Lord Throckmorton is holding her off to the side, out of sight of the royal guard. She's opening her mouth silently, as if she's trying desperately to cry for help, but is unable to force any sound past the barrier of Lord Throckmorton's arm pressed too tightly against her throat.

He's strangling her, I think. *She could die while all of us are standing here arguing about who truly has the royal lineage. . . .*

I didn't finish looking around for a weapon earlier, when I thought I was going to have to defend Harper. I look again. The fireplace poker that Desmia might have used to defend me is too far away, behind the huge cluster of soldiers. I have no time to run for it. The only weapon-like object even remotely near me is the harp, lying a few paces away, where Lord Throckmorton cast it aside.

I'd protect you. . . .

With what? Your harp?

My nasty, mocking words to Harper echo in my mind, mocking me now. But I'm already rushing forward, closing the distance to the harp. I scoop it up in my hands, first raising it by the strings, then transferring my grip to the solid wood frame. I lift the harp high, then bring it down hard on Lord Throckmorton's head.

He crumples to the floor, losing his grip on Desmia.

31

Silence. Utter silence.

And then Harper says admiringly, "Wow. That worked really well." As if I've just cast my fishing line particularly far; as if I've managed to skip a stone on the pond more times than he.

But Harper's words break everyone else's paralysis. Everyone begins to talk at once.

"Did you see . . ."

"Can you believe . . ."

"Does this mean . . ."

"Thank you," Desmia whispers as she gasps for air.

The captain of the royal guard rushes to her side.

"Princess!" he exclaims. "Did he hurt you?" He seems to take in the extreme coloring of her face, though the purple is beginning to fade. "Was he . . . trying to kill you?"

"I don't know," Desmia whispers.

The captain glares down at Throckmorton's unconscious

form sprawling in his pool of ermine cape.

"He would have passed it off as 'She died of fright, at the terror of being discovered as a fake,'" the captain mutters, almost to himself. "Or 'Her sins caught up with her when her deception failed.'"

"I—I—," Desmia stammers.

"He's done that kind of thing before, I think," the captain says darkly. "It's always been so convenient, how so many of his enemies have died, and he's managed to avoid any blame. . . . We always thought we had to believe him, because he was the princess's own adviser. . . ." He motions the other soldiers forward. "Men! Carry this traitor away!"

They jump to obey him immediately. It takes five men to lift Lord Throckmorton.

"I—I'm not actually completely certain that he killed my parents," Desmia says. "That just came to me—all the pieces seemed to fit."

The captain nods at her abruptly.

"Then we will find the proof, if there's proof to be had," he says. He begins pointing to one soldier after another. "You, go interview Lord Suprien; you, go interview Lord Tyfolieu; you, round up all the palace workers who were here at the time of the king and queen's deaths, and ask them what they saw. . . ." He bends down on his knee, bowing before Desmia. "I promise you, Princess, we will have the investigation that we should have had fourteen years ago, instead of the one Lord Throckmorton oversaw. . . ."

I don't hear the rest of this exchange, because Nanny is folding me into a hug.

"Cecilia! You were so brave! But"—still holding on to me, she leans back, studying me carefully—"what happened to you? Your head in that bandage . . . your dress in tatters . . ."

"I'm fine," I say. I swallow a lump in my throat. "But I don't think I'm really the true princess, after all." I can barely whisper this. Somehow it shames me to admit this to Nanny, as if it lessens what she did in raising me, as if it reflects badly on *her*.

"Of course you are," Nanny says. She glances over her shoulder, where Sir Stephen is leaning forward to pat my shoulder. "Sir Stephen—"

"I believe everything can now be told," Sir Stephen says gently. "That awful night fourteen years ago, when the assassins came, the king died instantly. But the queen . . . lingered. As one of the king's royal knights I was appalled that we had failed to protect our monarch. But I wanted to do everything I could to protect his wife and child. I went to the queen, secretly, and she told me there was no longer any hope for her. But she laid you in my arms—you! Her child . . ."

I groan.

"Sir Stephen, I mean no disrespect, but that's what all the knights say."

"Eh?" Sir Stephen seems jolted to be stopped in the midst of his story. "What's that?"

"Weren't you listening a few moments ago when all the knights were shouting out the names of the other girls as the true princess?" I ask. "Lydia, Sophia, Ganelia, Fidelia, Porfinia, Rosemary . . ." I know I'm leaving out several of them, but I think I've made my point.

Sir Stephen glances toward his fellow knights, all sitting up and staring toward us. They're listening too.

"Why, yes," Sir Stephen says. "Of course I heard them. But they were only pretending, doing an admirable job of shifting eyes away from you in a dangerous moment." He bends down rather stiffly, until he's on one knee, his head bowed. "My brother knights, I honor your service to the true princess, your bravery, and the courage, too, of these fine maidens. . . ." He gestures toward all the other would-be princesses.

"Get up, Stephen," Sir Roget mutters. "We have a bit of a problem we need to work out before anyone starts with the proclamations."

Sir Stephen blinks confusedly at the other knights. Harper's mam appears silently at his side, and the two of us help him back into a standing position.

"It would seem that our zeal for secrecy went a bit too far," Sir Roget explains. Now he's addressing the other girls and me, even more than Sir Stephen. "We were the Order of the Crown, the king's own knights, and after the king's death we told everyone we'd disbanded. But we kept meeting, secretly, to discuss the future of the kingdom and our plans for reinstalling the true princess when it was safe."

"But you couldn't even agree on the true princess's name?" I can't help asking incredulously.

Sir Roget looks at me sadly.

"We were so terrified—you have to understand, we'd just seen our monarch slaughtered—and some of us suspected that there might be a traitor in our midst," he continues. "So during our meetings and in our messages to one another we never said where the true princess was, we never discussed who had her in his care, we never called her anything but the true princess. . . . Even when we were hanging in the torture chamber, we were so careful to speak no names, for fear of being overheard. Until you came to rescue us . . ."

I'm beginning to see what happened. The knights were brave and loyal and true, but they were also idiots.

Behind me Harper begins to laugh.

"You're kidding, right?" he says. "Each one of you thought you knew where the true princess was, and you were teaching her about being royal and everything, but what, eleven of you were dead wrong?"

Sir Roget regards Harper with an air of injured dignity.

"I'll have you know, young man, that our suspicions were not unfounded," he says, with a strict, scolding tone in his voice. "That man—the so-called *Lord* Throckmorton— was one of our number. We knew him as Sir Eldridge, and I think he sent spies after us after our last meeting, because it was then that the men appeared to carry my dear Lucia away. . . ." He pats the hand of the young lady sitting next to him and wipes away a tear before turning to Sir Stephen. "As I was being captured, I tried to get word to my fellow knights, to call for help, not knowing that they were also being taken from their hiding places across the land, they and their . . . maidens." He glances a little disdainfully at the cluster of other alleged princesses.

Sir Stephen blinks.

"I—I didn't know," he murmurs. "And all this time I was wondering why none of you responded to *my* calls for help, when the soldiers searched my house, when Cecilia vanished. . . ." His eyes narrow, and I can almost see him applying Rule One of How to Handle Vast Quantities of Surprising Information in a Crisis Situation. ("Hold back your emotions. Focus on getting facts and deriving logical connections.") "But why?" he asks. "Why did Lord Throckmorton strike now, when it's fourteen years since the king and queen died, since the true princess went into hiding . . . ?"

He squeezes my hand, and everyone is silent for a long moment, presumably all wondering the same thing. Then Desmia clears her throat.

"Because I challenged him, I think," she whispers. "The peace delegation arrived from Fridesia, and Lord Throckmorton wanted to kill them all—"

Behind me, Ella gasps in horror.

"—but I said no, we would listen. And I did this in front of all sorts of other advisers and lords, so—I couldn't believe it—what I said happened." Desmia is shaking her head as if she's still amazed at her own bravery and the results. Then she looks down at her hands, going pale again. "But after that he began threatening me."

So Desmia did have a knight of her own, along with the palace and the beautiful dresses and the throne. But her knight was Lord Throckmorton, an evil, plotting man. I decide I'm not jealous at all. I put my arm around Sir Stephen's stooped-over shoulders and give him a gentle hug.

"So who really is the true princess?" asks one of the other girls—Sophia, I think—as if that's all she cares about. And as if, somehow, she's still absolutely certain it's her. "Maybe if we all brought in our royal objects, our proof, and had an expert look at them to determine . . ."

I swallow a lump in my throat.

"Then it's not me." I force the words out. "I don't have any royal object."

I look around at all the other girls. They've been in a dungeon, and they're all dressed in simple, peasant clothes, just like I always was. But none of them have the stains and the rips in their clothes that I have; none of them have bandaged heads. Somehow they've all still managed to look regal and haughty and proud. Any of them could switch dresses with Desmia and instantly look like a princess.

I'd need to scrub the mud from my legs and the cobwebs

from my hair and the dried blood from my hands—and even then I'm not sure I could carry it off.

"Eh? What's that you say?" Sir Stephen mutters. I think his deafness has gotten worse since the last time I saw him, at Nanny's cottage. Or maybe he's just following Rule Three of Ways to Deal with Delicate Situations. ("Play for time if you have to. Do anything to delay the moment of decision until you have all the information you need.") He clears his throat. "Royal object? Why, Princess Cecilia, of course you have one!"

"I do?" I say.

"Naturally!"

I think about all the objects in Nanny's cottage: the glass bottles, the spoons, the wooden table, the threadbare blankets, the kettle, the pot . . . the fish-scaling knife? No, everything at Nanny's was ordinary peasant ware. Except . . .

"You mean my books?" I ask, remembering the elegance of the gold leaf, the delicacy of the vellum pages.

"We all had books," one of the other girls sneers.

"Until they were taken away," Ganelia says sadly. I decide I like her best of all the other girls. I don't care if she has leadership skills or not.

"No, no," Sir Stephen says impatiently. "Not those." He seems surprised that I haven't figured this out. "You had the royal harp."

The royal harp? What? Has Sir Stephen gone senile as well as deaf?

"Uh, Sir Stephen? I never had a harp," I say cautiously. "I think I would have noticed something that big sitting around Nanny's cottage. . . ."

"Exactly," Sir Stephen says, as if I've made some incredibly astute observation. "I knew I could never leave something that conspicuous with you, because I was afraid the local villagers might guess who you were. For three days and nights as I rode my horse away from Cortona, with you and the harp tucked into my saddlebags—desperate, terrified, always in fear that your identity might be discovered—I was also racking my brain about what to do. I couldn't store the harp in my home, because it might be seen there, too, and link me to the true princess. I couldn't simply discard the harp, because it was the last reminder you'd have of your mother's love, and"— he glares a bit at his fellow knights—"I feared someday you would need it as proof. And then, out of the night, as if by providence, a woman appeared, begging me, 'Please, kind sir, do you know music? Can you give my son music lessons as he grows?'"

"Harper's mam," I breathe.

On the other side of Sir Stephen I see that Harper's mother, strangely, is blushing.

"Aye, and you were such a fine music teacher," she murmurs. "Teaching me so I could teach my lad. I couldn't believe my good fortune, you *giving* me the harp, and then giving me the lessons for free. . . ."

"Weren't you afraid that that would endanger Harper?"

I ask sharply. I shoot a glance back at my friend.

"Yeah, I thought those harp lessons were going to kill me," Harper mutters.

I shake my head impatiently.

"No, because then he was associated with the royal harp," I say. "Then the evil forces might have hunted him down—"

It is strange how anxious that thought makes me feel.

"He was a male child, not a female," Sir Stephen explains, in that same overly patient voice he always used when he thought I was taking too long to understand algebra. "There was no danger that someone would think he was the princess."

I think about how everyone in the village always whispered about Harper's mam, wondering where she'd gotten the harp and how she learned to play. Truly, I'm not sure anyone ever asked her directly, because she always seemed so sad. Who would want to add to her pain? Or maybe the entire village just wanted her to stay a mystery, so they'd have something to speculate about.

"It was a calculated risk," Sir Stephen says. "The harp would be nearby, but not actually in the same cottage as the princess."

"Thanks a lot," Harper mutters. "Thanks for ruining my childhood." He's wandered over to peer down at the harp, which fell to the floor with Lord Throckmorton. Nobody has bothered it to pick it up or set it right. I'm almost expecting Harper to give it a kick, just like all those other annoyed, angry, hateful kicks I've seen him give it over the years. Instead he kneels down and pats it, like it's a beloved pet that's about to die.

"Uh, Eelsy?" Harper says. "I think you just broke your own royal object."

I look down, and the harp does look shattered. The frame is twisted and warped, and splinters stick out where the wood cracked against Lord Throckmorton's head. A few strings have popped off.

"Can't it be fixed?" I ask, because now it's not just my friend's harp; it's also the last remnant of my mother's love for me. If I believe that story.

Harper plucks a string, which gives a forlorn, out-of-tune peal and then falls off.

"Oops," Harper says. He bends closer. "What's this?"

He's pulling a tightly coiled scroll of yellowed parchment out of the cracked frame. As soon as he's freed it, he begins unrolling the page.

I read over his shoulder as each word comes clear: "'Last words . . . and . . . confessions . . . of . . . Charlotte . . . Aurora . . . Serindia . . . Marie,'" I say. I gasp as Harper unrolls the last bit, and three more words appear: "queen of Suala."

32

Within seconds everyone is clustered around me. Even the feeblest of the knights somehow manages to leap up from the bed and crowd in close.

"Now, now, give the young lady some room," the captain of the royal guard scolds, and at least then everyone edges back a little so I can breathe. I see that the captain is looking at me with new respect—because the queen's note came out of *my* royal object?

I am still having trouble breathing, and it has nothing to do with the people crowded around me.

"That is the queen's writing," Sir Stephen says, peering over my shoulder at the parchment document. "I remember it well."

The script is perfectly formed, and completely free of blots. Of course.

"Read it out loud," Nanny urges.

"'I, Charlotte Aurora Serindia Marie . . . ,'" I begin, and

then stop, because I'm thinking, *She had the same middle names as I do! Does that prove anything?* I can't decide if I should point that out.

"Oooh, *my* middle names are 'Aurora Serindia Marie,'" one of the other girls says.

"So are mine," practically all of the other girls say at once. Even Desmia.

Okay, no big deal, I think. Obviously all of the knights had the same idea, passing along those names.

I take a deep breath, and keep reading:

I, Charlotte Aurora Serindia Marie, queen of Suala, being of sound mind and much less than sound body, feel compelled to put pen to paper to tell my tale. I am certain that I have little time left, and even now I fear that I may be dooming others to a fate as dire as my own. But whosoever shall someday read these words, please know that I have never had anything but the most hopeful and merciful of intents.

I begin my tale in happier days, when my husband, King Bredan the Third, took the throne of Suala at the death of his much beloved but long-ailing uncle. Though my husband ruled with a fair and kind hand, a small number of jealous rivals were determined to stir up discontent, and they challenged his claim to the throne. Of greatest concern, they said, was the fact that my husband and I were yet

childless, though we had been married for more than
two years.

So it was with great joy last September that I
told my husband that he could announce to all of
Suala that I was with child. In the ensuing months
I dreamed often of the coming child and paid much
less attention to the troublesome affairs of state.
I wanted nothing but to be around children; my
greatest joy was to visit the children of Cortona in
their homes, in their schools, even in the orphanage.
But it disturbed me to think that my child would
be dressed in the finest clothes, eat the finest foods,
receive nothing but the finest care, while many of
the children I saw were barely able to survive. I
asked my husband for more money from the royal
treasury for the orphanage in particular, as the poor
motherless children there broke my heart. But alas,
the royal treasury had been depleted by the war with
Fridesia, the same war that has consigned so many
children to their orphaned state. My husband and
I fell into a harsh dispute, the most serious of our
marriage. It was with heavy heart that I fought
with him, day after day, but my joy knew no bounds
when he began to take my side. What followed was
a time of many meetings and negotiations for my
husband, as he planned to do everything he could to
end the Fridesian War.

"What?" Ella explodes behind me. "But—if that was fourteen years ago, that never—"

"Let's hear the rest," Sir Stephen says, blinking his wise old eyes at her.

I look back at the parchment, and read on:

> *We announced the birth of our child, our beloved daughter, on April the thirtieth, a day of great rejoicing and celebration throughout the kingdom.*

"Doesn't she say the baby's name?" one of the knights interrupts.

"Did you skip over my name?" a girl asks. "You did it on purpose, didn't you—you're trying to cheat, you—"

"If I was trying to cheat anyone," I say through gritted teeth, "don't you think I would have pretended the queen wrote my own name in there?" I hold up the parchment for all to see. "Look. It doesn't say the princess's name at all, just"—I swallow a lump in my throat—"just 'our beloved daughter.'"

There are a few moments of jostling—everyone trying to see the parchment—and then they all fall silent.

I go back to reading.

> *Alas, I have come to the sad part of my tale, sadness upon sadness. I can hardly bear to write this; the quill trembles in my hand. Such suffering as I have known, in such a short span of time . . .*

Two nights ago a man entered our royal chambers. In the darkness I could not see his face; I heard no utterance of his voice. All I saw was the flash of a sword's blade, and then my husband lay dying, and I . . . I was mortally wounded as well. The life ebbs from me with each word I put to paper.

I believe the killer was a man known well to us, a man my husband and our royal guards (who were also slain) would have trusted. I believe my husband must have recognized the man, because Bredan cried out, as he expired, "What? More blood spilled over Fridesia?" I can only conclude that the killer opposed my husband's plans to end the war; I am heartsick that my persuasions may have led to my husband's death, when my intent was only to prevent the loss of other lives.

I would weep for my husband, my Bredan, but there is not time for that. My time on this earth is coming to a close; soon enough I will meet Bredan in heaven, along with the others I have loved and lost. I need only a few more hours of courage, and then my pain will end.

Beginning at daylight the morning after my husband's death, the knights began to come to me, secretly, alone. The Order of the Crown, the assembly of knights most loyal to the king, is made up of thirteen men; thirteen times I heard a whisper

beside my deathbed: "Your Majesty? How can I
protect the princess?"

What was I to do? Whom could I trust? What
if any of those men were traitors?

I sent them all away. I told them to come back
the next day. I prayed that I would have a next day,
just one more day in which to make my decision, to
take action.

"Wait a minute," Harper interrupts. "Did I miss something? Where was the baby princess during all this? How did the king and queen keep the assassin from killing the princess, too? See, that's something I've never understood about—"

An entire roomful of knights, would-be princesses, and guards all turn on him at once: "Shh!"

"Keep reading!" Nanny begs.

I obey.

I thought of the children at the orphanage, all
those poor, motherless babes I'd seen lying in rickety
cribs, crying after food that was never enough.
Though my other attempts to help have led to nothing
but tragedy, would it be wrong, in my last actions,
for me to try to provide for at least some of them? A
knight in possession of an infant he believed to be the
princess would surely treat her well, would he not?

I sent a trusted maid to the orphanage director.

*I asked for baby girls, only those young enough
that they could pass for newborns. It seemed
providential—a sign of divine blessing upon my
plan—that the maid returned with exactly the right
number of infants.*

"You mean—the queen gave out *orphans?*" Sir Roget
demands, sounding appalled. "She passed off common babies
from the orphanage as the true princess?" He turns to the girl
he must have raised, the one who is at his side holding him up.
"Except for you, of course, dear Lucia, because you really are—"

"Perhaps you would let Cecilia finish reading before you
draw any conclusions?" Sir Stephen asks in a barbed voice.

Sir Roget shrugs and nods his consent.

I go back to the parchment.

*Now I am lying here listening to thirteen happy
babies cooing in the royal nursery—such a glorious
sound! Such a sound to heal a shattered, grieving
heart! But I am beginning to have my doubts about
my plan. I will tell each knight to keep each child
hidden, to keep her safe above all other goals. I know
the knights are disbanding the Order of the Crown
and going their separate ways, and this will keep the
girls from ever meeting. I will tell each knight that the
girl in his care must never attempt to sit on the throne
as long as there is any danger—and I believe there*

will always be danger. I fear our land will be marked
by turmoil and bloodshed for generations to come.

And yet, and yet—perhaps these girls can be
happy? Perhaps they can be nurtured and loved;
perhaps they can grow to become lovely, strong young
ladies, as others cannot?

Perhaps some good can come out of evil, some
joy from all my sorrows?

Or perhaps . . . I fear even to write this. I have
not forgotten that I am not certain that all the knights
are trustworthy. I have not forgotten that the evil and
greed for power that led to my husband's death has
not been expunged from our kingdom. I pray that I
am not consigning any of these girls to a worse life
than she would have had in the orphanage.

Strangely, it is Desmia's face that my eyes stray to at that
moment. She stares back at me, an indecipherable expression
on her face. I go back to reading.

I pray that these girls will never be used as
pawns in political games, as I have sometimes been
used, as queen. I pray for them quiet lives out of the
public eye, their sorrows few, their joys many—and
all of their emotions kept to themselves, not thrown
out for the entire kingdom to see.

And yet, I fear . . . I fear . . . Is the darkness

I see before me only because my eyes grow dim?
Does any hope remain? I must believe that hope
remains . . .
    I am writing out thirteen copies of this letter.
I shall tell each knight that I will send one royal
object with the child in his care. These are objects my
husband has used for sending out spies; each object
contains a secret compartment for hidden messages.

"Hey, Cecilia, guess what!" Harper says. "That means you didn't actually have to break open your harp to get your message out!"

How can he make jokes at a time like this? I don't even bother looking up.

    I will leave it to God's will—to his providence?
to fate?—to determine when and if my messages will
ever be found. I think of you—whoever you are—
there in the future, reading this, and I hope you do
not judge my actions too harshly.

"Isn't she ever going to say who the actual true princess is?" the captain of the royal guard asks impatiently.

"Yeah, why would she wait so long to reveal her big news?" Harper agrees.

"Well, maybe because she thought it would be *obvious,* because the true princess would be so clearly different from the ordinary orphans," one of the girls says. I don't know her name—I decide I don't want to know anything about her.

"Or maybe she'll just say that she gave the true princess to the most trusted knight, the man she was sure would never be a traitor," one of the knights says. "The queen always liked me."

"Can't you just skim forward a bit, until you come to the princess's name?" another knight says. "Just look for 'Porfinia'; it's P-O-R . . ."

I gasp, and that silences him. I'm already reading ahead. I've already read quite far enough.

"What is it?" the royal captain asks. "Can you see—who's the true princess?"

I look up at all those hopeful faces, all those self-satisfied, self-assured, all-too-certain faces.

"None of us," I whisper.

33

A tumult breaks out in the crowd. In an instant I see the certainty and confidence on just about every face turn to astonishment, disappointment, shock. Two or three girls begin to wail. They hide their faces against their knights' shoulders, though the knights themselves are reeling. They look as though I have delivered a worse torture than the rack, than the thumbscrew, than the executioner's pike.

"You mean, it really was Desmia all along?" the royal captain asks.

"No, not even Desmia. She came from the orphanage too," I say. I glance toward the pale-faced girl. "Sorry."

She winces.

"I think . . . I think Lord Throckmorton knew," she whispers. "I used to have a crystal globe that he took away from me . . . I saw it in his office later, cracked open . . . And after that he always looked at me like . . . like . . . ,"

"Like he'd read your copy of the queen's letter?" Ella asks gently.

Desmia nods. Her shoulders slump; she sways unsteadily, standing alone. I feel so sorry for her that she has no knight to cling to, no grandfather figure to comfort her from the most devastating blow of her life. I am glad to see Ella step forward and put her arm around Desmia.

Desmia looks grateful too. But then she quickly glances back toward me, bafflement spreading across her expression.

"Then . . . did the queen give the true princess to her trusted maid?" Desmia asks.

"A maid—pshaw!" one of the knights grumbles.

Desmia ignores him. "If none of us is the true princess, who is?"

"Just listen," I say. I resume reading, though it is difficult to do so. My eyes blur; my voice shakes.

Perhaps you are wise enough to deduce how much I've left out of my story. I've left this part for the last, because it is so hard to write about—even harder than writing about my husband's murder, my own impending death. Can you not guess what else I have to tell you? Must I pour my bleeding heart out onto the paper thirteen times?

I must, I know. I must be clear, for the sake of all the girls.

The night of my beloved daughter's birth, even as the entire kingdom celebrated, my child did not breathe. Though she emerged as perfect and beautiful

as any child, she never took a breath. I held her in
my arms, willing her to open her eyes and look back
at me, willing her to draw air into her lungs, willing
her to live! But she did not. . . . When the royal
physician finally took her from my arms, I went
wild with grief, and the physician gave me a heavy
draught, to blunt my pain and send me into sleep.

When I woke to myself three days later, I
found my grief unabated—nay, multiplied. For my
husband had feared to tell our overjoyed kingdom of
the child's death, lest his subjects begin to believe that
the monarchy—and thus, all of Suala—is cursed.
(Are we?) I see now how much he feared, and the
accuracy of his fears. But I could not care about the
monarchy when my heart was already overflowing
with sorrow. My husband forced me to stand on
the royal balcony, holding a blanket cleverly folded
to look as though it enclosed a child—when really
there was nothing there. My husband had the royal
physician sent into exile. My husband acted as though
he had everything under control.

Perhaps he was a bit wild with grief, himself.

I do not know if my husband would have
someday announced the child's death, when the
politically expedient moment came. Or mayhap we
would have turned to the orphanage—as I've done
now—for an impostor princess. But I tell you,

now that I've heard these girls cooing in the royal nursery, I will be able to look each knight in the eye tomorrow and tell him, with all sincerity, "This is my child. Please take care of my child." As far as I am concerned, these girls are all my children now. They stand in place of the children I would have had, had I been allowed to live.

If these girls are not my children, then what do I have to leave behind? What has my life been worth?

When I stop reading, it is so quiet in Desmia's chambers that I swear I can practically hear the tears rolling down Nanny's cheeks.

"That poor woman," she murmurs. "That poor, poor woman."

She lapses back into a respectful silence. It feels as though we're all at the queen's funeral, mourning her life, mourning the sorrows she was never able to get past.

Then the royal captain moans, "Poor Suala! That's what you should say!"

Harper's mam, who knows everything there is to know about respecting grief, whirls on him.

"How can you say that? At a time like this? When we've just found out that that poor woman . . ." She sniffs, unable to go on.

The royal captain all but rolls his eyes.

"When that poor woman—what?" he says sarcastically.

"Practically guaranteed that Suala would be plunged into civil war? If she wanted to pass off a fraud, she should have picked just *one* girl, preferably one who looked a lot like her and the king, so no one would ever suspect. And then—"

"She wanted to help as many girls as she could," I say, forcing the words out through a clotted throat. "She wanted to save us all."

I'm thinking that, really, she succeeded. Mostly. I can look around at all the other girls and tell that they've been well-loved, well cared for. Except for Desmia, who became Lord Throckmorton's pawn. . . . I wonder if he did find the queen's letter in Desmia's royal object. Or if he figured out that there were twelve other "true princesses" just from spying on the other knights, and didn't care whether any of the princesses were authentic, as long as he could use them for his own purposes. It really doesn't matter.

None of us are pawns now.

"Humph," the royal captain grunts. "I've got daughters. I've seen them nearly scratch each other's eyes out when two of them want the same boy. And now we've got thirteen girls who are all going to want the same throne, but none of you actually deserve it."

He's glaring at us all, as if to steel himself for the coming battles.

"I've had reason lately to research royal law," Desmia speaks up, in a trembling voice. "It says that anyone the dying monarch designates as heir is, by law, the heir."

"Oh, so you think you have a greater claim than the rest of us?" one of the other girls argues. "Sure, as if we'll all just go away now, back to our little villages, while *you* get to stay in the palace, wearing silks and satins, eating feasts, being courted by handsome princes from other kingdoms. . . ."

Except for the prince part, this is so close to some of the resentful thoughts I had about Desmia, back when I was at Nanny's, that I'm jolted. It sounds so . . . nasty, spoken out loud.

But Desmia seems jolted too.

"No," she says quickly. "I don't mean I have a greater claim. I mean that *all* of us are princesses. The queen said so. Read that last part again, Cecilia."

It takes me a minute to grasp what she means.

"Uh . . . um . . . here it is. I think this is what you want," I say, fumbling with the parchment. "The queen wrote, 'As far as I am concerned, these girls are all my children now.'"

The royal captain releases another disdainful snort.

"You can't have thirteen princesses ruling as equals!" he scoffs.

"Why not?" I say.

Everyone is staring at me. I stare right back. Desmia and Ella both have faint smiles on their faces, as if they can guess what I'm getting at. Most of the knights and girls look puzzled, but a few are beginning to arch their eyebrows as understanding overtakes them. Sir Stephen and Nanny look proud. Harper looks gobsmacked. And Harper's mam just looks sad, like she always does—no, wait, even she is starting to look a little hopeful.

The royal captain shakes his head.

"I don't have time to explain palace protocol to you," he says scornfully. "Or monarchical authority, or divine right, or—"

"I know all about palace protocol," I retort. "And monarchical authority. And I don't believe you can invoke divine right, not when King Bredan was killed by a *man*, but anyhow I've been studying this stuff all my life! And so have the other girls, so we're ready. Of course we could rule as equals—there are thirteen of us, so there'd always be someone to break the tie. Or . . ." My gaze falls on Ganelia, the one who claimed in the secret stairways not to have any leadership skills. "Maybe we wouldn't rule as equals; maybe it would be better if we all just specialized in what we're best at. Ganelia could oversee building in the kingdom, and Rosemary is good at ordering people around, and everyone loves the way Desmia waves on the balcony"—Desmia's smile turns down a bit, so I rush to add—"and she knows more about royal law than anyone else, and . . . what are the rest of you good at?"

"Lucia knows every principle of leadership inside out," Sir Roget volunteers.

"Sophia can speak four languages," Sir Anthony says.

"Fidelia is an expert strategist," Sir Alderon adds.

The knights go on endlessly bragging about their princesses—not would-be princesses anymore, not with competing claims, but *real* princesses, ready to work together. I feel Sir Stephen's hand patting my shoulder.

"Well done," he whispers. "I believe this is exactly what the queen would have wanted."

The royal captain throws up his hands, cutting off the litany of praise.

"All right!" he says. "I surrender! It's indisputable: Suala has thirteen princesses—thirteen brilliant, talented, educated, beautiful princesses. We shall be the envy of the entire world!"

Epilogue

I stand in the tower room where Harper and I were once imprisoned. The door behind me hangs open, so I don't have to worry about being trapped. But I'm not facing the door; I'm facing the window. I'm watching the scene in the courtyard below, where dancers swirl and the crowd cheers and twelve jeweled crowns twinkle in the blaze of lights.

I hear footsteps behind me.

I turn around and see a handsome young man in a fine dark suit with gold trim at his collar and cuffs. Then I blink and notice the freckles. It's Harper.

"Hey," he says, "I've been looking for you everywhere."

"Then you should have looked here first instead of last," I say, and I'm proud of myself that I can say something like that to Harper, in my old, familiar, joking way, when he looks like he does, and when I myself have a crown on my head and a shimmery ball gown draped around my body and delicate, bejeweled slippers encasing my feet.

"You're missing your own party," Harper says.

I shrug.

"There are twelve other princesses down there," I say. "Who's going to notice one more or less?"

He opens his mouth, and I'm sure he's going to say something like, *Well, I did. Don't I count?* And then he's going to get all prickly and offended. So quickly, before he has a chance to say anything, I slug him in the arm and say, "Except you, of course, and you're probably just looking for a way to escape your mam. Right?"

A strange expression crosses Harper's face, and I see that I've misread him again. I have no idea what Harper was going to say.

He steps across the room and joins me at the window.

"Pretty fancy party," he mutters.

"Uh-huh."

For a second the two of us just stand there regarding the swirling dancers and the twinkling lights and the way all of it is reflected, again and again, in the mirrors that the palace staff put all around the courtyard. The palace types surely do love their mirrors.

"So," Harper says. "Now you have everything you always wanted."

"I guess," I say.

"Sure you do," Harper says. "The crown, the dresses, the *power* . . ." He grins. "I hear you even changed the game of chess."

This is true, sort of. Sir Stephen says there's a new variation of chess being played in the land, where pawns can become queens if they travel all the way across the board. But it's not like any of the other princesses or I ordered that change. It just happened.

Harper's grin deepens.

"Not to mention, now you've got shoes that aren't made of cloth and covered in mud. . . ."

I crack a smile, but it fades quickly.

"It doesn't feel the way I thought it would," I mumble.

"What—do the shoes pinch, or something?" Harper asks. "You can always ask for a new pair, or get them adjusted, or—"

"It's not the shoes," I say, though they do pinch. So does the crown, actually. I can't ever forget I'm wearing it.

"Don't tell me you're mad because you have to share being princess," Harper says. He's almost glaring at me. "Not when it was your idea."

"I'm not! Honest!" I say. "I'm still kind of stunned that we got any power—I don't think we would have, except that all the advisers and ministers were arrested. There's nobody else left to rule. And really, it'd be a lot harder if I *didn't* have anyone else to share things with, even though Sophia does get on my nerves, acting like she's the only one with good ideas, and Marindia—don't get me started on Marindia!—she has these really great ideas, but she'll never bring them up in our meetings, and so we'll argue for hours, and then at the very end, as we're walking out,

Marindia will just whisper, 'Well, how about doing things this way?' and it's exactly *right*, and then—"

"You're all still adjusting," Harper says. I can tell that he didn't follow me away from the celebration just to hear me talk about our hours and hours of meetings.

I look over at Harper, and in the dimness of the tower I can't really see him. I can't tell if he's the handsome young man who appeared in the doorway or the freckle-faced boy I've known all my life. Maybe that's why it feels safe to confess, "I think my problem is, I always thought that taking up my crown would be my happy ending—my happily ever after—and . . . it's not."

"You're not happy?" Harper says, and there's something extra in his voice that I don't stop to analyze.

"Oh, I don't know!" I say impatiently. "I don't really mean that—I mean that it's not the *ending*. It's just the beginning. Lord Throckmorton and all his conspirators are locked away, and the other princesses and I are safe, and we got that cease-fire on the Fridesian border, of course, but now we've got to negotiate the peace treaty, and make it fair and solid, without cheating either side, and without leaving anything so vague that the two kingdoms start fighting again. And we've got to figure out what to do about all the soldiers coming home, how they're going to adjust, and now the agriculture minister is saying there's going to be a bad crop on the western side of Suala, and so we've got to worry about that, and . . ." I grimace. "You can make fun of me if you want to. I guess I really did think that being princess would be nothing more than sitting around eating bon-bons and looking pretty."

"You do look pretty," Harper whispers. And for a second it seems like he's going to reach out and take my hand, and lean in close and tell me exactly how pretty I look, and then I could tell him how handsome he looks. But I guess I'm wrong; I guess my eyes were tricked in the dim light. Nothing happens.

"Porfinia's prettier," I say. "And you know Desmia's better at waving from the balcony, even though we're all taking turns with that now." I'm mostly just babbling, filling in the little space that came between us when he didn't reach out and take my hand. But something clicks—I do want to tell him this. "And Florencia is much better at studying the kingdom's budget than I am, and Adoriana has this talent for arranging flowers, and Elzabethl knows how to talk to the servants to get them to do exactly what she wants, and I swear, if we ever have to fight another war, Fidelia's the one I'd want planning the strategy, and . . ." I draw in a breath that's somehow turned ragged and pained. "Really, everyone else is better at being a princess than I am!"

Harper stares at me. His jaw sags, and his eyes bug out.

"You really think that?" he asks.

I nod. And then I'm annoyed with myself all over again, because tears have begun to prickle in my eyes. Harper brushes one of the tears off my cheek—such an amazingly tender gesture. But the effect is ruined, because at the very same moment he snorts.

"You are such an idiot," he says. "If all the others are better princesses, how come you're the only one Lord Throckmorton never caught?"

"You know," I say. "Only because I ran away. I came to Cortona before he had a chance to catch me. Remember?"

Harper nods, and in that moment he looks almost like Sir Stephen trying to lead me through a geometry proof.

"So you were the only one brave enough to come to Cortona," he says. "The only one who wasn't willing to let another girl be sacrificed for you. Don't you think that counts for anything?"

"Well," I say, "I wouldn't have come to Cortona if *you* hadn't talked me into it."

Harper grins, and even in the fancy suit the mischievous, freckle-faced boy I've always known shines through.

"Okay, so you should get points for having the good sense to be friends with me," he says.

I almost give him a little shove, our old way of relating to each other. But he is wearing that fancy suit. And something else is buzzing in my brain. A bit of alarm.

Harper's still talking.

"And *you're* the one who rescued all the knights, who then rescued all the other princesses," he says. "I can't take any credit for that one. And you tried to make sure that Ella rescued me. And you're the only one who dared to defend Desmia against Lord Throckmorton."

The way he's talking, I'm starting to think differently

about the fact that on the day we discovered the queen's letter the other princesses looked like princesses, while I was covered in muck and cobwebs and blood. Those weren't signs of shame. They were battle wounds, badges of honor. I should have worn my rips and stains proudly.

But I'm wearing a ball gown now. A ball gown and a crown and silver, jewel-covered slippers. And I was so busy with the coronation this afternoon and the peace negotiations and the agricultural reports before that that this is the first time I've seen Harper all day.

I turn and face him squarely.

"What about you?" I say quietly. "You were brave too. You tried to rescue Sir Stephen and Nanny and your mam. You were willing to walk all the way here, to keep me safe, even though you knew you might be carried away to the war. Don't you think you deserve credit for all that? Or some . . . reward?"

Harper looks away from me, out toward the party.

"I got to see you crowned princess, just like you were supposed to be," he says. He's speaking so softly I can barely hear him. He runs his hand through his hair, making it stand up all over the place in a familiar way. Then he turns back to me, a slight frown on his face. "And Mam says I can be her assistant."

That reminds me of the other big news in the palace. Even though Sir Stephen and Nanny and Harper's mam never got to play in the music competition, Harper's mam evidently talked to a lot of the other musicians while they were waiting behind the stage. She apparently made so many good suggestions for their performances that she was offered the job of palace music instructor.

Harper's frown deepens.

"So if I wait a million years until she retires, I could maybe even become the head harp teacher myself, and then finally get to play the way I want to," he says.

As expected, his mother is not thrilled with his new method of plucking the harp strings as quickly as possible.

"I seem to remember promising you the job of Lord High Chancellor of Fishing Ponds," I say. I hesitate. "But . . ."

At the same time Harper says, "Except . . ."

"You first," I say.

"No, no, royalty before commoners," Harper says.

"No, I insist! You—"

"What are you going to do, order me to talk, because you're the princess?" Harper asks brusquely.

I take one look at his face and decide not to, even in jest.

"Okay! Okay!" I say. "What I was going to say is . . ." It is amazingly hard to make myself speak. I whisper. "'But I would miss you.'"

Harper looks down.

"And I was going to say, 'Except it wouldn't be any fun alone,'" he says. "'Without you.'"

Neither of us seems to know where to look after that. I peer down at the party again, at the blur of lights and mirrors. Then I stare at the stones of the tower, each one held apart from the others by a thick layer of mortar. Or joined by mortar, depending on how you look at it.

Then, somehow, I'm gazing right into Harper's eyes.

And what I see there—it's like seeing everything at once. Why Harper didn't want to play a love song in front of me. Why he stopped wanting to be a soldier, even though he still said that he did. How many times he's wanted to hug me but held back. Why Ella thought that my feelings for Harper were like hers for Jed. And . . . how easily I could lose him.

"Maybe I could go with you," I offer faintly.

The corners of Harper's mouth curve down again.

"You're a princess," he says. "Princesses don't have time to concern themselves with fishing ponds."

"We wouldn't just have to look at fishing ponds," I say. "We could go around inspecting the countryside, gathering information about everything. And maybe we could travel to Fridesia, too, for the peace negotiations. And . . ." I feel a little shy, mentioning this. "And to go to Ella and Jed's wedding."

Harper kicks at the stone wall nearest his feet.

"We're almost fifteen," he says. "We get too much older, it'll be scandalous, you and me traveling together. . . ."

"Why?"

"You know," Harper says. Once again he won't meet my eyes. "A man and a woman, not married . . ."

"Well, then," I say, "I guess we'd have to get married."

My heart pounds like I've just done something incredibly brave—walked all the way from our village to Cortona, say, or run through an alley full of rats—rather than just speaking seven words.

"You're a princess," Harper says harshly. "I'm nothing. You couldn't marry me."

"Oh, yeah?" I say. I reach out and grab Harper's shoulders. I begin shaking him back and forth. "You make me so mad with all that 'I'm nothing' talk! I'm a princess only because some maid plucked me out of a rickety bed in an orphanage—"

"And the queen said you were a princess, and Sir Stephen taught you, and you walked all the way to Cortona—"

"And you walked all the way to Cortona too!" I protest, shaking his shoulders harder. "And you're good and strong and smart and true, and the best fast harpist in the land—"

"Which means nothing—"

"Harper, you grinning fool!" I say, giving him the hardest shake yet, almost a shove. "If we can make up the rules as we go along to get thirteen princesses instead of one, don't you think we could bend the rules a little to let you and me get married?"

I've stopped shaking his shoulders, but I'm still holding onto him. I'm not quite sure how it happens, but somehow my arms slide down, around his back, and his arms come up hesitantly to circle my waist.

"I didn't think this could ever happen," Harper says in a husky voice. "Because of your fate, and mine—"

"Harper, we have choices, too!" I say, leaning back to look up at his face. "I could push you away, or you could push me away, or I could give up the crown, or you could get a crown, or we could just kiss each other, or, I don't know, there are a million other things that could happen, a million different choices we could make right now. . . ."

Harper is standing very still.

"So what's it going to be?" he asks quietly.

In answer, I rise up on my tiptoes. He's already bending his head down, moving his lips toward mine. And then, well, I haven't exactly studied this, but I'm pretty sure that ours is not the most expert kiss in Sualan history. It's a little hard to figure out how we should tilt our heads so our noses don't bump. But the kiss is a promise, a vow.

Come to think of it, it doesn't really matter that ours is not the most expert kiss in Sualan history. It's still the best.

Harper takes a step back, and he is grinning, but not foolishly.

"Is *this* our fate?" he asks.

"It is now," I say, grinning back.

Far below us, down in the courtyard, the band has shifted into another song. The cheerful music floats up to us, each note full of hope, promising only good things for the future.

Harper sweeps into a courtly bow so smooth and perfect that I'm sure he's been practicing.

"Your Majesty," he says. "May I have this dance?"

I nod and then giggle, ruining my regal air.

"Up here or down there?" I ask, pointing down toward the courtyard.

"Whichever you prefer," he says solemnly, holding out his hand.

I take his hand and wrap my arm around his waist, and we begin to waltz in our former prison—because really, it'd take so long to walk down all those stairs that we'd miss the whole song if we tried to go to the courtyard. As we spin and twirl to the music, I think about how I used to be so certain about who I was and what my future would hold. And now I'm sort of promised to be married and sort of in charge of the entire kingdom—with twelve other girls—and so much of it has been a complete surprise. The queen couldn't possibly have understood what she was starting when she sent her maid to the orphanage. Sir Stephen couldn't possibly have understood what he was starting when he gave Harper's mam my royal harp. And Harper and I didn't know what we were starting when we began walking toward Cortona.

Who can know their own fate? Who can do anything except make the best choices they can and hope it all works out?

"Best choice," I whisper in Harper's ear. "This was the best choice."

"Dancing here instead of in the courtyard, you mean?"

he asks. "Or . . ." He looks a little dizzy, and I know he's thinking about how many choices the two of us have made, leading us here, to this moment. Leading us to our fate.

I smile up at him.

"All of them," I say. "Every single one."

Here's a sneak peek at the third book in Margaret Peterson Haddix's The Palace Chronicles

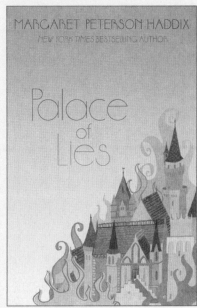

DESMIA AND HER TWELVE SISTER-PRINCESSES ARE FINALLY RULING Suala together, as a united front. All seems to finally be well, and Suala seems to have gotten its happily ever after at last. But Desmia, trained by a lifetime of palace intrigue, is not so sure. She desperately wants to believe everything will be fine, but she can't help but see danger around every corner.

And then the unthinkable happens, and Desmia's worst fears are confirmed. Now, without the support of the sister-princesses she's grown to rely on or the trappings of royalty that she's always taken for granted, Desmia must find the courage to seek out the truth on her own terms—and determine the course of two kingdoms.

Thirteen crowns glistened in the torchlight of the throne room. Twelve were newly forged, ready to be placed on the heads of the Sualan princesses whose identities had been kept secret their entire lives until now.

The thirteenth crown was mine.

I was the princess everybody knew about. The one who'd grown up in the palace, the one who stood on the balcony every day at noon and waved to the commoners crowded into the courtyard below.

The one who had always lived in danger.

Cecilia, beside me, jostled my arm in a completely unregal way, countering the effect of her satin dress and ornately upswept brown hair.

"This is so exciting!" she practically squealed in my ear. "I've been dreaming about this day forever! It's exactly like I always imagined it! Only, you know—not."

What she'd always imagined was replacing me.

For almost all of her fourteen years, she'd believed that she was the one true princess of Suala. But she had to remain hidden because her parents, the king and queen, had been assassinated, and the evildoers were still abroad in the land. Her own life was still at risk. And so, to protect her, there was a decoy princess on the throne, a mere commoner whose life didn't actually matter.

She believed that I, Princess Desmia, was an impostor.

Every single one of the eleven other newly discovered princesses—Adoriana, Elzbethl, Fidelia, Florencia, Ganelia, Lucia, Lydia, Marindia, Porfinia, Sophia, and Rosemary—had grown up believing some version of that story herself. Each one thought that she (Adoriana, Elzbethl, Fidelia, etc., etc.) was the true princess; I was the disposable fake.

They had all been lied to.

But then, so had I.

I had always believed that I was the one and only true princess. I knew nothing of the others' stories. I knew no tales of decoys and secret royal bloodlines. I knew only to fear assassins and pretenders and impostors who might show up with fake claims to my throne.

In one sense, it had turned out that all of us were impostors.

In another sense, every single one of us was right: We were all true princesses. Just not the way any of us had believed.

At least, we're all going to be true princesses now, I thought grimly as all thirteen of us fanned out across the back of the throne room, ready to step forward for the official coronation.

Was that right? Was that fair? Would the others all have been safer staying in hiding? Or—going back to it?

Of course they would, I thought, and for a moment my heart pounded as if I were the one stepping out into unfamiliar terrors and demands for the very first time.

"Psst, Desmia," Elzbethl hissed behind me. "How do you do that thing with your feet, where it looks like you're gliding when you walk? How do you keep from tripping over your dress?"

I sighed.

"I don't know, Elzbethl. It just . . ." If I said, *It just comes naturally,* that would be cruel, because nothing involving grace or coordination seemed to come naturally to Elzbethl. But I had learned how to walk like a princess so long ago I didn't remember it. I was probably taught with my very first steps. Elzbethl should have learned too. "I guess you kind of slide your feet. Don't lift your knees too high."

"Thank you," Elzbethl said, too loudly for the solemnity of the room ahead of us. "Thank you so much."

Her eyes were wide and awed, just like Cecilia's, just like all the other girls'. I could hear whispers down the line: "Did you think our crowns would be so *shiny*?" "I can't believe I'm wearing a silk dress. Silk!" "Oooo, is that courtier over there winking at you or me?"

They might as well have all been blind. They were like little kittens that didn't have their eyes open yet. They peered into the throne room, and all they could see was glitter and gold. They looked at the assembled crowd in their own silks and satins, their own velvets and gold-threaded brocade, and the only things my new sister-princesses saw were beauty and adoration and pride. They didn't see any of the scheming or conniving or greed. They didn't see any more lies.

They thought all the danger was past.

The royal trumpeters sent out a series of blasts on their horns. It was the same royal refrain that had announced Sualan royalty for generations. I had been hearing it all my life, but the others gasped and gaped.

"Hear ye, hear ye," the royal herald announced from the front of the room, from beside the newly arranged lineup of thirteen thrones. "Presenting . . . the thirteen princesses of Suala."

The other girls around me stood frozen, overcome. It would be unroyal and undignified for me to poke Cecilia in the back and hiss, *Proceed!* But for a long moment I feared that I would have to resort to that. Finally Adoriana, in the lead, stepped forward and began stumbling toward the thrones. After only a brief pause, Cecilia bounded up behind her. I waited a decent interval, then followed along.

"I still don't get how she does that gliding thing," Elzbethl whispered behind me, probably to Fidelia.

I resisted the urge to turn around and see how Elzbethl would fare strolling (or, more likely, galumphing) down the long purple carpet leading to our thrones. Faces leered out of the crowd at me, and I catalogued the expressions behind their expressions.

Was that man secretly working for Lord Throckmorton all along? I wondered, my gaze lingering on a particularly pompous, preening face. *Should we have arrested him, too?*

My gaze shifted to the next minister, the next adviser, one after the other.

What is that one plotting now? How about that one?

The other girls thought we had nothing else to worry about. After all, we'd triumphed over our worst enemy, Lord Throckmorton—and put him and his minions under lock and key. The other girls had never lived in a palace before. They didn't understand how new enemies could spring up overnight. Or do their evil in secret for years. I'd seen that happen too.

Elzbethl distracted me from my thoughts by stepping on the hem of my dress.

"Oh, sorry! I'm so sorry! I got too close, didn't I?" she cried, turning a tiny *faux pas* into a spectacle for the entire assemblage to gawp at.

I turned, partly to make sure there wasn't any damage to my dress, partly to get her to stop screeching.

She backed away so dramatically that she almost fell over.

I gave my most gracious bow.

"It is no matter," I said softly. "I pray, put it from your mind."

I didn't say, *And, from now on, watch where you're going!* Even though I was thinking it.

I turned forward again and kept walking toward the thrones.

Behind me I could hear Elzbethl giggle nervously and recount to Fidelia, "She was even nice about it! Back in my village, when I was pretending to be a peasant, the other girls would have punched me if I'd done something like that."

Truly? I wondered. But I was also secretly celebrating. *Yes, Elzbethl, that's right. Learn to be suspicious of false kindness.*

But did I want her to be suspicious of me?

This question absorbed me as we all settled onto our thrones, an array of glittering girls with a table full of glistening crowns before us.

It was unprecedented for so many princesses to be crowned—or, in my case, recrowned—at the same time. It was highly abnormal for princesses to rule at all, let alone multiple princesses who were all only fourteen years old.

We had jointly decided that becoming a kingdom with thirteen ruling princesses made more sense than having all of us designated queens. The others argued that we were making everything up as we went along, anyway—why not call ourselves whatever we wanted?

Secretly, I thought that they were all so happy to finally be able to call themselves princesses out loud, in public, that they didn't want to give up the title too quickly.

Was I being unfair? Were they really that shallow? How vulnerable did that make us all?

Why did any of us think this would work? I wondered in despair, as I stared out at the crowd. I was surer than ever that the assembled courtiers were all calculating and conniving. Was there a single person out there who wasn't scheming to take over Lord Throckmorton's old role as the power behind the throne—only with more princesses to manipulate?

I turned my head all the way to the far right, to the section where the delegation from the neighboring kingdom of Fridesia sat.

Ella, I thought in relief. *Jed. They aren't scheming. They're people I trust.*

It was ironic: Lord Jedediah Reston was the ambassador from Fridesia, and my kingdom had been at war with Fridesia for as long as I could remember. Until now. The other girls and I intended our first act as co-princesses to be signing a ceasefire with Fridesia. And then, as soon as possible, we planned to work out terms of a lasting peace treaty that would end the war once and for all.

Even though he was still technically my enemy, I trusted Jed. And I *really* trusted his fiancée, Ella Brown, who sat beside him clutching his hand and positively beaming up at all of us.

Does Ella believe thirteen girls can really rule as co-princesses? I wondered. *Or is she just being nice? Or just supporting us and Jed, because that's the way to get Jed's dearest dream of a peace treaty?*

So of course Ella and Jed had ulterior motives too. Did it even matter that their ulterior motives were noble?

The royal herald stepped to a podium near the center of the stage, between the thrones for Florencia and Ganelia.

"Be it known," he began, "that on her deathbed fourteen

years ago, Queen Charlotte Aurora designated not just one but thirteen baby girls as her royal heirs."

The other girls and I had struggled so over the wording of that sentence. Sophia and Fidelia in particular wanted to hide the fact that none of us actually possessed a drop of royal blood. The only thing that made us royal was the queen's secret deathbed writings. Otherwise, we were all of us just ordinary orphans—ordinary orphans raised by knights who were themselves tricked into believing we were princesses.

Why did it have to be my knight, Lord Throckmorton, who found out the truth first? I wondered for the umpteenth time. *So I was the one manipulated and preyed upon, instead of being protected and cosseted and ... and loved?*

Unexpectedly, tears sprang to my eyes. But I knew the trick to holding back tears: You stare at whatever you're afraid of and remind yourself how much worse it would be if you showed any weakness.

I learned that from Lord Throckmorton. For fourteen years, he was the one I feared most.